VENDETTA

DOMINION FIRST BLOOD

Series Book Two

RICHARD MANN

"Fabulous book! Science thriller with a feel of history. It pulled me from the first page. Plenty of action, adventure and unusual twists. The characters are masterly written and author's attention to details deserves a lot of praise. At times I felt like I was traveling in time and space and it reminds me Star Wars and Lord of the Rings. Highly recommend this book to all Sci-fi lovers. Looking forward to your next book Richard Mann!"

By Iryna Dudinaon 25 November 2017 | Verified Purchase

"An outstanding piece of work. Destined to be a classic. It's the best action adventure book I've read in years, gripping, edge of seat excitement, a real page turner. It's a mix of sci-fi action thriller horror and historical fiction...Frederick Forsyth and Bernard Cromwell on steroids..

This is quite a long book..but it needs to be. There is real depth on the characters.. they feel alive and real. I really love Cockney Vinnie the sexy femme fatale vampire lucia and the flawed complex hero Bullet Proof Pete. I felt I could relate to the characters. There are many funny moments (esp. When 2 tough SAS heroes dress up as women).

There's also an interesting love triangle but I won't go into it here as it will spoil the story. There is plenty of fascinating backstory....WWII and Roman times.i felt like I was there..i like the old fashioned chapter titles pictures appendices and history. Can't wait for book two."

By Dan 8 November 2017 Format: Paperback | Verified Purchase

"A tried and tested formula, aliens invade earth destroying and enslaving humanity. But this has an unusual twist. Humanity fights back with vampires as allies. A well-written book that will have you hooked from the first to the last page. It's reminiscent of Lord of the Rings in scope and adventure. Can't wait for the sequel."

By Celine 16 September 2017 Format: Kindle Edition | Verified Purchase

"Excellent effort by a new author!
Full of ambition and wide-ranging scope.
Something for lovers of Sci-Fi, action heroes and with vampires thrown in for good measure!"

By DejiDeal 15 September 2017 Format: Kindle Edition | Verified Purchase

"Although I'm not a big reader this book was very easy to read which kept pulling me closer and closer. The characters were very interesting and the plot twists and surprises kept the reader engrossed in the story, it's clear to see the author has put a lot of effort into the research that's gone into this book.

The quality of the book itself is also very good, however you wouldn't expect less for the price. This book has definitely peaked my interest in reading more books and I can't wait for the sequel."

By David on 5 September 2017 Format: Paperback | Verified Purchase

"What a vivid imagination the author must have. The story is so well laid out one has virtually to be arrested to put the book down. I will not go into the story here except to say that it covers the globe and ventures into space. I'm looking forward to book 2. Don't be long Richard mann." By Chris 22 August 2017 Format: Kindle Edition|Verified Purchase

This book is dedicated to my family
who are the rock of my life. To
my mother Patricia, you have always been there for us.

"Sometimes doing your best is not good enough.
Sometimes you must do what is required."
Sir Winston Churchill

"A time to love, and a time to hate, a
time of war, and a time of peace."
Ecclesiastes 3:8

Contents

Cast of Characters

Captain Peter 'Bulletproof' Morgan - SAS soldier / MI6 agent

Corporal Vinnie 'The Terminator' Carson - SAS soldier

Lucia - Vampire Elder and member of the Vampiri Grand Council

Count Cassian - Vampire Elder and Head of the Vampiri Grand Council

Jennifer Morgan – Peter's wife

Frank Wilson - US President

General Bill Scott - US Chief of Defense Staff

General Julian Grimbald - Head of US Space command

Professor Picard – Eccentric French Polymath

Father Sebastian Harris - Priest. Ex SAS

Sir Nigel Goldbroom – MI6 Chief

Ergtuk the 82nd – Sumeri Alien Clone

Herr Herg-Zuk – Sumeri Alien Emperor

Marshal Zurg-Uk – Sumeri Alien Defense Chief

Lord Grim-Uk – Sumeri Alien Narzuk SS Chief

Himm-Uk – Sumeri Alien Narzuk SS Deputy Chief

Gill Carson – Vinnie's wife

'Handsome' Mike - US Navy Seal

General Mike Schmitt – Sirius Defense Chief

Captain Duke Miller – CIA agent

Colonel Bradley – 21 regiment SAS Colonel

Colonel Stan Wight – Sirius base Colonel

Please note: The Appendices: Cockney slang table and Vampiri and Sumeri Alien command structure are at the back of the book. Additional material is available in the Special Edition.

"I imagine they might exist in massive ships, having used up all the resources from their home planet. Such advanced aliens would perhaps become nomads, looking to conquer and colonise whatever planets they can reach."

"To my mathematical brain, the numbers alone make thinking about aliens perfectly rational."

"The real challenge is working out what aliens might actually be like." "We only have to look at ourselves to see how intelligent life might develop into something we wouldn't want to meet."

"If aliens ever visit us, I think the outcome would be much as when Christopher Columbus first landed in America, which didn't turn out very well for the American Indians."

Professor Stephen Hawking

Chapter 1

SIRIUS SOLDIERS

SIRIUS UNDERGROUND COMMAND
BUNKER-MOJAVE DESERT

After three days with virtually no sleep, Peter is feeling refreshed after a good rest. He and Vinnie have both learned that the secret to a good night's sleep is to eat well and drink plenty of water, so as not to be dehydrated when you wake up. Vinnie is complaining to a technician that he cannot find any tea bags.

'I'm English—I don't drink coffee. Where's the tea?'

Peter produced some tea bags from his kit. 'Never travel without teabags.'

'Lifesaver. Yorkshire Tea,' replied Vinnie.

As Peter and Vinnie walk down a corridor Vinnie is stopped by a technician who looks at his torn trousers. 'What are you looking at mate?' asks Vinnie.

'Do you want some new pants?' asks the technician.

'You what mate? You want to look at my pants—are you a homosexual or somefin'?' Vinnie stands face to face with the technician. Peter smiles.

'Er no your pants are torn…' replies the frightened technician.

'Oh, you mean do I want some new trousers?' asks Vinnie.

'Yes, new pants.'

'These yanks don't talk proper English, Bulletproof,' says Vinnie. Peter lets out a guffaw of laughter and pats Vinnie on the back. Having Vinnie around cheers him up—takes his mind off Jennifer for a while. In their darkest hour, everyone needs a friend they can rely on, thinks Peter.

Every Frodo needs their Sam.

Vinnie and Peter in fresh military fatigues are in a TV room with other Special Forces soldiers. Like many soldiers who have seen a massive amount of combat, they have a wired look to their eyes, known as the 'thousand-yard stare.' Peter and Vinnie have it too—they have seen their fair share of combat in Iraq and Afghanistan.

And Yemen, don't forget Yemen.

The assembled soldiers are amongst the best of the best of the Elite Special Forces, chosen, like Peter, for the Sirius project. Peter waves to someone he recognises from his Iraq stint. They sup their tea while watching a training video on project Sirius weapons technology, and how to operate them.

"This is the PR7 Rifle. It uses electrically-driven, electromagnetic, rail gun technology. This gives a constant acceleration along the entire length of the device, significantly increasing the muzzle velocity. It does not use explosive propellant—it is a strictly kinetic weapon. Each projectile travels at 2000 mph with a muzzle velocity of 1000lbs, enough kinetic force, in one bullet, to take out an armoured vehicle. It takes a magazine of thirty 20mm uranium-enriched projectiles and is powered by a unique electro-mag battery which is inserted into the stock, here. It can also fire a grenade with a range of 1000 yards."

'Kinetic energy,' Vinnie raises his eyebrows. He has a natural interest in new rifle technology, being the best marksman in the regiment.

Peter has read a New Scientist article about a space-based weapon that was fired from a satellite orbiting Earth—a non-explosive, twenty-foot long tungsten projectile, which would hit earth travelling at Mach ten. Devastating. Project Thor or something. But a rifle? He has used the PR7 once before, at Buckingham Palace, but it would be good to get some proper training.

A Project Sirius officer addresses the soldiers.

'I am Lieutenant Ross. We will go outside so you can train on the weapons. Alien activity is low in this area, but we will warn you of any incoming.'

Peter and Vinnie are in the dry, arid Mojave Desert. There is a light breeze, but the desert air dries Peter's mouth. Peter looks up at the blue sky; a vulture is circling above. 'Nice place,' thinks Peter, as he gulps some water, and puts on his sunglasses. He examines his solid titanium PR7 rifle. He adjusts his sight, loads a grenade, aims and fired the grenade launcher, which takes out a bus—and half the hillside with it. A plume of dust fills the air around them. Peter rubs his shoulder, the recoil from the shot is ferocious—even though he has the strength of ten men, he feels the recoil.

'Use a pad for the stock, Vinnie, it's got a vicious kick,' says Peter. Vinnie nods and then destroys a tank with two shots from the rifle.

'Now that's what I'm talking about,' Peter admires his gun.

'Nice rifle,' says Vinnie, 'I think I'm in love,' rubbing his shoulder.

A siren sounds as Peter is about to fire another round. 'We've got incoming!' shouts the Lieutenant as soldiers run for the bunker. Peter just manages to dive into the bunker, and the huge steel door seals behind him as a black alien fighter flies past.

Chapter 2

VINNIE'S PAIN

SIRIUS UNDERGROUND COMMAND
BUNKER-MOJAVE DESERT

A technician looks at a bank of screens showing Sirius video feeds from around the world. Vinnie and Peter are standing behind him.

'Captain Morgan, we have an incoming feed from an X-37D over London.' The X-37D flies over a ruined Buckingham Palace; Vinnie and Peter are shocked.

'Glad we got Her Majesty away safely,' whispers Peter.

'God Bless the Queen,' replies Vinnie. Peter crosses himself and nods, recalling their conversations with the Queen and Prince Philip, now indelibly burned into his mind.

Next are pictures of toppled skyscrapers in the City of London, the Cheese Grater and the Gherkin lie in ruins, but remarkably the NatWest Tower still stands. The X-37D fuselage shimmers as the cloaking hides the ship from the alien fighters buzzing around the City. The X-37D slows down as it flies over Liverpool Street, then the East End of London. Vinnie looks worried.

'Looks like my street, they destroyed my local Pub; look Pete, the Blind Beggar. Where am I going to get a decent pint now?' says a distressed Vinnie. Peter's super-vision spots something, and his heart jumped as he points at the corner of the screen.

'Hold on there! In that crowd of women—it looks like Gill!'

Vinnie stands open-mouthed, then gets on his knees.

'Gill?'

The X-37D hovers over the street. Vinnie and Peter watch as Vinnie's wife, Gill, and a few other young and attractive women, are scanned, drugged and then taken away by Narzuks in black uniforms. Peter notices these particular aliens are fitter looking than the normal troops and have red armbands: *meaner and leaner.*

Gill wakes up and is waving her arms and screaming as she is taken onto a larger transport ship, but then is injected again.

Men and other, mixed-race women are ignored, or killed. Any who do not cooperate are shot where they stand. Bodies litter the streets. The ones who do cooperate are taken to a separate transport ship, to God knows where.

BLIND BEGGAR PUB - LONDON

Vinnie's gangster father Reg and his brother Ron are holed up behind the bar in the Blind Beggar Pub in Whitechapel. The buildings around are badly damaged, people wander around like zombies unable to comprehend what has happened to their lives. An alien ship has landed outside, and alien soldiers in black, followed by blank-looking troops in grey uniforms stream out of the ship. The aliens are shouting orders; Reg can hear the unholy barking of alien dogs. Vinnie's wife Gill hides, cowering under a table.

Reg looks at Gill, 'Gill, I won't let Vinnie down, I won't let them take you, love! Ron, the shotgun, quick!'

Ron gets the shotgun and throws it to Reg as two dogs jump through the door. Reg shoots with both barrels, and the dogs lie injured and howling on the floor. The pub doors disintegrate as a robot moves in for the kill. Ron fires a Kalashnikov at the robot, the bullets bouncing off in all directions, ricocheting around the pub, smashing glasses and furniture. Splintered glass and dust lie everywhere, Reg coughs on the dust, takes glass splinters from his arm, then reloads his shotgun. The robot returns fire, with its laser cannon, trashing what's left of the pub. Reg and Ron shoot in vain but are knocked unconscious by falling debris.

A Narzuk black-uniformed SS Stormtrooper comes in and grabs a shivering, dust-covered Gill, leaving Vinnie's father and uncle unconscious. The Narzuk injects her, and she falls unconscious, then he runs a scanner over her, and gets a green light. A robot carries her onto a waiting ship, along with other women.

Peter watches as his best friend shouts, cries and shakes his fist at the screen. 'You alien bastards! Leave my wife alone!' Peter puts his arm around him, as Vinnie crumbles like a child, sobbing.

The great "Vinnie the Terminator" in tears. He is here for Vinnie. He knows how he must feel—like someone has taken your guts out—as Vinnie sobs on his shoulder, Peter can do nothing but comfort his friend.

'But why do these fucking aliens discriminate?' thinks Peter. Separating out the women, rejecting mixed race and non-whites, shooting the rest, or transporting them off to God knows where. All these confusing thoughts run through his mind as he tries to comfort Vinnie; then his mind wanders to his own wife, Jennifer.

Is she safe? His heart skips a beat as the screen goes dead. The next thing they know the X-37D is north of London flying over green fields, then they see a black-walled camp, inside thousands of people are milling around, all in rags being segregated, separated from their children. Women are being herded into one building, while the men are being lined up near pits, then killed. They can see aliens in black uniforms, like the ones Peter saw in New York—the ones with red swastika armbands. The camera zooms in on a soldier who is being tortured by a Narzuk using a strange-looking metallic device. The terror is sketched on his face as the device drills through his skull, his eyes on stalks.

'Vinnie I'm going to make you a promise. When we have rescued Gill, we're going to go to that camp, rescue those poor people, and kill those fucking aliens,' says Peter, then crosses himself. Vinnie nods through his tears.

On a separate screen, another cloaked X-37D is flying over New York, over the towering 200-foot wall, over the thousands of people trying in vain to escape. Its cameras are zeroing in on Wall Street, onto a Sergeant, ordering troops to run away in retreat from clone aliens firing at them. The clone aliens in grey uniforms look different, thinks Pete, like copies, not quite real. The fighters pick off human soldiers as they are running. Peter shakes his head; it's a slaughter. How long can mankind last?

Peter looks as another camera on an X-37D zooms in on a remote country road in New York State. Thousands of dirty and exhausted refugees are carrying what possessions they can. They look dirty and dejected, as if they have lost all hope. A few have cars, but most have been abandoned. People glance nervously up at the sky, looking out for alien fighters.

Vinnie gets off his knees, wipes the tears from his eyes, and confronts Peter. They move to where they cannot be overheard. Vinnie has a fierce look in his eye. It is Vinnie's version of the thousand-yard stare, which made him the best debt collector in East London; it would scare the shit out of anyone.

'Bulletproof, what the fuck are we doing here, out in the middle of the fucking desert, when we should back in Blighty, finding Gill, being with our families and killing the bastard aliens?' Peter nods.

He looks at Vinnie, holding him by the shoulders with his own version of the thousand-yard stare, which would make Mike Tyson quake in his boots, and normal mortals run a mile, for he is the toughest and strongest soldier in the Special Air Service—even the officers avoid him.

Now he looks Vinnie in the eye.

'Vinnie, you're my oldest friend, sometimes things happen for a reason. I think we are meant to be here, out in the desert, in the States. It feels right to be here. I think here, we may find answers. I've been having these dreams, visions, like I was a warrior, not a modern war, but an ancient war, before the Middle Ages. I was dressed like a Templar Knight, a holy warrior, on a crusade, and I carried an ancient and powerful sword—not of Earthly origin Vinnie, but a holy sword, old as time itself. It was long and had a bluish tinge to the blade and a golden pommel. My middle name is Kay, also Cai, but I have another name; I hear it my dreams. Caius, yes that is it; I have been reading up on Kay. He was an indestructible warrior, that's why I am never hurt Vinnie, it's like something is going on, beyond me, beyond my control, like I am following a path.'

A look of understanding crept across Vinnie's face. 'Bulletproof…'

'Yes, Vinnie, that would explain why I have never been hurt in battle, not even a fucking scratch. It's unheard of Vinnie. That's why the rest of the blokes in the Regiment call me "Bulletproof Pete."

'Pete, old mate, I've never asked you why you never get injured, thought it would be unlucky, tempting fate, and all that. Maybe you are this Kay, Caius whatever your name is. It would explain a lot. You have always had an aura about you. At selection, Des and Artie couldn't believe you got through it so easy, like you had some magical power, and the lads in the regiment, well they think you can walk on water. I saw you on the carrier with that sword.'

'Things happen for a reason Vinnie. I've been sent here to find some answers, and by heck, we're going to get them. And we will find Gill, that's a promise.' He remembers the two creatures who saved them in New York. 'And find out who saved us in New York.'

Chapter 3

PEP TALK

Peter and Vinnie meet the base Colonel, Colonel Stan Wight, in his office. His grizzled face, burning eyes, silver hair, and lean body, show a depth of life, and military experience. He looks them up and down as he studies some briefing papers.

'Suppose you're wondering why you got dragged all the way from England to fight a war in a different country?' His gravelly voice has sincerity, thinks Peter. Yes, he would trust him, his growing intuition, his inner warrior, tells him so.

'It came from high up, very high up, I can tell you. Somebody must like you gentlemen.'

'What are we doing out here Colonel?' asks a puzzled Peter.

'Our troops have been decimated. We don't have the manpower to launch a full-scale attack on New York. Your intel confirms this. It's too well defended. It's a fortress, so that will have to wait. So, we're focusing on softer targets.' The Colonel smiled in admiration at his new recruits, the best of the best.

'I have a special mission for you, just you two. Your orders are to make your way to Los Angeles, their LA asset is less well defended than other cities. Find out their "raison d'être". Why are they here? And what can we do about it? So we can formulate a strategy. If you can kill a few aliens along the way, then so much the better. Dismissed Gentlemen, good hunting.' Peter and Vinnie look at each other.

'We normally work as a four-man team,' prompts Peter.

'Sorry, can't spare the personnel. Besides, I hear you two make a great team!' Peter knows the Colonel is trying to make the best of a bad situation.

'Will it be a night airdrop?' asks Peter.

'No, there's no air. We cannot use C130 or Chinooks, they'd get blown out of the sky. The X-37D's are all out on patrol. We lost another one yesterday. Sorry gentlemen, all we have is a Humvee.' The colonel looks apologetic, as if he is trying not to tell them it is a suicide mission.

'Mmm high risk, we will have to travel by night,' replies Peter.

'The Humvee does, however, use Sirius Technology: adaptive stealth armour—it hides the vehicle from infra-red detection,' Colonel Wight added, trying to sound upbeat.

'Will it work against the aliens?' Peter is curious.

'To be honest, we are not really sure,' the colonel replies, then he adds, 'We are counting on you, Captain Morgan.' They salute the Colonel then leave.

In a weapons storage area, they pick up some PR7 rifles and ten magazines each of ammo, each containing thirty rounds of uranium enriched bullets. Peter slots an electro mag battery into the stock of his rifle, supplying the kinetic power for the rifle—he is surprised how light it is.

They put on desert smocks and shemaghs (Arab) headscarves, the most suitable gear for the climate. In the webbing on the outside of their Bergen, they pack two PR7 magazines, for quick retrieval, the rest in the Bergen. Some PR7 grenades, water, and boil-in-the-bag rations are next. They still have some of their British rations, including treacle pudding, Vinnie's favourite, and curry, Peter's must have.

'Don't forget the Yorkshire tea bags,' says Vinnie.

'End of the world mate, if I forgot those,' replies Peter. They have Sirius-encrypted radios for comms, and some maps of the desert and Los Angeles.

They are carrying fifty pounds on their backs, unlike a normal SAS mission where their Bergen's could weigh over 100 pounds. They don't bother with claymore mines, or the normal kit they would carry, just the PR7 kit, and their food and survival kit. They were fighting a different kind of war.

They need to travel fast and be light on foot, so Peter focuses his attention on his belt kit, which has camouflaged webbing. PR7 ammunition, two water bottles, one metal cup, mess tin and handle, plastic bags, Silva compass, glass magnifying/burning lens, water purification tablets, medical kit, airway, hacksaw, safety pins, cotton wool, matches *(lots of those)*, fire stick, rabbit snares, NATO fishing kit, survival kit containing two-sided signalling flashcard, pen-knife, heliograph, fishing hooks online, needle and thread, condom *(for carrying water)*, razor blade, flint and steel, brass escape compass with luminous dial, detonators, mini-flares, maps, chocolate and a few rations.

Not forgetting Vinnie's teabags, of course, he will never hear the end of it if he forgets those. To most people, this would seem like a lot of kit, but when you are out in the wilderness, a simple fishing hook and line can mean the difference between dinner, or no dinner, survival or no survival.

'Vinnie, did you check the encryption codes for the radio?'

'Yes, I did. Twice. Works fine. Unlike the British radios,' Vinnie replies, muttering enough swear words under his breath to make a drill Sergeant blush. Peter's mind drifts back to Yemen, and the hurried and poorly planned mission to fight the Yemeni terrorists.

Unforgivable.

They could have died. He thinks about Baz and Mad Mike, then his mind comes back to the present.

Chapter 4

BREAKFAST IN THE DESERT

They packed their gear inside a Humvee jeep—heavy armoured, effective against improvised explosive devices, but not very fuel efficient. Peter looked at it.

'Prefer the Pinkie to be honest, but when in Rome.'

'Do as the Romans do,' replied Vinnie.

Peter had always preferred the Pinkie, the lightweight Land Rover, dating back to World War Two, recalling the amazing exploits of David Stirling, the founder of the modern-day SAS. He completed daring missions in the North African desert against the Italians and Germans. Stirling became a legend. Everyone in the regiment knew the history of the SAS. The Pinkie had a reinforced chassis and extra fuel tanks, but it was open top, so there was no protection from enemy fire, unlike the Humvee, which was built like a tank. The Pinkie had a hard suspension, which gave a bumpy ride, and a sore arse, unlike the comfortable Humvee.

'We will be a sitting target of course,' said Peter.

'Of course,' replied Vinnie, admiring the comfortable seats and stereo.

'We need to run dark. I have the passive night vision goggles.'

'Yep,' replied Vinnie, thinking of the music he could play on the vehicle's sound system.

'And silent,' Peter looked at Vinnie, who looked disappointed.

Peter looked sympathetic, he loved to listen to Led Zeppelin himself, 'They're bound to pick up the vibrations.'

'No sense of humour, these aliens,' said Vinnie.

'Yep, no sense of humour. Then again, they will pick up vibrations from the Humvee anyway, so what's the difference?' Peter weighed up the pros and cons.

'Know what? Fuck it, Led Zeppelin, it is,' Peter put a CD into the player with his favourite tracks on. Kashmir started playing. They both smiled, they were in good humour as they listened.

They packed their gear into the Humvee, which was still inside the compound. Vinnie took the first turn to drive, as a large steel door, opened to the desert. Vinnie drove slowly forward, they had their PR7 rifles close by, with the safety on, in case of negligent discharge—you never know, they could hit a bump, and that would be the end of the Humvee, and themselves. They drove out into the desert, Peter wound down the window, and cool air flooded in, the sky was lit by the moonlight as they listened to the lyrics.

Peter sang along to Robert Plant as they made their way through the desert. Stars do seem to fill my dreams—am I a traveller of time and space? Maybe. His dreams were of various ages in time—Roman, Medieval and modern times.

He looked up at the moonlight. Ideal, thought Peter, plenty of ambient light, as they wanted to drive under cover of darkness. Dark and silent, as only the SAS and Pathfinders operate. It took balls of steel to drive with no lights on, so they wore passive night vision goggles, and the moon lit the way. If the moon hid behind a cloud, the NVG would be essential.

Peter pressed the amber Adaptiv button on the dashboard, hoping it would work, which then turned green..

Vinnie made his way through the desert, avoiding obstacles for a couple of miles, until they hit Route 66. Peter double-checked his sidearm, another kinetic weapon, the PR1, with twenty tiny rounds, but still with enough power in one bullet to go through three men before stopping.

Bring it on, you alien bastards. Jimmy Page's guitar solos rang in Peter's ears as they drove through the cool night of the desert; 1970's rock and roll, a decade of genius, then it was gone. 'Wonder if the aliens listen to music?' he thought. No, they all look soulless.

He had his grab bag on the seat next to him, in case it all went to rat shit. It contained non-perishable food, water purification tablets, a fire stick and matches, water bottle, waterproofs, and maps—enough to survive 72 hours.

Vinnie drove from the desert onto Route 66, and as they made their way, they could see a rabbit, staring at them in the middle of the road. 'Stupid rabbit,' said Vinnie.

'Run dark and quiet,' repeated Peter. Vinnie turned down the volume on the stereo, now playing Celebration Day, and went smoothly through the gear shift. He knew the drill, they had done it often enough during gigs in Iraq. The moon went behind a cloud, and they adjusted their night vision goggles. It was midnight and Peter felt sleepy.

'Wake me at 0200,' Peter grunted before he fell asleep. As he dreamed he had a vision of walking on grass, it was warm and he was wearing a toga, he was walking hand in hand with a beautiful woman with curly black hair – she had something about the gypsy about her, wild and passionate. The stars shone above him as he kissed her red lips, then they looked above at the stars, entranced at their magical beauty. At 0200 precisely, Vinnie nudged Peter awake.

'Anything to report?' The image of the woman strong in his mind.

'Nah, just some stupid coyotes crossing the road.' They stopped the Humvee, letting it idle, as they looked up at the sky, the shining stars, and the moon, the cool night air brushing their faces. It was peaceful and quiet, and at any other time, they would be enjoying it, but they were pensive.

'Gill, where are you?' Vinnie stared up at the sky.

'I know mate, but let's find out what these alien bastards are up to first, shall we?' Peter lit a cigarette, which he shared with Vinnie. Peter blew smoke rings, which he knew would amuse Vinnie, and cheer him up a bit. In the distance, Peter thought he could see a moving star, possibly an alien fighter, on patrol as he puffed out smoke rings. The woman – she seemed familiar, was it the woman who rescued them?

'Let's get going.' They clambered back into the Humvee, Peter driving this time. Peter let Vinnie sleep past the two-hour wake-up call. As he drove, he could see the light increasing, rising in the east over the mountains. Vinnie jolted awake, rubbed his eyes, and looked around.

'Why didn't you wake me?'

'Don't need much sleep,' Pete replied, which was true, he could go for days sometimes without any sleep, reinforcing his reputation as Bulletproof. He parked the Humvee, behind some bushes, doing his best to conceal it amongst the sparse brush in the desert.

'Let's get a brew on,' smiled Peter.

Peter's smile encouraged Vinnie, as he dug out his camping stove boiled some water and added some boil-in-the-bag sausage, egg, and beans to the water. Vinnie would normally do it, but he wanted to cut him some slack. They sat with their backs against a rock, supping their tea, and eating their boil-in-the-bag rations.

'Meal fit for a king,' Peter smiled.

'Fit for a king,' Vinnie replied.

As they sat there, the sun rose from the east, rising majestically over the mountains, bathing the desert in a golden light. Everything was quiet and peaceful; the chaos of the last few days seemed a million miles away as they hungrily ate their breakfast. A coyote strolled past, licking its lips as he saw their food; Vinnie shooed him off.

They sat there for a while absorbing the soft warmth of the sun on their faces after the cold desert night air. The peace and quiet of the desert reminded him of Yemen somehow. A small bird hopped along and looked at Peter; he smiled as he threw it a few breadcrumbs. This was good, thought Peter, one of those special moments, savouring the peace before the storm hits.

'Vinnie.'

'Yes, mate.'

'In a strange kind of way this war is a good thing. War brings people together. It brings out the best and worst in people. And it doesn't matter if you're a tramp or a billionaire, black or white, Muslim or Christian, the alien bastards are a common enemy. Maybe some good will come out of this.' Vinnie nodded as he enjoyed his breakfast.

'Vinnie.'

'Yes, mate,' replied Vinnie slurping his tea.

'Did you know my father was in the service?' said Peter drinking his tea and dunking a biscuit.

'Yep. You told me.'

'But I never found out how he died, it was all hush-hush. Until now.'

'What do you mean?'

'You know the meeting I had with Sir Nigel?'

'Yep.'

'Sir Nigel used to be his commanding officer.'

'Get the fuck outa here!' said Vinnie, nearly spilling his tea.

'Frank was a sniper in A Squadron. A good one. Took out a war criminal in Bosnia. Then he took a shot in the back himself. That's how he died. Sir Nigel carried him to the exfil.' Vinnie nodded, understanding.

As Peter began to fill in the rest of the story to Vinnie he began to feel a sense of closure, about his father. He was starting to square things away and talking to Vinnie about it made him feel better somehow.

'I think in a way, Sir Nigel feels responsible,' added Peter.

'For your father's death?'

Peter nodded. Then he had an epiphany. When he was young, maybe seven years old, his father used to call him Kay, sometimes Cai, his middle name, telling him about a great hero named Kay, one of King Arthur's knights. He smiled, remembering his father's laugh and animated storytelling. Maybe he knew what he would become one day. Was it in the blood?

They put on factor fifty sun cream and sunglasses as Peter dug out his map and GPS, working out a plan. 'Going for a tom tit,' grunted Vinnie who strolled off behind a rock. Unlike standard SAS mission procedure, on a Black Ops mission, they would not be putting it into a bag and carrying it - everything was different now.

They would need to think outside the box.

Chapter 5

ROUTE 66

'We make our way down Route 66 to the edge of Los Angeles. If we get spotted and it goes noisy, we ditch the Humvee and go firm. Our objective is to remain hidden for as long as possible, do surveillance on their ship movements, try and get inside one of their ships, and find out what we can. We send a daily sitrep at 4 pm, switching radio channels every day. If we don't report at 4 pm they will not rescue us, were on our own.'

'High risk, little chance of success, bring it on,' said Vinnie peering at the sky. Peter was quiet and edgy. They had pushed the bounds of probability by not being spotted yet; his muscles tensed and his jaw tightened.

Pre-battle mode.

'Ice cold in Alex,' said Peter.

'Ice cold in Alex,' replied Vinnie.

They set off again in the stifling heat of the desert, but after four hours driving they were nearer to the outskirts of Los Angeles, and they became more nervous. Vinnie slowed down as Peter scanned the blue skies above with his Sirius binoculars, which can see five miles in any direction. Peter's senses kicked in as adrenaline pumped through his body. His heart was beating faster as he heard a noise behind him. He jerked around and sees a black fighter hovering a hundred yards behind them.

'Fuck! Floor it Vinnie—floor it!'

Vinnie put his foot hard down as the 6.2-litre V8 engine kicked in, smoke squealing the tyres. They were on the edge of Los Angeles now, and they raced past buildings. Pete checked his PR7 rifle and wound down the window. Peter knew when the fighter craft would fire.

'Watch that pothole!' cried Peter.

'What pothole?'

The Humvee launched in the air as it hit a huge pothole, and they hit their heads on the ceiling.

'That one!' replied Peter.

The Adaptiv button flashed red and started beeping.

'Shit!' said Peter, then 'Hang left Vinnie!'

Vinnie wrenched the steering wheel left as the fighter fired, hitting the road where they were one second ago. They went down a road by an industrial park; the fighter turned and followed them, and then fired again. It missed them by inches—the laser blast destroying some parked cars, which flew into the air, landing in front of the Humvee. Vinnie narrowly dodged a flaming car but clipped it, and the Humvee swerved, as he tried to regain control.

'Fuck it!' cried Vinnie as he fought the steering wheel.

'I got a plan—max it Vinnie, max it!' shouted Peter.

As Vinnie floored the accelerator, he could see a dead-end looming three hundred yards ahead.

'When I say NOW slam the brakes on!' shouted Peter. Two fifty, two hundred, one fifty. Vinnie glanced at Peter, panic in his eyes.

One hundred yards.

Eighty.

'NOW!' cried Peter.

Vinnie slammed the brakes on, the Humvee screeching to a halt, Peter felt the g-force of the seat belt on his chest, like an F1 driver braking at a corner, or like being the passenger in an F22. The Humvee left great, black tire marks behind it as its tires screeched. As it slowed, in the space of one second, he unclipped his seatbelt, grabbed his PR7 rifle, loaded a grenade into the launcher, and jumped out as the alien fighter flew past a few feet above their heads.

He got on one knee, balanced the stock on his shoulder, took an intake of breath, calmly got the cross wires of the fighter in his sights, and fired. There was an enormous explosion, as a split second later the grenade hit the fighter's shields, flames shooting everywhere. Peter fired another, then it went out of control and smashed into a nearby warehouse, demolishing half of it, debris flying everywhere.

Peter was blown back by the blast but got up unhurt. It blew the Humvee back several feet and cracked the front windscreen. Vinnie looked at him. That blast should have killed him.

He really is bulletproof.

Chapter 6

SMELLY ALIENS

They strolled over to the downed fighter, Vinnie had his PR7 rifle ready, safety off. Peter drew out his PR1 hand pistol, ensuring he had one in the barrel, as they crept near the smoking fighter. They jumped as a cat ran out from behind some debris, then crept closer. Life seemed to pass in slow motion as an alien ran out, laser pistol in his pale green hand, his personal shield activated, shimmering, like water.

The alien smiled, showing his razor-sharp teeth.

Just as the alien was about to fire Peter fired off three rounds from his PR1 sidearm, hitting the alien's shield with tremendous force, knocking him to the ground. A split second later, Peter was on him and punched his lights out, his shield having no effect. The alien stopped moving.

'Wipe that smile off your face you alien bastard!' said Peter looking at his PR1. He nodded, 'nice handgun,' he thought. 'Shame we don't have enough of them—I will blame that on the accountants.' He turned around and Vinnie nodded in approval. He stood over the dead alien. It looked the same as the one in Buck House: black eyes, green skin, sharp teeth—then a smell hit him.

'They don't use Lynx Vinnie—they stink!'

They stood outside the smoking, ugly, black fighter aircraft, waiting for more aliens, but there were none. Whoever had designed the alien fighter had had a bad day at the office, Peter thought, as he peered inside. He knew the risk from radiation from previous "close encounters" so Peter nodded to Vinnie.

'Get the suits from the HV.' In a moment, Vinnie was back with the biological and radiation suits they had picked up from the base before they left, and the two men put them on. Vinnie stood guard while Peter walked one step at a time inside the craft, looking out for any nasty surprises, and chatting to Vinnie on his comms link. 'This ship seems different from the other one, Vinnie,' Peter said, recalling his close encounter on Salisbury Plain. 'Those aliens seemed, well, more friendly and polite. Not like these ugly bastards, going around kidnapping our women, for God knows what purpose,' he thought. Inside were black panels with strange lights. As he walked further, he could see two dead aliens lying on the floor.

'Two dead aliens, probably died on impact.'

Peter took some photos on his Samsung mobile, the camera worked, the problem was charging it, but he had a portable charger with him. There was no electric power anywhere, except back at the Sirius base, as the invaders had destroyed the infrastructure, no electricity, no water, no nothing. 'People don't appreciate how lucky they are,' Peter thought, 'people take so much for granted. Take away people's electricity, water and Wi-Fi, and there's chaos.'

The suit had a mini-Geiger counter built in, but it showed very low levels of ionising radiation.

In the cockpit area where the two pilots were, there were large smoking panels. Peter took more photos; as he did so, he noticed some devices on the floor. He picked them up and put them in his bag—maybe the guys back at Sirius could find out what they mean. But as he put the devices in his bag, he noticed something. He walked back outside the craft, which was starting to smoke—billows of black smoke, and then flames billowing from it.

'Back to the HV, hurry!' said Peter. They ran back to the Humvee; Peter took off his BioRad suit and looked at Vinnie.

'Vinnie, have a look at this mate.' Peter pulled out one of the devices. On the panel was a picture of a plane, a jet fighter. Above this was a series of numbers and strange shapes.

'Looks like a fighter Pete, one of the Yank fighters,' Vinnie studied it.

'An F22, if I'm not mistaken.' Peter had been on enough US airbases during his missions for M16 and the SAS to know his aeroplanes.

'Yep, you're probably right mate.'

'The F22 is amazing, I had a ride in one once, by a US top gun pilot. They called him the "Red Baron." Nice guy.'

'These numbers above it?' Vinnie saw smoke coming from the fighter out of the edge of his eye. 'We'd better get inside.' As they entered the Humvee the fighter exploded.

'Let's get out of here, else ET's mates will be along, to see who blew up their fighter,' Peter suggested. Vinnie drove the Humvee back down the road, looking for a safe haven, Peter keeping an eye out for any more alien patrols.

'Think I prefer ET, much prettier than these ugly bastards,' grunted Vinnie, thinking of Gill.

'How dare they—how dare they!' cried Vinnie. Peter could see that Vinnie was upset. Apart from himself, Vinnie was the hardest, toughest guy he knew, plus a proper East End gangster to boot. But he had a heart of gold, a real diamond geezer. And he loved his wife, he could tell, by the way he talked about her.

'Let's find somewhere to lie up for a bit,' said Peter, trying to sound comforting.

As they got closer to the centre of Los Angeles, near Cypress Park, they could see the massive shape of an alien ship; not the mothership, but still a mile wide, and casting a shadow over the centre of downtown Los Angeles. Ugly, black and foreboding. Functional and evil-looking. Peter was wondering how difficult it would be to get on the ship. Vinnie drove down a side turning and into a deserted garage. There was no one around, not a soul. They drove in; Peter closed the large metal door and locked it.

'We need to have a Chinese Parliament,' said Peter. Vinnie knew the score, even though there were just two of them, all members of an SAS team, regardless of rank, could have an equal say on what happens in any mission. Even though Peter was a captain, he always listened to Vinnie's advice, even though he didn't always want to hear it.

But that's what real friends do.

'I'll get a brew on,' said Vinnie. While Vinnie was busy making the tea, Peter laid out a large folded map of central Los Angeles and its environs, on the bonnet of the Humvee. He switched on a roof light and studied the map. Vinnie brought over two steaming mugs of tea, Yorkshire Tea, and Peter's favourite biscuits.

'Do we go back to base or proceed with the mission?' suggested Peter.

'We do have some useful intel,' replied Vinnie.

'Yes, that's true. But we haven't found out what they're up to yet, have we?'

'No, we haven't, and I would like to kill a few more aliens if that's all right, Bulletproof.'

'Take it as granted. I want to find out their weaknesses—something we can exploit.'

They stood in silence for a moment, knowing what they must do.

Peter looked out the garage door at the sky, it was nearing dusk.

'Shit, we missed our 4 pm sitrep!'

Peter grabbed the secure Sirius comms device, typed in a message about their intel, on channel 14, to the Sirius base, and then pressed send. When he pressed send it would be encrypted and sent into a tiny data burst, lasting for 1 thousandth of a second, thus ensuring it would remain secret—*at least he hoped it would*. He suspected that these bastards already had the F22 codes, what else did they have?

'Do we ditch the Humvee?' asked Vinnie.

'It's getting dark now. We will take it for a few more miles, run dark, then ditch it.'

They reorganised their kit, ready for a quick exit if they needed one. They drove slowly out of the industrial park with lights off, but as they turned a corner, they could see the bright lights of two alien fighters, hovering 400 yards away as if waiting for them. They stopped the Humvee, staring at the lights. Peter's heart pounded, it was too late to reverse, they had been seen.

'Do you think they've seen us?' whispered Vinnie. Peter's sixth sense kicked in as he realised the danger.

'Vinnie, get your kit, and let's get the fuck out!'

They grabbed their Bergen's and stood on the pavement, looking for an escape route. Ahead was blocked by the two fighters, behind them was too open, to the right was a high fence and wasteland. The only way they could go was back the way they had come. They legged it with full Bergen's back to the industrial estate, their hearts pounding, adrenalin coursing through their bodies. As they ran, they heard an explosion, as the Humvee was blown to oblivion.

They felt the heat and force of the explosion on their backs as they ran. They could hear the whining motors of the fighter craft getting closer, no doubt looking for revenge for the ship they downed earlier. Their eyes darted back and forth in the darkness, looking for an escape route. Peter's night vision was excellent, like a cat, as he scanned the area. He was alive, in the moment, senses working at full capacity, adrenaline pumping away. He saw a door slightly ajar in a building fifty yards away. He could hear the fighters approaching fast—they didn't have much time.

'Follow me!' shouted Peter, as he ran for the door with Vinnie close behind him. They charged through the door into darkness, tripped over, and lay flat on the floor, which was just as well, as intense beams of light scanned the doorway. Two seconds later, the fighters moved on. They stayed motionless for two more minutes until it was clear the danger had passed. Vinnie closed the door and shone his torch around the place. It was dirty, with rubbish in a corner, but it was dry. There were some stairs on the right, leading downwards.

'Have a look down there. I will see if we have any bogies on our tail,' Peter ordered, as he stood guard by the door, scanning the area for activity. Vinnie came back up the stairs and gave Peter a thumbs-up. Satisfied they wouldn't be disturbed, Peter locked the door tight as they carried their Bergen's down into a cellar and set up camp for the night. As Vinnie boiled some water, Peter looked through his rations.

'Oy Terminator, how about Lancashire Hotpot followed by Treacle Pudding?'

A big grin came across Vinnie's face. Peter knew that would cheer him up. Besides, he didn't know when they would eat again, so they took the opportunity to fill their stomachs. Peter looked at Vinnie as he stirred their meal on the stove.

'Those numbers on that alien device, the one with the picture of the F22.'

Vinnie nodded. 'I reckon that was an encryption code, I've seen them before, top secret, of course, I've been around enough US airbases and seen enough M16 documents to know what's going on. The F22's have shields Vinnie, developed from alien technology. They captured downed spaceships and adapted the technology. The shields on the F22s should be able to stop any missile, or alien laser blasts. It was some famous professor who developed the technology after many others failed. The code is unbreakable, apparently.' Peter sipped his mug of tea. 'Fractal encryption code, that was it.'

'Unless the aliens have the codes, of course,' said Vinnie, giving a loud belch.

'Yes, unless the aliens have the codes, which would leave our F22's open to attack,' repeated Peter. He thought about their current situation, trying to balance all the risks and opportunities. Ideally he wanted to tab through the night, under cover of darkness, until they reached central Los Angeles, but Vinnie was exhausted, and Peter had taken only two hours of sleep the previous night; despite having the stamina and constitution of a rhinoceros, even he was tired.

'Let's get a good night's kip Vinnie, we'll be better for it.'

Chapter 7

BLEAK HOUSE

In the morning, they awoke refreshed and ready for action. They looked at the map again, then packed their gear, and looked outside. It was a bright and sunny day in Los Angeles with a cloudless blue sky, 'Why doesn't everyone live in Los Angeles?' Peter thought. They could see a dirty, bearded, tramp walking past with a shopping trolley full of carrier bags. He looked at them with absent eyes, drank from a bottle, then went on his way.

They made their way out of the industrial estate and took the road into central Los Angeles, peering all around them, maintaining a 360 view. It was five miles to the centre, their target location. They stood rooted to the spot as they saw the alien spaceship. It cast a shadow over the heart of Los Angeles, a mile wide, and ugly, black and foreboding. Like it didn't belong—which it didn't, of course.

Peter remembered his childhood in Merthyr Tydfil. There was an old house just outside of town—derelict, dark and foreboding like the Welsh weather in the wintertime. Bleak House, it was called, nobody had lived in it for years, the last occupant being an old woman, always dressed in black. Rumour had it she was a witch.

Nobody would go near it, especially the kids as they thought it was haunted. Peter used to walk past it on his way to school, he looked at it out of the corner of his eye, into the dark windows, imagining what horrors lay beyond. Peter and his schoolmates used to dare each other to stay in the haunted house on the hill for one whole night. As luck would have it, his new friend Vinnie, from London, came to stay for a few days. He told him about the haunted house, and he was up for it. So one Halloween Peter, Vinnie, and two of Peter's friends decided to stay in Bleak House for one whole night, telling their parents they would be staying with friends. First to leave was chicken and had to buy sweets for all of them for a month.

On Halloween night, dressed in their scary Halloween costumes, Peter, Vinnie, Jimmy, and Ray walked up to the gate. They pushed the heavy gates, which creaked and moaned, as they all gripped the iron bars, which felt as cold as ice, sticking to their hands. They walked up to the uneven and overgrown stone path, up to the dark and forbidding house, shadows dancing here and there. An old crow stared at them with beady eyes from the branch of an old withered tree. The air was cold and numbing, and when Peter exhaled, his breath was misty, and he felt the chill air in his lungs. As they drew nearer to the house, everything around Peter became quieter and more distant, and a cool shudder trickled down his spine. Ray said, 'Let's turn back—I'm scared,' but nobody made fun of him.

Eyes wide with trepidation, they pushed the old wooden front door open, and they walked into the hallway, the wooden floorboards creaking as they did so. They stopped every time the boards creaked, looking at one another. In the hallway was a painting of a thin, creepy old woman in a black dress, 'The former owner,' thought Peter. Her dark beady eyes seem to stare at him from behind layers of dust, penetrating his soul. He opened the door into the living room, and they crept across the bare wooden floorboards, which creaked and groaned, the dust getting into their nostrils and making them sneeze. As they walked into the room, there was an instant chill, as it suddenly became colder. They stopped and glanced around, knots of fear in their stomachs. Light streamed in through a cracked window from the full moon, casting eerie shadows on the walls. They could hear the sound of a cuckoo.

There wasn't much furniture, just one frail old wooden rocking chair, and of course, no electricity. They had some food, beer and sleeping bags, which they laid out on the floor—they were going to make a party of it.

'There be no ghost here,' said Ray.

'We've only just got here Ray,' said Peter.

'No such thing as ghosts,' blustered Jimmy.

Peter knew that was wrong because his mother told him she had once lived in a haunted house, and that ghosts were a normal occurrence. Every day there was a supernatural phenomenon, like plates moving on their own, or sudden chills, his mother thinking it was normal, which of course it wasn't. He thought his mother was psychic, she sometimes told him things about the future that came to pass.

Were his powers hereditary?

Did he carry the demons of his mother and father?

Peter was beginning to regret having entered the house on the one night in the year, when—his mother told him—the veil between this world and the next was thinnest.

Halloween.

He looked at Vinnie, who was grinning away, then his smile vanished, and his face went pale—quite white, in fact.

'Vinnie…what is it?' Vinnie was looking out the living room door, to the hallway. He was looking at the picture of the old woman. He pointed, his finger shaking, but couldn't speak. Peter looked at the picture, trying to figure out what was wrong. Head, face, neck, body.

The eyes. They seemed to have a particular intensity about them, as if staring, as if alive. Dark and piercing, those eyes. Peter kept looking, but nothing, then his heart skipped a beat as the eyes seemed to move, staring at him as if to say, "What are you doing in my house?"

Peter had never been so scared in his life. He couldn't speak; he and Vinnie just stared. His heart started pounding, then Jimmy and Ray also looked, laughing and joking, but froze. Peter was no longer looking at the picture of the old woman, which seemed to be alive, but at the old wooden rocking chair.

Had it moved? It could not be.

The atmosphere in the room seemed to get colder, and Peter's breath was like smoke as it came out of his mouth. He nudged Vinnie to look at the chair. They all looked in silence at the chair, which ever so slowly started to gently rock, back and forth, back and forth, all of its own accord. They all screamed at once, jumped up and ran out of the house, leaving their sleeping bags, and running past the picture of the old woman, who now seemed to be smiling an evil smile. As they ran out of the house, the front door slammed behind them of its own accord. They ran non-stop all the way back to Peter's house, out of breath, bursting out their story to Peter's mother, who scolded them, but gave them some food, then lectured them about never going back there.

As Peter and Vinnie made their way, down side streets, and alleyways, on their way to the centre, trying to stay hidden from patrol craft, they looked again at the massive ship, seeming even more ugly, black and foreboding. If it was possible for an inanimate object to look foreboding, and evil, it did.

'Bleak House,' said Peter.

'Yeah, Bleak House,' replied Vinnie.

Chapter 8

REMEMBER THE HOLOCAUST

Up until now, they had hardly seen anyone, but now, as they got closer to the centre, they started seeing refugees making their way out of the city, any way they could, carrying whatever worldly possessions they had managed to grab in their haste. It was not long before larger, alien craft landed; Peter and Vinnie watched as Narzuk SS, and others in grey uniforms come streaming out of the ships and start rounding up the terror-stricken refugees.

They began splitting up families, the women and mothers being separated from their husbands and children, there were scenes of panic as mothers were torn from their crying children. Peter and Vinnie watched in desperation from their hiding place, as a pretty, young, white mother was separated from her daughter, the father holding his daughter tightly, trying to fend off two tough-looking Narzuk Stormtroopers, who were trying to take him. They knocked him unconscious, and dragged him away, leaving the daughter alone and crying. African-American men and women and several Jews wearing kippahs were separated into another group, as well as disabled people.

The three groups were taken onto separate ships. Tears were shed as families looked at one another, not knowing when they would see one another again. The children were left in a group to fend for themselves; crying and sobbing, looking frantically for their parents. Cold-looking Narzuks were rounding them up.

Lord Grim-Uk stood with his brother Himm-Uk by a black transporter ship, watching the tragic scene in front of them. 'Brother, how is the harvesting proceeding?'

'We have 1,000 human women in this batch brother,' replied Himm-Uk enthusiastically.

'Take them for processing. We need more to achieve our target. Place some scanning machines here on the ground, it will be quicker,' ordered Grim-Uk.

'Yes, brother.'

Lord Grim-Uk smiled as he surveyed the latest batch. He popped a pill into his mouth, and red veins appeared in his eyes as he toyed with a carved figure around his neck depicting a god, black and grotesque—he would pray to his patron this night that all goes well.

'How's your history, Vinnie?' tears were in Peter's eyes, trying hard not to look at Vinnie.

'Pretty good mate, I watch the History Channel.'

'I cannot believe what I'm seeing. Remember the holocaust?'

'Yeah, it's like the holocaust all over again,' it was Vinnie's turn as his eyes watered, looking straight ahead.

'It's the same ones with the red armbands,' said Vinnie. Peter remembered the creepy-looking alien officer with red-veined eyes that he had seen in New York. His sharp eyes thought he recognised him in the distance, standing near the ships. He must be their leader.

'We've got to stop these bastards,' Peter seemed to grow in stature, his Caius alter-ego, showing itself.

As the ships took off, they went in three different directions. Peter remembered the Nazi atrocities, the dark history of the Second World War. The Jews were taken on trains to Auschwitz, from Poland, France and all over Europe, never to be seen again.

Exterminated.

The men who weren't Jews were put in slave labour camps to help the German war effort, and the children, they suffered, because they had no mother or father. Many Jewish children were lucky and hidden away by the French Resistance in orphanages. Some even escaped to Switzerland.

But these women, what did the aliens want them for?

'We've got to stop them!' said Peter again.

Vinnie was thinking about Gill, and where she was now—in some alien camp somewhere, or on a ship? 'We will stop these bastards, by hook or by crook, or my name's, not Vinnie the Terminator.'

'We will find a way, Vinnie, for my name is Caius,' Peter said.

'You're Bulletproof Pete,' replied Vinnie.

'I am also Caius, the ancient warrior.' Vinnie hoped he wasn't having a schizo moment, what with all the stress they had been under.

As they looked, a little girl was standing there crying, holding her teddy bear, her blond curly hair blowing in the breeze. She ran around in desperation, searching for her parents. Tears flowed from her eyes as she searched in vain.

Chapter 9

SHIRLEY

'We can't leave her Pete!'

'No, we cannot!' his warrior blood rising. The little girl reminded Peter of his young daughter, and his thoughts immediately went back to his family home in Wales.

Were they safe?

Were they still there?

All of these thoughts ran through his mind as he looked at the little girl. There were still some Narzuks hanging around, including one creepy-looking alien in a black uniform. Fit looking. Peter was looking at the girl, and for the first time his heart skipped a beat, as he saw what looked like a Swastika symbol, but in a circle, on a red armband.

She was in danger.

He was in warrior mode now, as he watched the creepy Narzuk SS officer walk up to the little girl, and touch her with his hand, the pale green skin peeling a little. The girl screamed louder, as the alien turned off his force-field, then went to grab her, in one swift moment Peter aimed his PR7 rifle, set it to full-auto, and from a hundred yards, shot the creepy alien, blowing his head clean off its shoulders, the head bouncing on the ground.

'Vinnie, cover me!' he ordered. Peter ran at tremendous speed and agility at the young girl, while Vinnie calmly unleashed hell on the other unsuspecting aliens. Three Narzuks were blown to smithereens as he fired a grenade, two others were blown in half by the brutal power of his PR7 rifle. The rest of the aliens scattered, as Peter picked up the girl, and ran back to Vinnie in their hiding spot within the ruins. Vinnie packed their gear in a hurry.

'This wasn't part of our mission!'

'No, it wasn't!' Peter replied, but he decided to let fate take its course. Their mission was now compromised, and now they had extra baggage, 'Que sera sera,' thought Peter, 'whatever will be, will be. Such is fate.'

'You could have taken them sooner, with your speed and agility, you could have attacked earlier; you're too cautious,' said Vinnie.

'Maybe you're right,' said Peter.

'Maybe it's time to become your alter-ego, this Caius matey, whatever his name is,' Vinnie gently suggested. Peter nodded, the Caius alter-ego was becoming more dominant in his personality—the visions, the dreams, his demeanour. Maybe it was time to fulfil his destiny. He remembered the sword, the magical holy sword, of the Archangel Michael, "only call it at times of great need" said the priest, reading from the Book of Borossus. He supposed he would know when the time was right—when there was no other choice, but what were the risks? Would he control the sword, or would the sword control him?

Peter and Vinnie looked around, looking for an escape route. They had already alerted the alien forces by Peter's attack, so they didn't have much time. The little girl started crying again.

'What's your name, little girl,' asked Peter gently, as he dug around his pocket looking for a Mars bar.

'Shirley, what's yours?

'I'm Peter, and this is my best friend, Vinnie.' Vinnie made a funny face, and she started laughing. Peter gave her the Mars bar, and she smiled at him. She looked sad again.

'They're bad aliens aren't they?'

'Yes, Shirley they are bad aliens.'

'They took my mummy and daddy!' Shirley cried.

'Me and my friend Vinnie are going to sort them out, okay?' Peter said as he hugged her, the humanity in his soul rising to the surface, a tear in his eye.

But could he save the whole world?

Vinnie looked up and saw two alien fighter craft converging on their position.

'Bogies, two o'clock!' Peter looked at them, and something changed inside of him, he became resolved.

'I'm fed up with running Vinnie, let's kill some aliens!' he said, as he put Shirley down.

'Rock on.'

'I will take one o'clock, you take two o'clock. Hurry, they're locking their weapons.' Peter could see the laser cannons from the fighters glowing orange, charging—ready to fire. In the space of two seconds, they had retrieved grenades and loaded them into their PR7 grenade launcher and taken aim. By the third second, they had both fired, and the shells exploded against the alien shields in a blaze of flame and noise, knocking them off course, both now heading for earth.

'Fireworks!' shouted Shirley in joy, jumping up and down. The fighters were heading straight for them, doomed to crash. Shirley stopped jumping and stood there frozen, eyes wide with terror as the fighters converged on them. The adrenaline pumped through Peter's veins as he searched for an escape route, looking left and right. He carried Shirley as they sprinted from their hiding place - the remains of a multi-story car park, broken concrete, and steel rods all around them.

As they ran out of the car park, the two alien ships crash-landed nearby, in a blaze of flames and flying debris. Before them was a large square, and nearby was Rio de Los Angeles State Park, where the larger alien ships had landed. It was a Latino neighbourhood, but they couldn't see many people now, maybe they were all hiding.

They decided to head for the park, for the ships that were there had already left for their destination. When they got there, it didn't offer much cover, it was mainly low-lying bushes, but it gave them a chance to rest up and decide what to do. They had the extra baggage too—Shirley—though if truth be known, Peter liked her, she reminded him of his daughter.

As they sat there, catching their breath, a group of Buddhist monks with orange robes walked past, a look of calm serenity on their faces, as if they were on a Sunday picnic. They stopped when they saw Peter and Vinnie and bowed. Peter stood up and bowed—it seemed the right thing to do.

'Hello,' said Peter, to an old bald, monk who had a look of calmness and peace on his face, an island in a sea of chaos. 'I could learn from him,' thought Peter. The old monk looked at him, and smiled, but said nothing, still studying Peter.

'Where are you heading to?' asked Peter. One of the younger monks replied.

'We are heading for a monastery in Hacienda Heights.'

'Won't you get caught?' asked Peter.

'No, the aliens do not touch us, they leave us alone.'

'Why?' asked Peter curious as to the reason. The wise old monk who had been studying Peter spoke for the first time.

'They are afraid of us because we are men of God. From what I can perceive, God has turned his back on them. I can see the darkness in their souls. I have seen them commit many atrocities, worse than the Japanese during the Second World War. They are most ungodlike.' He looked Peter in the eyes.

'My name is Rinpit - I am from Tibet.' He smiled as he shook Peter's hand, a look of understanding came across his face, which Peter shared. Here was a wise old man. In a way he reminded him of the priest in his visions, not the physical features, but the sense of calmness. Rinpit also reminded Peter of the Dalai Lama; a pure reflection of calm, love, peace and kindness. Time seemed to stop, and all around him seemed obscured.

'My name is Peter,' he said as he held the old monk's hand. The monk nodded, then became more urgent. Peter felt like he was in a confessional.

'Peter, I can see into your soul, my friend. You are on an urgent mission.'

Peter nodded. The monk became earnest.

'You have been chosen to undertake a difficult task. You are the one, the one to save humanity from destruction. But you are unsure of yourself.' Peter nodded.

'You must fulfil your destiny. Everyone is counting on you.' Peter looked at Vinnie, who nodded.

'I know…' Peter hesitated. 'I know I must become Caius, this Eternal Warrior.' Peter felt a great weight of responsibility fall on his shoulders, and he wasn't sure if he could do it, as he hung his head.

'You can do it,' Rinpit insisted, Vinnie and the monks nodded and bowed to him. This was the moment: he must commit, Peter thought. They all stood there for a while until Rinpit spoke again.

'We must go…the aliens will be coming soon.'

'What about the girl?' asked Peter.

'She can come with us, we will give her sanctuary.' Rinpit held Shirley's hand, and she smiled as he gave her a sweet from his pocket.

'If you don't mind we will tag along for a bit, then split off,' replied Peter. Rinpit nodded. They made a strange sight, a line of monks in orange robes, a little girl, and two fearsome, filthy-looking soldiers walking out of the park and back onto the streets of Los Angeles. As they walked down a side street, there was a group of Narzuks standing around, molesting a woman, who turned when they saw the group. They switched on their personal shields, made as if to go towards them, then backed off when they saw the monks, a look of concern on their faces.

Peter ran at lightning speed towards the three aliens, a look of utter determination on his features, in Caius mode, dodging the alien laser blasts, then he was upon them, retrieving his titanium knife and slicing through their shields with brute strength and then butchering them. He wiped the green blood on his jacket and helped the woman up. 'Come with me,' Peter half carried her back towards the group.

'One more for you,' Peter said to Rinpit. The monk smiled and nodded. When they got to the end of the street, Rinpit stopped and turned to Peter.

'We go this way. Goodbye my friend and remember your destiny.' Peter and Vinnie watched as they walked away. Shirley turned around, then came running up to Peter, and he kneeled as she gave him a big hug. He kissed her on the head, then smiled at her. She smiled back.

'Don't I get one?' asked Vinnie, Shirley gave Vinnie a big kiss, then she ran back to Rinpit.

'At least Shirley will be safe…what about my Gill?' Vinnie hung his head. And Jennifer thought Pete.

Chapter 10

INTO THE MAELSTROM

Vinnie rubbed his chin, with three days stubble.
'You look like shit,' Peter said looking at Vinnie.
'So do you mate.'
They both laughed, for they knew what lay ahead.
They clasped hands, laughing in the face of death.
'Strength and honour.'

As they looked up, they saw, almost overhead now, the monstrous shadow of the black, ugly spaceship, over a mile above them, with its deep grinding vibration, as it slowly rotated around downtown Los Angeles. As they looked at it, a section of it appeared to be moving, then broke apart from the main part of the ship and fell to earth. They opened their mouths as the spaceship debris fell, now growing larger, it had to be a hundred feet wide. Peter tried to judge where it would fall; he only had a few seconds to make the calculation.

It would fall into the park.

They watched as the huge section of spaceship fell into the park with an almighty crash, sending a shockwave through the ground, like an earthquake, as the concrete underneath their feet rippled and cracked, bits of the spaceship flying up into the air, some landing in the street fifty yards from them.

Vinnie laughed, 'Don't fink they build their spaceships very well.' Peter thought 'He's right, another weakness. Poorly built ships, perhaps built in a hurry.'

An indication of desperation.

And they are afraid of monks, perhaps priests as well. Another weak point. Peter thought there was more to do before they could complete their mission, but he was beginning to get the measure of these alien invaders.

'I want to kill some fucking aliens!' said Vinnie. That was it, thought Peter, time for some payback. He smiled as they loaded fresh magazines into their PR7 rifles and PR1 pistols, making sure the grenades were within easy reach in the webbing of their rucksacks. Spare magazines for the PR1 they put in a trouser pocket, and two spare PR7 mags in the webbing of their rucksacks. A large swig of water and a Mars bar and they were ready. Peter adjusted his Kevlar body armour, even though he was "Bulletproof Pete," he wasn't going to tempt fate. Peter and Vinnie grinned at one another,

'Let's give them hell,' replied Peter, 'Yes, Caius, let us go forth,' smiled Vinnie.

'Once more into the breach dear friends,' laughed Peter, his deep voice booming.

'You and your poetry!' laughed Vinnie.

'Henry V – Shakespeare!' corrected Peter.

They edged closer to the maelstrom of central Los Angeles. Even though it was daytime, they were in semi-shadow because of the grinding, black beast above them. Fighter craft were flying above. In the distance they could see skirmishes between other troops and the aliens. As they got closer, they could see the regular army fighting units getting the worst of it, being forced to retreat. They could see one poor, injured soldier on his own, stranded behind a pile of concrete, trying to hide from the advancing aliens.

Peter and Vinnie were 300 yards away, they could hardly bear to watch as four white alien robots, armed with laser cannons, created carnage, regular soldiers fleeing for their lives; four were blown to kingdom come as the two friends watched.

It was like watching a Vietnam War video. But worse.

'We must do something,' shouted Peter, above the noise, looking at the lone soldier.

'I will take out the robots, you take out the company of bogies behind them. Peter loaded a grenade into his PR7 grenade launcher and aimed the sights in the middle of the advancing robots. He fired, and a second later there was a huge explosion as the shell hit one of the robots, which fell back, then fell over, incapacitated. Another robot's arm fell off, and it went around in circles, in confusion. But the other two robots turned slowly and gazed in the direction of Peter and Vinnie as if they had been bitten by a mosquito and now wanted to swat it. A few, angry-looking Narzuks, the elite alien fighting units, wearing the swastika symbol Peter had seen earlier, turned in their direction. They directed the large number of blank-looking clones to attack them. There were about 100 clones for every Narzuk.

Chapter 11

WHO DARES WINS

'Now we've stirred up a hornet's nest!' shouted Peter as they hid behind a pile of bricks and rubble. Narzuks and clones alike returned fire with their laser rifles, which ripped into the debris in front of them, sending dust and grit into the air. Peter and Vinnie coughed as the dust entered their lungs and  blew into their eyes. They put on their desert scarves to protect them from their worst, but their eyes watered, and the pounding continued in front of them.

'Let's kill these bastards!' laughed Vinnie, in a shout of joy felt by all warriors in the thick of battle. Peter laughed, as he recalled older memories of the ancient warrior, within him, waiting to get out, Caius, Caius. The joy of battle, the joy of victory.

The smell of blood, the smell of victory.

'Victory or bust - Who Dares Wins!' Peter bellowed.

They now threw caution to the wind, fighter craft patrolled the city, above and around them smoke rose from destroyed buildings. Peter and Vinnie, were fighting pitched battles with the clone aliens, who greatly outnumbered the black-uniformed Narzuks.

'Those bastards look different: their eyes they look blank, like zombies,' observed Peter, as he took out ten of them with his PR7 rifle.

'Yeah, know what you mean,' replied Vinnie.

They took cover behind a wall.

'Remember when we were kids, shooting rabbits in the hills!' Peter shouted.

'Yeah, it's a rabbit shoot!' replied Vinnie.

'Not like rabbits though. Every time we kill an alien, that's one more bastard alien they can't replace. Got him!' as Peter took out a group of clone aliens with a grenade.

They ran around a corner, only to see a group of Narzuks cutting up a human. They watched as one alien cut open a man's skull and retrieved the brain, then they ate it, taking turns. Then they sliced off his penis and ate it with their razor-sharp teeth, the man's blood spurting everywhere. Peter and Vinnie could not quite believe what they were seeing.

They aimed their PR7 rifles and shot at the aliens, who disintegrated, and a section of a building was also taken out. Peter ran up to the half-eaten man, who was whimpering in agony, begging for death. Peter retrieved his PR1 pistol and finished him off.

'Poor bastard,' panted Peter, as he closed the eyes of the man. 'Rest in peace,' he continued, and crossed himself.

'These aliens make terrorists seem like nice people in comparison,' he thought.

'I hate these fucking aliens, they really pen and ink. I can smell 'em from 'ere,' replied an angry Vinnie.

'Bet they don't use Lynx Vinnie!' Peter replied, laughing as he fired a grenade that took out half a building, four clones and a Narzuk officer. More patrol craft are moving in now and homing in on their position. Peter was aware that the tide was turning against them.

'Cry God for Harry, England, and Saint George!' The battle rage ran through Peter as he took out half a dozen aliens, but more alien craft were landing, and more troops were gathering.

Vinnie fired his PR7 rifle and took out another group, their shields failing. Vinnie crossed himself,

'That's for the Queen—God bless her!' Another unfortunate group also get the worst of it. 'That's for my Gill! They're ugly bastards, these aliens; got a boat race like a cow's arse.'

'Wouldn't win a beauty contest, would they Vinnie?' Peter replied.

Vinnie fired at a fighter, hitting its shield and pushing it off course so that it crashed into an already-demolished building. Aware of the alien troops gathering around them, Peter and Vinnie examined the fighter craft, not bothering with radiation suits, as there wasn't time. They found two injured aliens inside but were looking for anything they could use, anything that would tell them anything about these alien interlopers. Peter took photos and picked up what looked like a communication device from one of the aliens. There were strange characters on it, like an early form of Arabic. He was fluent in Arabic and had studied ancient Arabic as part of his degree course, but this was different—like hieroglyphics—more like ancient cuneiform. Symbolic. But this was an alien spacecraft, so how come the language was even remotely familiar? There were many questions to be answered as he stowed it in his Bergen.

They ran out of the craft and saw alien troops advancing, as well as some Narzuks in black uniforms, and many more grey-uniformed clones, closing in for the kill.

Were they pushing their luck too far? They had been lucky so far, but a storm was gathering around them. They hid behind a wall, and took a swig of water, breathing heavily. 'Too exposed,' thought Peter, but there was nowhere else to run. He looked at Vinnie, who smiled back.

Peter recalled the SAS motto, "Who Dares Wins."

'Who Dares Wins!' shouted Peter recalling all the battles and all the conflicts he and Vinnie had been in, which all flashed before him in a few seconds. Was this how it was going to end?

A massive laser blast from two robots blew them and their fragile protective wall into the air. Peter felt like the world was moving in slow motion as he and Vinnie flew through the air, arms flailing, then he hit the ground with a thud; he was winded. He coughed as he lay there: live or die, that was the choice.

Live or die. Options, options.

Vinnie was unconscious but looked alive; blood on his forehead. Peter could hear the guttural alien shouts of the Narzuk troops, SS Stormtroopers, and others, as they advanced towards them—maybe to take them and torture them in some godforsaken torture chamber on one of their ships. Then something happened inside him: something stirred, the soul of the Eternal Warrior.

'I will not die today, no thanks, not today, for I am Caius, the Eternal Warrior, and I will succeed, I will win the day,' his voice boomed. Peter stood up, filthy and bleeding from various cuts. He looked for his PR7 rifle, frantically searching, but the solid titanium weapon lay crushed under a large piece of concrete: it was fucked. All he had was his PR1 handgun—not much good against the advancing robots.

Double fuck it.

Chapter 12

SUMMON THE HOLY SWORD

His mind raced for a solution, as he recalled the Angel in the desert, and his words. The aliens edged closer, sure of their prize, the Narzuk SS officer, his thin face wearing a tiny smile, thinking about what he would do with his prisoners. He egged on the grey-eyed clone troops to follow.

Peter's mind entered an altered state: he knew instinctively how to do this, for he was Caius, the Eternal Warrior, come to defeat the alien menace, for that was his purpose, his mission, in this incarnation.

He cleared his mind, picked up some dirt and rubbed it into his hands, earthing and balancing himself before he spoke the invocation.

His mind wandered, contacting the dimension beyond time. Time itself seemed to stop, the robots and aliens in front of him, frozen in the moment. He had a vision of a large silver sword, with a golden pommel and jewels—amethysts—embedded into the pommel.

'Caliburnus!'

'Caliburnus!'

'Caliburnus!'

Three times he said the words, as he closed his eyes, his mind focusing on the sword, and when he opened them, he was holding it in his hand. It felt heavy, powerful, and it vibrated with enormous power, as it gave off a blue light—all around him was a blue light. It was one of the seven holy swords of Prince Michael, Lord of Angels. For indeed it was an object of immeasurable power, which could only be wielded by one such as Caius.

'The sword will give you power, strength, and the will to succeed and conquer your enemies,' he remembered the Michael's words.

As Peter admired the blade, it vibrated in his hand, the power running through his body; he felt invigorated. And yet he was not alone, for there was another entity standing beside him, a figure in blue and purple robes, he had a smile so beautiful, and he radiated such raw power, such infinite love, that Peter knelt before him, in silence. He now had a sense of the power and majesty of God. His will was being done through him.

As the being laid his hands upon Peter's head, he felt a rush of power to his body, he now felt at peace with the world, as the energy surged through him. Michaels' eyes flashed a fierce blue, and then he witnessed an emotion: infinite power, limitless and unstoppable, and when he looked up again, the entity was gone. He now stood, his eyes shining blue, and as he raised his sword the atmosphere changed. Dark clouds gathered as the sword shone like the sun and lightning sprang from it. Thunder rolled in the distance as the aliens stood back frightened, a strong wind blew as he raised the glowing sword.

Vinnie was stirring as he stared at Peter with his sword, surrounded by blue light.

'Caius,' whispered Vinnie weakly. He looked at Peter and was shocked by the change in appearance, as if he had aged, and grown larger and stronger, more malevolent—then he fell unconscious again.

Now Caius was back in the current dimension, back in Earth time, and the aliens were advancing towards him, menace etched on their faces. The evil-looking Narzuks, a mixture of SS and others, looked at him, egging on the numerically-superior clone troops first. They looked at him holding his sword, why would these humans use such primitive weapons? The grey-eyed clones held back, afraid.

The two robots advanced, now towering above him, over ten feet tall, they raised their arms to crush him with one blow.

Of its own volition, the sword moved upward at lightning speed, then it came down on the robot's arm, slicing it clean off as if it were made of butter. The robot looked at him in shock and surprise - it wasn't programmed for this. Its logic circuits went into overdrive, as it reversed back toward the oncoming aliens, who now looked in awe at the sword, and stopped in their tracks, unsure of what to do.

In a split second, Peter had swung the sword around again and plunged it into the other robot, sparks flying everywhere, as the sword shredded the robot's outer metal armour, and pierced the innards, until the point came out the other side. Then it collapsed with an electronic grunt. There was silence as the Narzuks and clones looked at him in shock and awe. Who was this human who had defeated two of their indestructible robots? They hesitated, but it was too late, for Peter, now Caius the warrior, was running at lightning speed towards them, the sword blazing like a blue sun. Lightning sprang from the sword, incinerating two clones.

The aliens were now frozen in terror, the ones at the back dropping their weapons and fleeing, as Caius advanced. The aliens stood no chance as Caius sliced through them like they were made of matchwood. He showed no mercy, for they showed no mercy to humans, committing diabolical acts in the name of their unholy cause. His sword and body were covered in green blood, and when he had finished, all the aliens lay dead, but then the world started spinning, he felt weak at the knees, and Caius blacked out, falling to the ground. When he came to, the sword had gone, and he had a splitting headache. He was Peter again, and Vinnie was kneeling beside him, offering him water.

'Well done mate. You are Caius. Those aliens are terrified of that sword!' Peter got up slowly, his head still pounding, as if he had just drunk a bottle of whiskey and then passed through a black hole and came out the other side.

'When I wield the sword, I am Caius, Vinnie. That is my secret name, but now I am Peter again. The sword has a very strong will Vinnie, almost a mind of its own. It's difficult for me to control it, that's why I blacked out...I feel weak. Help me up.'

Vinnie helped Peter to his feet, then slapped him on the back, which made his headache worse. They looked around them; there were no aliens, but some fighter craft were approaching in the distance.

'Time to get back to base.' Peter sighed, his heart heavy.

Chapter 13

ESCAPE TO MOJAVE

MOJAVE DESERT

Peter and Vinnie have escaped from the streets of Los Angeles, which are now overrun with alien soldiers and patrol craft. They find an old jeep on the outskirts of the city, which Vinnie hotwires. They hide the vehicle in an abandoned garage until dark and get two hours' kip.

At midnight they leave the relative safety of the garage and drive travelling along the highway in the pitch black; lights off and navigate using night vision goggles. Every hour or so an alien patrol passes along the freeway. They switch off the engine and wait, hoping and praying they are not seen.

Peter is reviewing the last few days' events in his mind.

Have they failed in their mission?

Have they found the 'raison d'etre' for the invasion?

Certainly, the aliens have completed a military victory. Normal weapons are useless against them. The Sirius technology is effective, but the Sirius force is too small, and the weapons are too few to make a difference.

Everything is in a state of chaos.

They are kidnapping women, no doubt, but why? They have retrieved some communication devices, maybe they will give up some answers. There is a Nazi connection—the human general in

Central Park and the supreme race speech, *what the fuck was all that about?* They also seem afraid of Rinpit, the monk, which is odd, *"God had turned his back on them,"* he said.

Why?

They need a strategy against the invaders—before everyone is dead, and the planet is overrun.

After four hours driving through the night, they arrive at their destination: the Mojave Desert. Dawn breaks over the horizon; a beautiful sunrise of golden orange over the mountains. The jeep suddenly splutters, jerks forward and stops. Peter looks at the fuel gauge.

Out of fuel.

He looks at his GPS. They are still thirty miles from base. They get out and stretch their legs. Peter stands in silent awe at the natural beauty and peace of the desert, there is something spiritual about the desert. He remembers Yemen and his transformational experience, as he watches the sunrise in silence, then sits down with his back against a Joshua tree and gets out his map.

'This is the only place in the world where Joshua trees grow. Isn't that amazing Vinnie?' he says, sounding chirpy.

'Do you have any more fun facts, or can we get back to base now?' replies a grumpy and tired Vinnie. Peter looks at the map again and decides to be cheerful, just to wind him up.

'This way. Keep your eyes peeled. Cheer up Vinnie, it's a lovely day for a walk.' Vinnie grunts as they make their way on foot, carrying Bergens with their valuable cargo through the desert scrub. Peter, of course, takes it in his stride, having the constitution of an ox, but Vinnie is miserable.

'I'm not carrying you, Vinnie, this isn't Yemen,' teased Peter.

They have only gone a mile or so when Peter's sixth sense kicks in. He stands rigid. Something is approaching—he can see it in the corner of his eye, a fast-moving black, ugly object, flying low and fast.

'Three o'clock—move!' They look around desperately for cover, where there is none, here, in the open desert. The alien fighter craft seem to be homing in on their position—*the shape gets bigger every second.*

They are sitting ducks.

Then Peter's eagle eyes spot a depression, in the landscape, and runs like a man possessed. His heart pounds, hoping the fighter won't spot them. They run a hundred yards looking this way and that— then they see a natural trench below them and almost fall into it.

Chapter 14

HANDSOME MIKE

They landed in a pile and looked around them as the black object passed overhead. They were surprised to see other soldiers in the trench. They had the glassy faraway stare of soldiers just out of combat. Exhausted and disorientated.

'Who are you?' said Peter.

'I'm Mike—my friends call me Handsome Mike. I'm a Navy Seal,' said a soldier in US Special Forces gear.

Peter and Vinnie looked at each other. Vinnie was grinning this time.

'Ugly bastard if you ask me,' Vinnie grinned wider.

'You're not so pretty yourself,' Handsome Mike replied.

'I'm Peter, this is Vinnie. We've just survived a shit storm in Los Angeles.'

Mike looked them up and down, and immediately recognised them, for what they were, Special Air Service, they had that look about them, absolute confidence, thousand-yard stare, hard as nails, built like Bruce Lee, especially this Peter fellow. He had heard about them— a gentlemen to their friends, and a nightmare for their enemies.

'What are you doing all the way out here?' Mike asked, curious.

'Long story,' replied Peter.

They all smile as Peter sat next to Mike in the trench.

'What happened to your unit?'

'We were ambushed in Orange County. Radios are dead, can't raise them. The last I heard they were somewhere in Santa Monica.' Peter smiled, he liked Handsome Mike.

'Let's get a brew on, things always look better after a cup of tea,' Peter's mood was improving.

'Best idea all morning,' agreed Vinnie.

'Do you have any coffee?' asked Mike.

Vinnie looked hard at him as he retrieved his supply of Yorkshire Tea.

'No, we don't mate.'

As Vinnie boiled some water in a mess tin, Peter retrieved his old, battered metal teapot from his kit. He washed it out and, put some tea bags in, as Vinnie poured in the boiling water, while Peter stirred with a spoon. Handsome Mike watched in fascination at the tea ceremony taking place. They sat around relaxing, sipping their tea—Vinnie slurping his. Peter looks at him.

'Don't slurp your tea.'

'I ain't slurping my tea,' Vinnie was annoyed.

'Vinnie, The Queen won't invite us to Buck House if you keep slurping your tea,' Peter winks at Mike, who smiles.

Peter grins in return, 'Can't take him anywhere.' He thought he should introduce himself properly.

'I'm Captain Peter Morgan.' He would never reveal his regiment, but it didn't seem to matter anymore, 'Special Air Service.'

Vinnie chipped in. 'Also known as "Bulletproof Pete," 'cos he's never been shot and the toughest guy in the regiment. And I'm Vinnie.'

Peter chipped in.

'Also known as "Vinnie the Terminator."

Peter looked at Vinnie as he dunked his biscuits.

'Vinnie likes killing aliens.' Vinnie's face grew red.

'I hate the fucking aliens. I want to kill all of 'em.'

Vinnie retrieved his biscuit from the tea. Mike looked at Vinnie then at Peter.

'They took his wife,' Peter whispered. He could see Vinnie was visibly upset, so he tried to change the subject.

'Mike, was there something about the aliens that seemed familiar? The uniforms, I mean.' Mike looked thoughtful.

'Now you come to mention it, they reminded me of the Nazis those uniforms, kinda creepy.' They all nodded.

Peter's Sirius Comms device started bleeping.

'Drink up lads. Back to base: objective Sirius Bunker.'

'Where is this base, Bulletproof? We were trying to locate it, but our Captain is missing—he knew where it was,' Mike asked.

'Need to know Mike. Safer that way. Follow me. Try and stay in the shadow of those rocks.' Peter thought the fewer people knew the location of the Sirius bases the better. He could imagine these bastard aliens had excellent interrogation techniques which even the SAS may not be able to resist. He looked up and behind him.

'We had better hurry, looks like a sandstorm is coming.'

'I can't see anything,' muttered Handsome Mike.

They left the relative safety of the trench. A few other soldiers followed Behind them in the distance they could see a brown wall of sand moving towards them, like a tsunami. As the wind started to rise, they could hear the sound of an alien patrol craft. Peter shouted.

'Dive for cover!'

He suddenly had a waking dream—a vision. Phobetor, the Greek god of nightmares had a grip on him, and he couldn't move—his limbs frozen—as the alien craft approached.

'Move yer arse!' shouted Vinnie.

But Peter could not move. His fellow soldiers shouted at him as swirls of sand blew around them before the tidal wave of sand hit. He had a vision of a warm Mediterranean sun, walking up a volcano over hard, brittle lava rock, and a blue sky above him. It was hot, and the air was dry. He coughed as he inhaled sulphur, and smoke seeped from cracks in the mountain. There was a woman with him. Those piercing blue eyes – was it the same woman who had rescued them? She touched his arm - a look of fear in her eyes. Fear for him, and what he had to face.

Up ahead there was a dark cave, but he did not want to go in, for his stomach was gripped with fear. He stood there motionless staring at a dark cave—black and forbidding, daring him to enter—he

remembered the feeling he had as a boy when he cowered under the bedsheets wondering what monsters were hiding in the wardrobe. But this was not imaginary - *there was something in that cave.*

And it terrified him to the bone.

Chapter 15

SAND STORM

Vinnie pulls his friend back into the trench. When the alien craft has passed, they make their way through the desert, Peter leading. But the soldiers have trouble keeping up with his rapid pace. As they look around, the sandstorm hits them like a tidal wave, and they cover their faces trying to breathe. They walk at 45 degrees against the wind and sand, putting desert scarves around their faces to keep out the grit from their eyes and mouth. Peter uses his locator device through the fog of dust and sand to find the base. One soldier falls, exhausted. Peter picks him up and helps him back up to his feet. They continue to trudge through the storm, but it is too much for the other soldiers.

'We're out of water!' shouts Handsome Mike above the storm.

'At least we have cover from the bastard invaders thinks Peter, 'they cannot fly in this.'

The sandstorm rages, obliterating their view and stinging their eyes. The storm seems to get worse. They bend double against the wind, trying to make progress. Mike points to a rock, and they shelter behind it, which gives them some cover. They rest up for a bit. Peter and Vinnie hand Mike the last of their water; he nods thankfully as he puts the bottle to his cracked lips.

After about an hour or so the wind stops, the storm passes, and the sky is clear. They struggle to their feet and look around them; the desert has changed. Peter understands how it is so easy to get lost in the desert; everything looks the same, and disorientation occurs through heat, lack of water and food. He thinks about the miraculous Bedouin man who saved them from the desert in Yemen. He needs to save these men: *it is his duty.*

He switches on his Sirius locator device and leads the way once more. One man collapses through heat exhaustion, so Peter carries him on his shoulder. Handsome Mike looks on in amazement at Peter's strength and stamina, considering he is also carrying a fifty-pound Bergen on his back. What he doesn't know is that it carries valuable cargo, valuable intel about the alien menace.

'How much further, Bulletproof?' asks Vinnie looking around at the state of the soldiers.

'Nearly there—one more hour,' says Peter checking his locator device. The sun blazes above them; there is not a cloud in the sky. Vinnie's mouth is as dry as a bone as he helps a soldier who staggers and falls. He has a vision of the Blind Beggar, in London, now that is a watering hole. He imagines downing an ice-cold lager. Vinnie now carries the delirious soldier on his shoulders.

'How much longer Bulletproof?' he asks again.

'Nearly there,' Peter looks back and stops.

'We had seven men when we left the rock—now there's only six.' Vinnie looks behind him. He is right, they have lost a man. 'Fucking careless' he thinks, but it is easy to get disorientated in the desert.

'Sorry Bulletproof,' Vinnie's head is down, he has been walking near the back, but has been pre-occupied with helping another man. He hasn't noticed the injured straggler. Peter shakes his head again. After another half an hour, they reach a large rocky outcrop, standing out from the desert. The party of soldiers leans against it or collapses onto the desert floor, wiping their faces of the sand and dirt.

Peter examines the rock, like an expert burglar trying to crack a safe, then he stops, and slides back a panel. He places his eye against the panel, and a retina scanner scans his face and eye. It beeps, and a green light comes on.

He enters his personal Sirius ID into the locator device, which returns a six-digit code. He enters this scrambled code into the panel, something beeps, and the rock face moves back to reveal a steel door. A friendly female voice sounds.

'Now speak your id code,' say the voice recognition security system kicking in.

'Morgan, Peter. Sirius ID A0777ZA. Confirm.'

'ID confirmed,' comes the friendly reply. The steel door slides open to reveal a cave-like structure. Vinnie shouts, 'Incoming!'

'Hurry, move your arses!' shouts Peter. 'Too much security' he thinks, as they all tumble into the cave, coughing and laughing with relief, as the thick steel door closes behind them. They are met by the base commander Colonel Stan Wight, who shakes Peter's hand. He likes the Colonel, who has an old wisdom about him, in his grizzled features. The Colonel looks at him as if he were looking at a God.

Chapter 16

HOW WAS IT OUT THERE?

'Captain Morgan, we received your coded messages, HQ are very interested in talking with you.'

'Colonel, these men need medical attention!' Peter replied. The colonel shouted some orders, and medical orderlies rushed to help the men.

'Thanks for your help, Pete, we would have died without you.' Handsome Mike shook his hand.

The colonel looked at Peter, were the rumours true— was he really bulletproof? And yet he seemed more concerned about saving these men than personal glory. There was something special about this man, something noble: *something good.*

Maybe there was hope after all.

'I need to speak to HQ. I found some devices on an alien craft,' smiled Peter.

'How was it out there?' asked the Colonel, genuinely interested.

'Like Armageddon Colonel, like the end of the world. We've got to stop these alien bastards.'

The Colonel nodded concerned.

'Son, we haven't heard from any of our Sirius units, you're the first combat soldiers we've seen return from a mission.' They stood in silence for a moment, trying to scrounge an ounce of hope out of the situation.

'I will arrange transport to take you to Sirius HQ,' said the colonel breaking the silence.

'Transport?' Peter asked.

'Yes, an underground train system,' the colonel replied.

'Yes, but Sirius HQ is in Virginia.'

'It runs underground for 2,400 miles.'

'And I thought the Channel Tunnel was a big project,' quipped Peter. They were in the mess, piling their plates full of burgers, eggs, and chips. Peter drinks a pint of water and then orange juice, to rehydrate himself after their ordeal in the desert.

'We will sleep on the train,' grunted Peter taking a bite out of his third burger. 'Your eyes look like piss holes in the snow,' he joked.

'Yeah, I'm cream crackered.' replied Vinnie.

They had a quick shower, stuffed some rations into their Bergens, and replenished their water bottles, before making their way down the corridor, to a lift. A security guard opened the doors and got in with them, pressing the level -3 button, and they went down three levels. An exhausted Peter and Vinnie walked out of the lift, out onto a platform cut out of the rock and soil and climbed aboard a sleek-looking train. It reminded Peter of a Japanese bullet train.

They found two very comfortable recliner seats and took another swig from their water bottles. Vinnie looked at his friend, clinging to a shred of hope.

'What?' asked Peter mouth still dry.

'You're our only hope now Caius, our only hope against these alien bastards. You must promise to help me get my Gill back.'

'Promise mate.' Peter closed his eyes, tired to the bone, the effort of carrying a fellow soldier and fighting the storm over 15 miles of desert had taken it out of him. And he had hardly slept in three days. Even Bulletproof Pete had his limits.

Peter was dreaming. He and Jennifer were walking in the Brecon Hills, hand in hand. It was a beautiful, sunny day. The birds were singing, the flowers were blooming, the grass was a wonderful lush green. He could feel the sun on his face as he looked at her perfect features, her brown hair flowing over her shoulders as from his pocket, Peter produced a ring, got down on one knee and asked Jennifer to marry him. She seemed to emit sunshine as she kissed him, then yelped in delight and put her arms around him, her brown eyes sparkling. It was forever, he decided, as she kissed him again. 'I love you,' she beamed. At that moment she looked like a Greek goddess—Aphrodite, rising from the sea in a scallop shell; the personification of beauty, a demure and gentle smile on her lips. Godlike, shining with an inner light. Peter woke up as the train moved off and recounted his dream. Would he ever see her again? Then he looked at his friend Vinnie, who seemed lost in thought as the train quickly accelerated to its top speed of 500 mph.

'Don't worry mate, we'll get her back. I'm just glad Jennifer's safe in the Brecons. They will never find her there,' he said brashly.

Chapter 17

THE CENTURION

Peter was dreaming. He was going back in time to a former life. He was a young man; he had been promoted to centurion in Julius Caesar's army, and he was responsible for one hundred men. They were good men—battle hardened and disciplined, and most of all loyal: *they would follow him to the death.*

He was in an officer's tent preparing for battle, his hard muscles rippling beneath his tanned skin as he put on his armour and sheathed his short sword. He glanced across at his superior officer, tribune Atticus, who was responsible for a cohort, part of a legion consisting of six centuries. Atticus saluted him.

'Caxus, strength and honour.'

'Strength and honour, Atticus. May the Gods be with us today,' he replied in his deep voice, his blue eyes shining.

'Yes Caxus, may they be with us,' he said as he sipped some wine and offered some to Caxus—who declined. Atticus scratched his balls as he grumbled,

'The sooner we get out of this flea-infested hell hole the better, Caxus. This heat vexes me.' Then Caxus had a brainwave.

'I will let my men cool themselves in the Nile, so they will be ready for battle.'

'Good idea,' replied Atticus as he laid out battle plans on a papyrus, wiping his brow from the heat and dust which blew inside the tent.

'Caxus, we are short of officers, you will lead my cohort the morrow.'

'Six hundred men', thought Caxus. Atticus looked Caxus in the eye, looking for any sign of weakness, or trepidation, but there was none—*his promotion was well deserved.*

'Caxus, our emperor Julius Caesar is horrified that his brother in law, Pompey was murdered by the miserable agents of Ptolemy. Even though they were at war, he loved and respected Pompey and wants revenge. We are combining with the Egyptian forces of Cleopatra to defeat Ptolemy.'

'Cleopatra is the sister and co-regent of Ptolemy?'

'Yes Caxus.' Atticus pointed at a map. 'His forces are based here, just South of Alexandria, ten leagues distant. Our main forces will be led by Julius Caesar; you will travel north by night up the Nile and hide your men in the bulrushes. Then when Ptolemy attacks you will come out of hiding and attack his army from the rear. He will not be expecting this.'

'By your command Atticus,' Caxus saluted his tribune. At that moment Julius Caesar walked in and talked to Atticus—regal, statesman-like and clever. Caxus's heart pounded as their great general talked and banged his fist on the table. 'The legions of Mithridates of Pergamum and Antipater from Judea are delayed by two days: *we must hold out till then!*'

'By your command Caesar,' said Atticus bowing. Then Caesar looked at Caxus, smiled, and walked out abruptly. Atticus was anxious as he looked at Caxus. *They both knew their plan had to succeed or they would all die.*

It was midnight, and Caxus and his cohort of men, fully rested, fed and bathed, walked in silence to the waiting boats. A cavalry soldier dropped a spear, clanging on the wooden deck of the longship. His comrades looked at him sharply; it was rumoured there were enemy spies in the camp. Secrecy was paramount; if the enemy found out their mission it would all be over. They would be defeated. Caxus walked up to the clumsy soldier and kicked him up the arse, making him fall headfirst into the Nile, coughing and spluttering.

Their ship was a wooden galley ship with a single row of 25 oars on each side powered by galley slaves; he wanted his men rested, *not rowing oars.* They got underway and slid silently through the water. He had ordered that no fires be lit, and silence be maintained. There were six galleys, each with a hundred men, who either slept or whispered as they navigated up the Nile. He could not sleep; *he never slept well before a battle* as he walked down the side of the wooden ship, feeling the cool breeze on his face, looking up at the stars as they twinkled in the night sky. All was peace and beauty.

The morrow would be different. Caxus recalled battles in a hot and dusty landscape, spears and shields: running, cries of anguish, cries of conquest, clashes of shields, the smell of blood, then lying in the dust after the battle looking at a blue sky, the vultures circling above. But he survived the last battle. He would not predict the outcome of the forthcoming battle but would let nature take its course: *he left it to the gods to decide.*

He saw his friend Virgil, rough and bearded, sharpening his short sword. 'The sooner we beat this bastard Ptolemy, whatever his name is, we can get back to Rome—and get out of this heat!'

'Virgil, imagine us toasting our victory in the Athena in Rome, and it will be so.' Caxus smiled at his oldest friend and recalled their happy times in the *immundas popina*, drinking and partying with bare-breasted women. Virgil had a faraway look in his eye, as he smiled, burped and farted. Caxus laughed, and slapped Virgil on the back, then walked to the prow where the air was cleaner.

Caxus woke with a start. The sun was rising over the Nile, and his men were stirring. The morning air was still, silent and peaceful. The peace before the storm. He walked over to Virgil, who was already dressed for battle.

'Wake the men, I want them in battle order!' Caxus ordered, then added, 'Hide the boats among the bulrushes on the west bank, then wait for my orders.' He knew surprise was their secret weapon; he walked along the wooden deck, among his men putting a finger to his mouth, warning severe punishment for those who disobeyed. He crouched down and whispered with Virgil, eating some bread and water in the morning sunshine. Six centurions, each responsible for one hundred men, now gathered, as agreed on their commander's boat. Caxus stood and looked at each one in turn, gauging them. They did not flinch. They were all good, battle-hardened soldiers, veterans of several campaigns, and bore the scars to prove it.

'We have traveled past Ptolemy's army,' said Caxus.

'How far?' said one centurion.

'We are now at their rear. They are one league distant.' Caxus pointed, then added, 'to the South.'

'We must wait until Caesar engages them in a full-frontal assault. Meantime we creep up from the rear in a pincer movement; then we attack. We must put fear into their hearts, then we will win.'

Virgil and the centurions nodded and saluted their commander. 'We MUST maintain the element of surprise, else we are meat for the vultures. Virgil…' At that moment a soldier from Gaul who had been caught drinking wine the previous evening, dropped his sword on a metal plate, which clanged loudly in the still morning air. Incensed, Caxus walked up to the quaking soldier and kicked him in the balls, then grabbed him by his battle tunic, and looked into his tearful eyes.

'Any more trouble from you, soldier, and you will spend the rest of your miserable life in the salt mines. You go in the front line!' Caxus ordered, then threw him onto the wooden deck of the galley.

They climbed in silence out of the boats and started wading through the cool Nile water into the rushes by the bank. Caxus had ordered ten men to stay behind on each boat, but the rest of his men now hid amongst the reeds and rushes below the banks of the Nile.

Waiting for the moment.

Caxus and Virgil crept up the muddy bank to the desert above. A mere fifty yards away Caxus could see the tail end of the enemy, the stragglers. Some enemy soldiers in their chariots trundled past, carrying spears and arrows, their chariots generating a dust cloud. Each chariot was pulled by two horses. Caxus counted two hundred chariots, each with two men carrying spears. Each chariot stored arrows and spears – a mobile fighting platform. And they had a blade attached to each wheel to dismember the enemy; *a terrifying weapon.*

Behind him he heard a loud cough among the reeds and rushes. He looked at Virgil in horror; then they crawled back several yards, praying not to be seen.

The nearest chariot stopped.

Caxus's heart thumped as he lay still as stone. A charioteer wearing a helmet and dark makeup around his eyes looked at them. Another chariot stopped. Four of the enemy were now looking in their direction.

Searching, listening.

Caxus lay rigid, daring not to breathe, as the wary Egyptians looked at them. Caxus touched an idol on a string around his neck, and prayed to the war god, Mars. The warriors in their chariots seemed to stare for an eternity, then they trundled on behind the main force: the Egyptian army of Ptolemy.

Caxus breathed a sigh of relief and looked at his friend, Virgil. They waited until the rear of the enemy was half a league distant, then he and his men moved out of the reeds and rushes and crept along the bank of the Nile, Caxus leading, using whatever cover they could find. They could not walk in open desert, since they would be spotted. They followed Ptolemy's army, silently and discretely, swords drawn.

Waiting for the moment.

The sand was blown by the wind in the silent desert. Only the sound of nervous horses being kept in rein by the charioteers reached them.

The tension was palpable; Caxus could hear shouting, about a mile distant, then more shouting; Egyptian voices, then the drumbeats of a Roman army—Julius Caesar's army. They would engage soon. Caxus held up his hand, holding back his men, timing his moment, for such moments can mean victory or defeat, a few small moments in time. Caxus picked up some sand and rubbed it into his hands, earthing himself, and saying a short prayer to the war God Mars. The roaring became louder, but they had still not engaged; they were throwing insults at one another.

'Caxus!' Virgil said in a loud whisper. Still he held his hand up, waiting for the right moment, for he knew it would not be long now, he could feel the tension in the air, like a brewing thunderstorm.

Then there was a great roar and the two mighty armies engaged, the Egyptians unaware of the impending attack from the rear.

'Attack! Attack!' shouted Caxus in his deep voice! Caxus's men ran like madmen towards the charioteers at the rear of the enemy, swords at the ready. The Egyptians were taken by surprise, Romans jumping onto the chariots and making short work of them. They could not turn their chariots around in time, for they were swamped by shouting Roman soldiers, hardened veterans of many wars, and they stood no chance. Soon half the charioteers were dead or dying, and vultures started to circle overhead.

The rest ran into the desert.

The rear of Ptolemy's army, the foot soldiers, now realised the danger as they glanced behind them, as a full cohort of Roman soldiers fell amongst them. The back of the Egyptian army was composed of young men, inexperienced in battle, and they did not put up much of a fight, as the Roman army slashed its way through, hacking and stabbing and lunging with their spears. Many deserted, disappearing into the heat of the desert, never to be seen again.

Ptolemy's army of six thousand men was now down to five thousand, with a thousand either dead or deserted. He looked ahead of him, to see Caesar leading a mere fifteen hundred men, but his confidence was waning; there was a disturbance from the rear. Ptolemy could hear shouts of anguish and anger and fighting. Who was attacking him from the rear?

He still had more than enough men to finish off Caesar - but he had not accounted for Caxus, who hacked and slashed his way through the enemy, his rippling muscles and expert swordsmanship making short work of surrounding soldiers, who turned away in fear when they saw him, like an enraged Greek god. But he was bleeding. His face and body were covered in blood and his left foot was injured, he had a slash in his side from an Egyptian spear, wielded by a giant of a man, who had thrust repeatedly, but then Caxus had deflected the spear point and driven his sword deep into the stomach of his enemy, who had dropped to his knees, clutching his stomach in agony.

The battle was being fought in the heat of the desert. Ptolemy's army was now down to four thousand men, Caesar one thousand, as the battle raged. Almost two thousand of Ptolemy's army were now attacking Caxus's Cohort of men in a furious battle, but the Romans were standing their ground through grit and courage. Caxus looked around at his men, he had lost one hundred already, good men, brave men. They were preventing the slaughter of Julius Caesar and his men, but Caxus might not hold out, his men were tiring under the ferocious onslaught by crack Egyptian swordsmen; they were running out of time.

They needed a miracle.

Then he heard a horn, a battle horn. His heart leaped. He could hear the stomp of a Roman army in battle march behind them and could see a cloud of dust in the distance. Then out of the dust, his heart leapt as he could see thousands of Roman soldiers—disciplined, fierce and ready for battle. One of his centurions ran up to him.

'The legions of Mithridates of Pergamum and Antipater from Judea have arrived!' he exclaimed in jubilation.

Ptolemy's army looked around in panic as they saw ten thousand men march towards them from the North, marching towards Caxus. Caxus saw a look of panic in the Egyptians' eyes, looking this way and that, looking for an escape route, to the east was the Nile, to the south was Caesar's army, to the north was Caxus's cohort and the approaching Roman army. Suddenly, the mood changed in the Egyptian army. Sensing defeat, thousands of the Egyptians dropped their weapons and ran east into the open desert.

Caxus dropped to the ground in relief, retrieving a bandage from a bag and wrapping his foot wound inflicted by an Egyptian spear. Soon the fresh Roman army marched past him and then proceeded to massacre the remains of Ptolemy's army, the rest running off into the desert.

Caxus shouted in joy as he saw his friend Virgil stagger out of the desert. They clasped hands and then walked to the Nile and bathed the battle blood from their bodies, catching their breath and resting on the bank. Further down the river they could see some Egyptians struggling to swim across the river. Some were nobility.

'These Egyptian bastards are not good swimmers,' laughed Caxus.

'We are stronger than them, Caxus.'

'Yes, we are stronger, we are Roman,' replied Caxus. 'Come, my old friend, let us find Caesar.' They strolled back up the bank and out of the hot, dry and dusty desert. They could see Romans on horses, and a Roman general. Bloodied and dirty, Julius Caesar, climbed off his horse, walked up to Caxus, and put his hands on his shoulders, looking him in the eye. Caesar had found him instead.

'Caxus, you are a friend of Rome. Come to my tent, we will talk.'

They were in the tent of Caesar, eating grapes and drinking wine. Amongst the throng of officers, Caesar walked forward with two other generals. 'Ah Caxus, let me introduce you to Mithridates of Pergamum and Antipater from Judea. This is the young man I've been telling you about.' The two men greeted Caxus warmly.

'Julius Caesar tells me you are a one-man army. You saved the day and saved our friend Julius.' Caxus smiled and bowed.

'You came in the nick of time, not sure how much longer we could have held out,' replied Caxus, as Caesar clapped him on the back. 'What became of the little shit Ptolemy?' asked Caesar.

'We saw him drowning in the Nile, my Lord.'

'They are not good swimmers,' said Virgil.

'And who is this fellow?' asked Caesar.

'This is my oldest and trusted friend Virgil, my Lord.'

'Any friend of Caxus is a friend of mine,' said Caesar as he clapped Virgil on the back—which made him burp loudly. Caesar looked shocked, looked at Mithridates and Antipater, then they all burst out laughing. 'Come, I have this special wine, Caxus, let us drink and celebrate our victory together.'.

'Have you seen Atticus?' asked Caxus. Caesar shook his head.

But then across the tent, Caxus saw a vision: a woman with jet black hair and blue eyes, and striking beauty, like a goddess. Her blue eyes smouldered with passion, like a wild Spanish gypsy. She stood motionless and looked at him, as his heart pounded.

'You look like you have been struck by lightning young Caxus. Do you like her?' asked Caesar.

'Yes, my Lord.'

He was dreaming again, he was wearing leather sandals and a toga, and there were stone buildings around him, people shouting as they sold bread and wine in the market stalls scattered along the street between dwellings. He was middle-aged and walked with a slight limp—an old battle wound earned fighting as a centurion in Caesar's army. He could smell fragrant fresh fruits and a multitude of herbs. There were displays of shellfish, fish and the smell of blood-red slabs of meat around, which buzzed with hoards of flies; this was summer, so there was no ice or snow from the mountains.

This was the Aventine Hill, one of the seven hills on which ancient Rome was built. He greeted a wealthy wine trader who bought wine from his lands in the north. They exchanged pleasantries and then he was walking up a hill. The air was cleaner here, he could feel the warm sun on his face. As he continued up the hill he came to his villa, surrounded by a stone wall. A guard in Roman military uniform stood sentry outside saluted him—one of his loyal soldiers—and as he got closer the thick wooden door was unbolted from inside and opened by the new servant girl. She smiled shyly at him, her brown eyes sparkled and he looked at her long hair flowing over her shoulders, like a Greek goddess. He looked at her for a moment, then beckoned to his wife, who was relaxing on a sofa in the garden, amongst the flowers and herbs.

He could smell rosemary as he walked up to her and kissed her soft red lips, tasting the red wine she was drinking, and looked into her eyes, her jet-black hair flowing thick over her shoulders. Her gown slipped showing one of her breasts as she kissed him. He cupped it in his hand; her eyes blazed with passion as their tongues met. Then he sat down, and the servant girl offered him some grapes.

He smiled as he ate them. Then his wife took some, the juice running from her mouth, as she took the girl by the arm, pulling her, and then kissed her on the lips. The girl giggled and Caxus could feel his passion rising as he watched them kissing and play-making, looking shyly at him; egging him on. 'Come join us,' said his wife to him as she took the girl's hand and walked through the garden, through the flowers and herbs, towards the bedchamber, hand-in-hand, laughing and giggling. They both turned around and smiled at him, his wife throwing kisses at him, like two goddesses on a picnic.

Chapter 18

MEETING OF MINDS

SIRIUS UNDERGROUND COMMAND
BUNKER HQ - VIRGINIA

Peter and Vinnie arrived at Sirius HQ and sleepily got through security, showing their Sirius IDs to the guards who checked their details. The complex was deep underground; everything carved out of the rock. Their voices echoed as they talked.

They waited outside a huge steel door which slowly opened. It was the thickest door Peter had ever seen—all of twelve feet thick. They were escorted to an elevator, sculpted out of the granite rock, that took them deep down inside the Sirius headquarters complex. Doors opened, and they were escorted to a large meeting room, where a lot of important looking people were gathered. Peter gestured to Vinnie to tuck his T-shirt in and comb his hair. General Scott looked at Vinnie with disdain.

Vinnie could be embarrassing sometimes, but Peter always covered for him. Vinnie was also the best friend you could ever ask for, and that was all that mattered in Peter's book. They were greeted by a smiling President Wilson.

'Welcome gentlemen, I'm President Frank Wilson, this is General Schmitt, Head of the Sirius project, and this is General Scott, Chief of Defense Staff. This is Smith from the CIA, and this is Professor Picard. Any sign of Fraser, anyone?' He looked around the room.

'We had an unconfirmed report that he was injured.' Scott grunted, as he looked Peter and Vinnie up and down.

Wilson gestured to Peter.

'Okay. Have a seat. Smith here from the CIA thinks very highly of you—your reputation goes before you it seems—he insisted you join us, which is why you're here and not in England. I'm told that you have been doing a great job, Captain Morgan.'

Wilson passed them some coffee and biscuits.

'Thank you, sir we try our best.' Peter's first impression of the president was that he was a decent, honourable man. But God, he looked tired—as if he was carrying an extra burden—Peter's sixth sense told him he was unwell.

Vinnie took a plateful of biscuits. His shirt was still hanging out as Peter introduced him.

'This is my friend, Corporal Vinnie Carson.'

Scott looked at Vinnie.

'Smarten yourself up, son. This is an executive meeting.' Peter was indignant. They had been through hell and back and here was this general, criticising his friend Vinnie. He was having none of it, his deep voice boomed, startling the occupants in the room.

'Vinnie, here, won the SAS sniper competition three years running, which makes him the best shot in the world. He's also saved my life more than once. We risked our lives to get these alien gadgets here!' Peter sat down. The stress of the last seventy-two hours had got to him; his eyes were watering. His blood ran hot, and shadows flickered in the corner of the room. The lights dimmed. The atmosphere seemed heavy, like a thunderstorm; then the lights came on again.

Everyone looked a little shaken as Wilson looked sharply at Scott, making a mental note to talk to him about his people skills, then took off his tie and loosened his shirt. The people around the table did the same. The president poured Vinnie and Peter more coffee.

'Welcome, Vinnie. Here have some coffee.' Vinnie was too polite to say he didn't like coffee, but he tried it anyway. 'Nice coffee,' he said.

Scott, straight-laced as ever and still with his tie on, looked at Peter.

'Captain, I understand you have found something on an alien craft.'

'Yes sir, we downed several of their fighter craft, including the one on the Ronald Reagan. We found this. It looks like a communication device.' Peter passed the device to Scott who passed it to a technician.

'Was it a difficult shot?' asked the president, looking at Peter and Vinnie. President Wilson was a master politician and orator. Peter now understood why he was so popular and why people wanted to follow him.

'Yes, it was, sir, moving targets always are….' said Peter. General Scott interrupted in mid-sentence.

'Mr. President, Chip found a similar device in Grimbald's office.' As Peter looked daggers at him. 'Bad move,' thought Peter.

'Try and figure this out, will you?' The technician walked away, but Peter thought he didn't look too confident. 'Give me the device,' said the professor. Peter leaned forward to speak.

'Hello Professor, aren't you the inventor of the encryption technology?' replied Peter.

'Mais oui, Monsieur Peter,' replied the professor staring at him. Was he the one in the book? His thoughts were interrupted by the general.

'How did you know? That's classified information!' replied General Scott, surprised how knowledgeable this captain was, but he had also heard the rumours about him. Maybe this Captain Morgan was their silver bullet.

Time would tell.

'I have a high-security clearance. I work closely with Sir Nigel from 6.'

Everyone around the room nodded in approval.

Picard looks at the alien device on the table in front of him, then picked it up, studying it.

'Ah oui, oui. These symbols here are not so different from ancient Sumerian…it is a communication device.'

'You understand this?' asked the president, shocked.

'Mr. President, I have seven PhDs—in archaeology, anthropology, philology, biochemistry, physics, mathematics, and electronics. I have a higher IQ than Stephen Hawking. I am not married, never found the time really.' The professor fiddled with the device.

'If I press this button here, ah yes, that's it.'

'Can you help us, Professor?' asked President Wilson.

'Mais oui, of course,' smiled the professor.

'Excuse me, professor,' Peter took an instant liking to this eccentric Professor, but he was interrupted by the general. Again.

'Professor, Captain Morgan of the British SAS recovered two devices from the alien craft, one of them is the communication device you're looking at. The other is some kind of encryption device.'

Peter retrieved the other device from his bag and handed it to the professor, who frowned as he examined it.

'Professor, the device has a picture of an F22 and a series of letters and numbers. I think it's an encryption key, and the alien device is a decrypter. It looks like someone gave them the codes.' Peter leaned back in his seat.

'That's what we figured Captain, our F22s were rendered useless against the aliens; our shields didn't work. But thank you, it's very useful intel,' replied General Scott, trying to remain calm.

'That sonofabitch Grimbald…' he muttered under his breath. 'Sonafabitch.'

'Sacre bleu! Young Peter here is correct,' said the professor taking a liking to this young, charismatic SAS captain. 'It is an encryption device—a decrypter, to decrypt codes from…an F22. It uses— non, it cannot be—it has decrypted the F22 code. Impossible!' The professor raised his hands in the air, 'they have the fractal codes! I invented the fractal encryption engine for the F22s!'

'Yes, we know the professor,' said General Scott his face turning slightly red.

'It cannot be broken, c'est impossible! The algorithms cannot be broken…unless.'

'Unless they have the key Professor,' Peter gently prompted.

'But who would have given it to them? This project was classified Above Top Secret?' The professor looked at the general, looking resigned.

'I believe someone gave them the codes Professor. All your hard work was for nothing. We have a traitor in our midst!' Scott's face turned redder as he took a pill from his pocket.

There was silence around the table.

Chapter 19

NAZI ALIENS

General Scott leaned forward, warming to the professor. 'Professor, I have a question, why didn't our nuclear strike work on their Chicago asset?'

'General, if you can imagine, these alien ships have to travel light years through solar flares, past black holes and all sorts of radiation. Their shields are built to withstand much more than a nuclear blast.'

'Thank you, Professor. Now…where was I? Ah yes, as I was saying, conventional forces.' Scott continued.

Peter interrupted, Vinnie smiled.

'The leaders of these bastard aliens are black uniformed, there's not that many of them. Most of the troops are grey-eyed zombies—the foot soldiers. There is something else though. Their uniforms—they seemed odd.' Peter paused.

'Reminded me of the Nazis.'

President Wilson put his head in hands.

'Yes, we have had similar reports. It is odd. They are obviously familiar with Earth history. Perhaps they are trying to emulate the Nazi ideology. But we suffer from a lack of intel, a lack of insight into their plans.'

Wilson looked at Peter, who nodded. Then the memory of New York hit him full in the face. 'What does this Grimbald look like?' Peter is curious. An aide displayed his picture on a screen.

'I know that face—he was in New York!' said Peter.

'You saw him?' Scott's neck went red as he stood up.

'Yes General, he was with the alien top brass. He's joined them I think. He was making a speech about his plan for a supreme race—a Nazi speech if ever I heard one.'

Scott sat down again, red-faced, lost in thought and muttering to himself. 'Why would they be wearing Nazi uniforms? Grimbald? Aliens? Doesn't make sense.'

'So Grimbald is in bed with the aliens. At least we know now, thank you, Captain Morgan. Anyway, we need to come up with a plan to fight back. There must be something we can do. What do we know about them already?' asked Wilson.

He leaned back in his chair and looked around the table. Most of the assembled attendees looked blank. Peter stood up.

'They have personal shields. The Sirius PR7 rifles can breach the alien shields, but only on full automatic. But that means we run out of ammo quicker. Normal weapons are useless against them.'

'God damn it! We just don't have enough PR7s—budget cuts. Ammo is short too. Carry on Captain,' said a frustrated General.

'I have seen them drink water, so their physiology can't be too different to ours. They seem to breathe oxygen like us, but they seem weak, their skin looks diseased on some of them,' said Peter.

'Poor DNA,' said the professor.

'We nearly got hit by falling debris from their Los Angeles ship. Their ships seem to be falling apart. Perhaps they were built in a hurry; who knows?' added Peter.

'Mmm,' Professor Picard scratched his beard.

'They're vicious bastards, and they show no mercy,' said Vinnie. General Scott and CIA director Smith smiled patronisingly.

'They have an agenda these aliens…' said Peter in his commanding voice.

Scott continued. 'The reports we have had indicate that they're kidnapping women and taking them onto their spaceships. Purpose unknown.' Peter had a sinking feeling in his stomach as he looked at Vinnie. 'They're killing the men and putting children and older men and women into camps they've set up.'

'Yes, we have seen the aliens splitting up families, women on one ship, men and children on another…also anyone who's disabled, African-American or Jewish they put on a different ship,' said Peter unusually quiet.

'Racial cleansing,' Wilson shook his head.

'Like the Nazis,' said a red-faced Scott remembering the stories of his grandfather—tales of Auschwitz; tales of terror.

There was silence around the table, then General Scott continued.

'We estimate fifty million dead in the United States alone, worldwide nearly a billion.'

'Why so many dead?' asked Wilson.

'It's not just the aliens. There's no power, fresh water, or fresh food. People are not surviving,' the general continued. 'Their technology is vastly superior to ours. Our Sirius technology has had partial success, but not enough.'

'Bill, what do we have left?' asked Wilson, desperate for some good news—*any good news.*

'Most of our army and air force bases are destroyed. The USS Ronald Reagan was sunk this morning. All but one of our carrier fleet is destroyed, the USS Nimitz—that's hiding out in the Arctic. The scattered remains of our army are in hiding. Navy Seals and other Special Forces units are still operating in isolated pockets but in greatly reduced numbers. Oh, and we have some F22s left in underground Sirius bases.' The general is straight-faced and sombre.

Peter whispered to Vinnie, 'Don't dunk your biscuits.' Scott continues.

'We have fresh Special Forces Reserves, Navy Seal units, and CIA personnel based here sir, and at a few other Sirius bunkers scattered around the world. I'm holding them in reserve. We haven't heard from our nuclear subs, but that's not necessarily bad news, they don't want to give away their position. Conventional forces…'

Scott was interrupted by a nervous looking aide.

'Excuse me, sir, you have some "visitors."'

Chapter 20

PETER MEETS A VAMPIRE

In walks Cassian and Lucia. There was complete silence as they stood there, their presence dominating the room.

'May we join you, gentlemen?' spoke Cassian with a deep Eastern European accent.

President Wilson sat open-mouthed. 'Yes, yes of course.'

General Scott stood up, looking with disdain at the ancient vampires. 'How did you get past security? This is a secure facility.'

'Years of practice, General Scott,' Cassian smiled thinly.

Wilson beckoned to the new arrivals. 'Please be seated. I must say I am surprised to see you again but welcome!'

They acknowledge the professor. 'Cassian, Lucia. I thought you were never coming!' beamed Professor Picard.

'Gentlemen, this is Cassian and Lucia. I'm hoping we can find some common ground together.'

'Preposterous!' says Smith from the CIA standing up. 'We don't make deals with vampires!' Scott nodded his head in agreement, turning red.

'Please,' said President Wilson, looking sharply at Smith.

Cassian and Lucia, were seated at the main table, the participants looked uneasily at the pair of white-faced, blue-eyed and fanged beings, who looked around the audience, returning the stare, gauging them one by one. Smith started sweating as Cassian probed his mind, unearthing his darkest childhood nightmares. Lucia stopped as she looked at Peter with the faintest hint of recognition.

Peter had never seen a woman so beautiful as Lucia. She had, soulful eyes, like those of a wild Spanish gypsy, deep and passionate. It was as if time had stopped. There was something about her he recognised; a distant, vague memory, just out of reach, but nevertheless very real. Peter's heart thumped as he had another vision, this time of an ancient land, and a city on seven hills, and a large wall surrounding it. Hyssop, lavender, and rosemary, the smell of them, the warm, scented air, and a woman, dark and mysterious.

Then the vision was gone. He felt a small stabbing in his heart. He clutched his heart as if clutching a wound. But then it disappeared.

Vinnie nudged Peter to pay attention. Peter came out of his trance, as if in a dream, but then his thoughts turned to his wife, and he felt a bit guilty. Deep in his heart, Peter loved Jennifer, he always had.

But this Lucia; she was magnetic.

Irresistible.

Cassian and Lucia stared pointedly at Peter as if searching for something. Lucia opened her mouth as if to speak. The telepathic link was very strong. Peter was aware of it, his sixth sense kicking in, pictures flashed in his mind as he stared at her. Lucia spoke telepathically to her master.

'Is he the one?' Peter could hear her thoughts.

'I am the one,' he replied. Cassian and Lucia locked eyes on Peter.

Cassian then stood up and spoke, his black medieval suit seemed out of time, but his wiry frame and thin face exuded terrible, hidden power. His blue eyes surveyed the room, looking into the frightened souls sitting around the table.

'We have not forgotten you. You underestimate how much we admire you, humans. We have come to help you.'

A hostile looking Scott stood up. 'Let me be blunt. Can we trust them, sir?' Looking at Wilson.

'Do you have any better ideas general?' Wilson threw his hands in the air exasperated.

Cassian and Lucia looked offended. Peter and Vinnie looked confused. A very frustrated president stood up. 'Bill, please, we need all the friends we can get at the moment!' Wilson opened his hands in a welcome gesture. 'Cassian, our situation is desperate. We need to find a way of fighting back. We need some sort of plan. How many of you are there?'

Cassian ignored Scott and looked at the president with his penetrating blue eyes.

'Mr. President, we bring many legions of Vampiri to da fight. They are making their way to your Sirius bases around the world as I speak.' Scott is enraged, his face reddening.

'The locations of those military installations are top secret!'

Cassian gave a hint of a sarcastic smile.

'You humans are transparent to us.'

Wilson is annoyed at his general, shaking his head.

'Let Cassian speak, General. Cassian, continue please!'

'Da aliens: First of all we can tell you what we know about them already, based on our past dealings with them. They are taking women for their filthy experiments and breeding program. The aliens, Da Sumeri, as we call them, are a dying race. Their DNA is failing. Most of their women are barren.' Professor Picard now spoke.

'Mais oui, the same will happen to the human race in a million years, our DNA will also start to fail. It was the subject of my dissertation for my anthropology doctorate.' Cassian continued.

'Thank you, Professor. That is why they have been kidnapping human women, picking da best genetic material and conducting experiments on them, trying to breed a new race—half-human, half-alien. I can tell you now, these women are suffering.'

Peter listened intently to Cassian, his heart beating faster, hoping Jennifer was safe in their home, hidden deep in the Brecon Beacons.

'My wife has been kidnapped by these alien bastards!' said Vinnie tears in his eyes. Peter put his arm around him, ignoring the rest of the meeting, then looked at Cassian.

'Cassian, we must do something, we must join forces. It is the only way.'

'God help us,' grunted Scott. The professor crossed himself looking sharply at Scott. Then he stood up.

'Young Peter is right - it is the only way. Humans and Vampires must unite!'

Chapter 21

MESSAGE FROM THE QUEEN

'Mr. President I almost forgot: I have a message from the Queen. She asked me to give it to you personally.'

'You met the Queen?' asked the president.

'Yes, we rescued the Royal Family from Buckingham Palace, and took them to a royal bunker,' replied Peter.

The assembled people around the table stared at Peter in absolute silence as he recalled the message in his mind, then spoke to his captive audience, his commanding voice booming around the room.

'Remember that it is in our darkest hour that we find the greatest courage. We British and Americans have always stood together, through thick and thin, through times of war and times of peace. We both uphold the same values of freedom and democracy, our abhorrence of tyranny and evil. We now stand on the brink of destruction. We must make a stand; we must find a solution.' Peter drank some water then continued.

'In the Second World War Britain stood on the edge of destruction, London was in ruins, the German invasion force twenty miles away across the English Channel. Thus began the Battle of Britain, where a few Spitfire pilots stopped wave after wave of Luftwaffe through skill, grit, and determination. If we had not been resolute, and instead wavered, just for a moment, and not found that extra ounce of courage, we would have lost. In the words of Winston Churchill, "Sometimes our best is not good enough, sometimes we have to do what is required."'

President Wilson smiled.

'A word fitly spoken is like apples of gold in pictures of silver.' He remembered with fond memories his state visit to England when he met the Queen and recalled how wise and knowledgeable she was, with a great sense of history. He had felt privileged to meet her. This was exactly what they needed, everyone around the table nodded, knowing what was expected of them, even though it may cost them dear.

Wilson sat silent for a while, then leaned forward and looked at everybody, examining their faces—wondering if they were made of the 'Right Stuff.'

'We can't change the laws of physics, so we have to find other ways to beat them,' said Peter. 'We have to think outside the box—do what is required, as Her Majesty says.'

Everyone was silent around the table, except Peter.

'This is unlike any war I have encountered before. We SAS are very resourceful, but we are at full stretch. We need a new approach. We need to fight another kind of war. We need to find their weaknesses.'

'I think therefore I am,' said Professor Picard. Everyone looked blank. 'Descartes: think from first principles.'

'I think what the professor is trying to say is that we have to forget what we knew before and start with a clean slate,' said the president.

'Exactly,' replied Peter nodding.

Everyone now looked at the two vampires, hoping they were their secret weapon. Cassian looked at Peter, his deep blue eyes penetrating his soul, but he was not afraid, for he was Caius, ancient warrior, the Eternal Warrior, incarnate to fight a new tyranny.

'Peter, isn't it? From the land of Albion—Britain.'

Cassian and Lucia looked deep into Peter's eyes, questioning. Peter nodded and returned the gaze.

"Was he da One?" thought Cassian.

'Peter, when you said '*Sounds like da Nazis all over again*,' you are right, in a way. Their intention is to become the dominant species on Earth. They want *dominion over Earth*—and remember, they drew *first blood* so feel no mercy for them—for they will have no mercy for you. You must be ruthless.'

Chapter 22

CASSIAN REMEMBERS

Cassian cast his mind back to the Second World War.
'I remember the Nazis; they were cold and heartless…much like da Sumeri alien filth. There are many parallels here. You don't know this, but during da Second World War, da aliens tried to build an alliance with the Nazis. Da Sumeri admired da Nazis—their strength, and technological advances—besides, with a population of only a few million back then, there were only a handful of good alien scientists. The Sumeri were desperate, they wanted da Nazi scientists for their despicable breeding program. They took some, but the alliance never materialised. Of course, now da aliens are desperate. Things must be much worse now.'

'Desperate people make desperate decisions,' reflected Wilson.

'Their desperation may be their undoing,' said Peter. 'Their ships are falling apart and their numbers are limited. What's this Grimbald like?'

'Poor leadership qualities; an ass kisser. Let's hope they make some poor decisions that we can take advantage of,' the president leaned back in his chair, hoping to find a chink in the aliens' armour.

'We will deal with Grimbald later. Continue Cassian, please,' said the president. Cassian paused, looking around the table.

Cassian looked at the professor, an old memory resurfacing.

'We were active during the latter stages of the Second World War. The war was on a knife-edge. The Nazis had many advanced weapons, and we knew if they had more time that they could win the war. So we invaded many Nazi secret bases at night. The French called us the "Résistance Noire" - Black Resistance.'

Cassian's mind went back to that time, dressed in black, infiltrating Nazi bases and attacking German soldiers. He remembered an underground hangar, a flying wing aircraft, and a large, strangely-shaped bomb. It had a skull and cross bones on it.

'A few more months and it could have turned out different. You may not know it, but we helped you win da Second World War. Anyway, I digress, Mister President.'

'Da alien genetic code is weak, and they will die out within one thousand years unless they rebuild their race. They are desperate. That is their weakness. They are far from home, every time you kill an alien or destroy a spaceship, that is one alien or spaceship they cannot replace. The war we must fight is a war of attrition, gentlemen. A guerrilla war, kill one here, one there. And find a way of destroying their spaceships. Da Sumeri are our ancient enemy, and we have decided to help you in this war. Our fates are inextricably intertwined, your fate is our fate, humans, and vampires. We will stand shoulder to shoulder with you.' Cassian paused for emphasis.

'We will stand with you in this war.'

'Things are looking up,' said Peter smiling.

'Excellent. Thank you, Cassian! I think we stand a chance with our new-found allies,' said a happier president.

'Why do you call them Sumeri?' Peter was curious.

'At da dawn of human civilisation, they started invading and integrating with your ancient civilisation of Sumeria, in what is now modern Iraq. Da Sumerians are your oldest race, and they originally lived in mud brick huts and were fisherfolk. All of a sudden, there were great advances in writing—cuneiform, mathematics, agriculture and architecture. Then they started building cities and ziggurats. Who knows whether they did it all on their own or were helped by da aliens? A mixture of both I think. Your bible talks of "The sons of God saw da daughters of men that they were fair."'

'The ones I have seen looked decrepit,' observed Peter.

'Some people confused da sons of gods were the aliens, though I would hardly call them shining. The real sons of God were the fallen angels who…fell from heaven and took wives for themselves.' Cassian looked sad, as if remembering something, then continued.

'But da ancient Sumerians paid a terrible price when the aliens started kidnapping them and experimenting on them. Da aliens drew first blood. That's when we stepped in. Anyway, that was then, this is now; back to da present. Mr. President, we have some limitations. We can move during da day, but not under direct sunlight; our skin must be covered. We prefer night when we can move unhindered, and our powers are greatest. Also, we cannot suck alien blood, as it is poison to us. We feed on human blood, animal blood when we cannot get human, so we would be grateful if you could make your blood banks available to us, as our supplies are short.'

'Agreed,' said the president.

'On da bright side, we are stronger and much faster than the aliens. Their physical condition is poor, much worse than when they first came to Earth 6000 years ago. They keep themselves alive with drugs and boosters. They are protected by robots and alien dogs.'

President Wilson leaned forward. 'I was curious, are these the Roswell aliens?'

'No, they were explorers, who happened to crash land on Earth. These filthy aliens are here to take over your planet!' said Cassian.

Lucia spoke, 'There is something else. These aliens have no moral compass: they do not subscribe to da Geneva Convention, so do not expect them to behave like humans, they do not have an ounce of compassion. Much like da Nazis.'

President Wilson looked pale. 'God help us. Thank you, Lucia. General Scott, I want you to coordinate ground attacks with our new allies against all known targets in the major cities. Take down their fighters and kill as many aliens as possible. We need to use stealth and guile. No frontal assaults.'

'Like the resistance during the Second World War,' said Peter.

Professor Picard looked thoughtful. 'Yes, exactly young Peter,' the professor replied, liking this young man. But was he the one?

'Cassian, I want you to stay with me, if that's okay, to command and control our combined forces and work with General Scott,' ordered the president. Scott nodded grudgingly.

'Agreed,' said a solemn Cassian looking at Scott, who looked around the table.

'I suggest we form small fighting units of eight: four Special Forces soldiers and four vampires. That way we keep the element of surprise.'

'We also need to find a way to get on their spaceships undetected. Any attempt to get on the ship via mechanical means will be detected. You will need to fly unaided. How about a balloon?' Picard added.

'I have a better idea. We could take you to their ships,' Cassian stood up.

'How?' Scott asked.

'We can fly when we transform.'

At that moment, Cassian transformed into a demon of the night. Large leathery wings emerged from his back, he grew two feet taller, his eyes turned red, and fangs dripped saliva. The room turned darker, and the lights flickered.

'I am Nergal, God of da Dead. The Sumerians worshiped me, and I protected them from da alien filth!'

Everyone sat open mouthed and terrified until Cassian transformed back to his normal self, but General Scott was visibly shaken.

'My God, Heaven protect us! I'm glad you're on our side.' He wiped his brow and coughed, 'Were making a deal with the devil.' Cassian smiled. Scott then looked at Peter.

'Captain Morgan, New York is a fortress, but our analysis indicates the Los Angeles ship defences are the weakest of all the ships, and you are our best soldier. I want you and Corporal Carson to go back to Los Angeles and work with the vampires to find a way onto the ships. Your precise orders will be sent by Morse code. Dismissed.'

'Yes sir,' replied Peter, then looked at Lucia who nodded. General Scott took a large map, laid it on the table and then discussed plans with Cassian. President Wilson shook Peter's hand.

'Good luck son. We have great faith in you.'

The same technician came up to Professor Picard with another alien device. He looked up at the professor.

'Er…we cannot work out what this is Professor Picard Sir. Could you have a look please?'

'It's Friday afternoon, nothing ever works on a Friday afternoon. Quantum physics, my boy. The brain is relaxing and not thinking about work but the weekend. That is why you cannot solve the problem.'

'No weekends off here professor,' Scott grunted.

The technician looked confused.

'I am a philosopher too. You need to focus more, then you will find your answers, my boy. Here, try this French roast,' said the professor as he clapped him on the back.

Peter was beginning to take a liking to this eccentric French professor—and the vampire Lucia. *The magnetic Lucia.* There was something about her. But what was the connection between the likable professor and the vampires?

Chapter 23

FORGING OF FRIENDS

Lucia walks up to Peter and Vinnie. They are speechless as she approaches them— totally captivated. Peter cannot take his eyes off her as she approaches them; her eyes are like blue diamonds. He stares at her, caught under her spell.

'Peter, do not be frightened, you show great courage. I will go with you.' She speaks in an earthy yet silky Eastern European accent which Peter finds fascinating. Peter's trance is broken as they are joined by Professor Picard, who smiles at Lucia, like father to daughter. Vinnie mutters something about being hungry and leaves.

'Lucia my dear, before you go, I need to show you how this device works.' Lucia returns the smile, as she puts her hand on his shoulder.

'Yes, uncle.' Picard instructs Lucia on the alien communications device. Still Peter cannot take his eyes off her.

'This button here to view the message, like so, this button to use the interface. Use these buttons to type the codes in. Now help an old man to his room, will you?'

Lucia then takes the professor's arm as she walks with him. She stares back over her shoulder and smiles at Peter. He is mesmerised by her charismatic smile, lost in a different world. He waits patiently for Lucia as she helps the professor.

Peter is ensnared by Lucia's charisma. He tries to shake his thoughts, but he is captivated by her. Those piercing blue eyes; it's like she is staring into his soul. Peter doesn't know it right now, but she will save him more than once. He is putty in her hands, such is her power over him.

'I love Jennifer,' he says to himself again and again, but Lucia is like a magnet, burning so bright, and he is like a moth to the flame. He has known her before, that's for sure - but where? When?

Cassian walks up to Peter and grips his hand, again looking deep into his eyes. Lucia arrives back and stands beside him.

'Thank you for saving us, even I cannot jump a two-hundred-foot wall,' Peter is grateful, remembering his rescue in New York.

Cassian and Lucia look at Peter with fixed stares as Cassian holds Peter's hand. 'He is da one,' Lucia speaks via telepathy to her master Cassian.

'He shall speak to kings, and show wisdom. it is da prophecy.'

'You are from Cymru?' asks Cassian.

'Yes, Wales.'

'You are a warrior—one of da elite?'

'Yes, I am in the British Special Forces.'

'You have special abilities: super strength, stamina, never get harmed in a fight?'

'Yes, they call me Bulletproof Pete.'

'Have you had any strange dreams? Think.'

Peter thinks about the vision he had in the woods near his home. Was it fatigue? Was it real? Cassian waits patiently as Peter collects his thoughts.

'I was in the woods, then again in the desert; an ancient place. Timeless.' Cassian nods his eyes boring through Peter.

'It would need to be.'

'There was an old man, a wise man, a priest. He was reading from a book.'

'What did the book look like?'

'It was black. Very large, very old—old leather.' Lucia nods and urges him on. 'What colour were the letters?'

'Gold. Large, gold letters.'

Cassian's eyes widen.

'What happened in da dream?'

'The priest—the old man—spoke to me. It wasn't the words, it was the meaning. The impression. There was also an Angel. Nine feet tall. Not human.' Cassian grew pale as he spoke. Lucia seemed to shrink.

'Prince Michael. What did he give to you?'

'Give to me? Ah yes, it was a sword; a flaming blue and silver sword.' Cassian and Lucia become more intense.

Peter rubs his forehead and looks at the strange vampire creatures before him.

'You know about my dream?'

'Yes, go on. What happened next?' urges Cassian.

Lucia's eyes are bright with excitement as she looks at this strong, powerful man, built like Bruce Lee with piercing blue eyes and powerful charisma. The charisma of a god. She licks her blood-red lips again. 'Then he gave me a silver cup, and I drank from the stream in the woods. Then I fell asleep. That was it.'

'Peter, you are more important than you think,' says a cryptic Cassian.

'You must fulfil your destiny.' Cassian looks at Peter, searching his soul.

'What do you mean?' asks Peter.

'We are in possession of an old book of prophecy. It was written by an ancient Greek prophet, Berossus. He foretold of a time when da skies would be aflame and fall in.'

"Flames of fire come down from the Sky and scorch da earth. The Gods come down from the heavens and create fear among the people. The nations are scattered, their buildings are rent asunder. Da people flee from the demons in their chariots in the heavens above. They get on their knees and cry unto God." Cassian looks again at the translation Picard has given him.

"But there is one who will come forth from the Isle of Albion, from Cymru, from the land of da mountains. A warrior with foresight and strength who will travel to da land of the eagles."

Peter nods. 'It all makes sense now.'

They are joined by Professor Picard and Vinnie, who is stuffing his face with food. The professor looks at Peter intently, studying him, wondering if he really is the one they are looking for.

Vinnie joins in looking at his friend Peter.

'Not as much as a scratch in all the battles we've been in. It's unheard of, no wonder he got the nickname in the SAS squadron of Bulletproof—he is fucking Bulletproof. He is also Caius—he told me so himself. You should have seen him on the carrier. Fearless.'

Vinnie looked at all the assembled group, chewing a burger.

'Christ knows how many body bags we've brought back from our missions abroad. Remember Iraq? Remember carrying Tom and Bill back to the helicopter? Bullets flying everywhere—not even a scratch on you. And carrying me single-handed through the Yemeni desert? Endurance in three hours. Your nickname is well deserved. I think the legend is true Pete—you just cannot see it mate.'

Peter is beginning to resign himself to being this mighty warrior, Caius. He shrugs his shoulders as he looks at everyone.

'I just want to live in peace and quiet with my family in Wales, if truth be known. Be a simple farmer.' 'Your destiny beckons, young Caius,' Cassian said gently. Lucia smiled and stood close to him – he knew those eyes!

They spoke to him telepathically. He knew her!

He could not help himself – he was under her power.

Chapter 24

CAIUS IS THE LEGEND

'Do not doubt yourself, Peter,' prompted Cassian.

'You are our one hope,' Lucia smiled touching his arm. She could not believe how lucky they were in finding this mighty warrior so quickly.

'It was no accident Lucia, we were meant to find him,' said Cassian, reading her thoughts.

They all nodded at Peter. He felt the weight of responsibility fall on him. 'I will protect you, Peter,' Lucia touched his arm.

'We all will mate, I won't let you down,' Vinnie put his arm around his friend.

'Thanks, Vinnie.'

'There is more, there is a legend,' continued Cassian reading from his translation.

"No one would be able to brave fire or water like him. Caius is attributed."

'He's never been shot or injured, it's unheard of in the regiment,' said Vinnie. Cassian nodded and continued.

"Cai is attributed with a number of further superhuman abilities, including da ability to go nine days and nine nights without da need to breathe or to sleep."

'He went five days without sleep once, on a mission. He can go a long time without sleep,' said Vinnie. 'But when he does eventually sleep, he can sleep for two days.' They all nodded. The professor stared intently at Peter.

'The ability to grow as tall as the tallest tree in the forest if he pleased and the ability to radiate supernatural heat from his hands.'

'It is early days,' said Peter, 'Maybe that is to come.'

Peter began to open up his heart and soul. It was beginning to dawn on him that all these events were not a fluke, but he was the one, the Eternal Warrior, incarnate for a special purpose.

'I am Caius.'

'Yes, my boy, that is the Latin version of Cai. You are the one!' beamed Professor Picard.

Lucia and Cassian nodded and stared at him.

'Da prophecy must be fulfilled,' Cassian's intense blue eyes bore into his soul. Peter was confused, but from what Cassian was saying, his dreams now seemed to make sense. But the responsibility—a saviour of the world, was he up to it? All he could think about was Jennifer.

'He can also fire thunderbolts from his arse,' joked Vinnie who was still eating. They all smiled and laughed, especially the professor who thought it was very funny.

'Caius, you are lucky to have Monsieur Vinnie as your friend,' chortled the professor.

Even Cassian had to smile at Vinnie's remark. 'You are a loyal companion, and a good friend, Vinnie da Terminator. You were meant to be together.'

'Tell me more about this sword Cassian,' asked Peter.

Cassian cleared his throat and continued. "Furthermore, it is impossible to cure a wound from Cai's sword."

'The sword. I have summoned the sword. It was a last resort,' said Peter recalling the ordeal, which nearly broke him.

'It would need to be,' said the professor, 'For it can only be summoned in time of great need. And only by the Eternal Warrior, who has reincarnated in you.'

'The effort of summoning the sword nearly killed me,' said Peter recalling the mind-shattering experience.

'It is a sword of unspeakable power Peter, or should I say, Caius,' spoke Cassian in awe. 'Da sword of Caius is ancient, before human history began. It was created by da Creator, and given to Prince Michael, one of seven.' If it was even possible, Cassian grew paler at that name. Lucia looked down in shame as Cassian continued.

'It is one of da seven holy swords of the Archangel Michael—the Lord of all Angels, the one who is like God. Da one, who…who cast us demons out from heaven. We admired da daughters of men, so we disobeyed God, and we fell to Earth so we could lay with them. God was angry with us.'

Cassian looked downcast, and shamed, as he recalled the experience. Cassian looked at Lucia, then at Peter.

'God turned his back on us, so I walked da earth, lonely and dejected. We were called The Watchers. Peter, imagine being disowned by your own mother and father and being ejected from your home; that's what it was like,' said Cassian, as though he wanted sympathy. 'I made Lucia, so there is some hope for her. But for me, no hope of salvation, for I am an original vampire. An original demon.' Cassian shook his head.

Sympathy for the devil thought Peter.

'Peter, read the book of Enoch from the Apocrypha,' said the professor. 'It is all there.' Peter nodded.

'There was a holy war among da angels, and we lost, for Prince Michael came, with his sword, his Holy Sword, and cast us into the pits, the deep dark, places of the world. None could withstand him, for he is all-powerful.'

'Michael is a prince among angels and serves the Holy One. The one who is called Jesus and sits at the right hand of God. We demons can contest His will, but we cannot deny his authority. The Holy One is supreme over all angels and demons. It is not what we wanted.' Lucia and Cassian looked pale and downcast, even for vampires.

'Carry on,' urged Peter, now understanding that he was talking to supernatural entities, but he didn't feel afraid, he felt that they were on his side, trying to help him. But Cassian and Lucia were silent.

Professor Picard cleared his throat and now spoke.

'You may call your sword only in time of great need. It will not always come, so I repeat, only in times of great need. It will give you power and strength, just call it three times and see it in your hand. 'You will know instinctively how to summon it—*that is in your DNA.*' The professor looked at Peter, studying him.

'It has been called several names, Caledfwlch, from the ancient Welsh. In early medieval times, it was called Excalibur. In Latin, the sword is called Caliburnus. Listen to your heart, you will choose the right name.'

'Caliburnus—that is the name I used, it felt right,' replied Peter.

'It has existed before the creation of the earth, before men, before the dinosaurs roamed the earth. It will give you power, strength, as well as the will to succeed and conquer your enemies,' said Cassian quoting from the book.

'But beware its power, beware it does not take hold of you!'

Peter nodded. 'It seemed to have a will of its own. It appeared to be controlling me, rather than me controlling it. It is a formidable weapon. I used it to destroy some alien robots. I cut through them like they were made of butter; there was no stopping me, but then I blacked out. I woke up with a tremendous headache. I felt weak—I have never felt like that before.'

'Mais oui, I think I understand,' said the professor. 'The sword comes from another dimension, mon ami. It is a supernatural weapon. You were partly in this dimension, and partly in the next. When you call the sword, a dimensional rift opens to allow the sword to enter into this Earthly dimension. It could only be wielded by one such as yourself, the Eternal Warrior incarnate, for it would destroy a mere mortal. The experience dehydrates you, and you may also lose salt and protein, that's why you get a headache. You were shifting between dimensions.'

'Professor, who was the priest in my vision in the desert?' asked Peter.

'It was Borossus himself dear boy, an ascended master who serves the Holy Archangel Michael.'

'What is an ascended master?' Peter's curiosity was piqued.

'Someone who no longer has karma, who has cleared and paid off his spiritual debts and Earthly karma, leaving the cycle of rebirth and incarnation. They have a very high vibration and live with the angels in Heaven young Peter.'

The professor put his hand on Peter's shoulder.

'How do you know this?' asked Peter as the professor shrugged his shoulders.

'I studied the Book of Borossus. All of it. There is much wisdom there. I deduced the rest, Mon Ami.' The professor repeated, *'Beware of the sword, beware it does not take hold of you.'*

Cassian looked at Peter. 'The alien filth would cover the land in darkness and enslave the human population. You are mankind's last hope; *our last beacon of light Peter.'*

'We will help you,' added Lucia, understanding the responsibility that lay on Peter's shoulders. But there was a tear in Professor Picard's eyes as he looked at Peter. The Book tells of a challenge he must win before he becomes Caius. *A terrible duel.*

He may die trying.

But now is not the time to tell him.

'What is it?' asked Lucia, sensing the professor's anguish. But he shook his head. 'Now is not the time,' he said gently.

'Professor?' asked Peter, noticing the change in his countenance. He was holding something back.

'You will be fine my boy,' the professor lied.

Peter thought about the sword. What was the saying? Absolute power corrupts absolutely. But could he control the power, and use it wisely? Or was the sword using him for its own ends?

Chapter 25

INTO THE UNKNOWN

It was midnight, and there was no moon. Lucia was carrying Peter up into the inky blackness towards the huge, creaking, groaning alien ship two miles above them. Below them, they could see the lights of fighter craft as they patrolled Los Angeles—*or what was left of it.*

It had been agreed by Sirius command that they would test this strategy of vampires flying Special Forces personnel up to the ship, gaining entry, and destroying the ship. If successful, they would adopt this tactic worldwide.

But how would they gain entry, Peter had asked repeatedly.

'Try using the comms device,' the professor replied, 'Lucia will help you.' They carried the alien comms device, but how would that help them?

As Peter stared at the red-eyed black-winged vampire carrying him higher, he wondered what attracted him to her. How could he love a demon?

As they neared the spaceship above them, a piece of it dislodged, and fell earthwards towards them. Lucia changed course just in time, nearly letting go of Peter as they climbed ever higher. Then they were on the ledge of the ship. The cold wind chilled their bones as Lucia transformed back to the black-haired, blue-eyed beauty that Peter found so fascinating.

They had a few feet of space on the windy ledge as they searched for a panel to attach the comms device to. Even though Peter had excellent vision he retrieved his torch, its high-intensity beam giving away their position. Cannot be helped, Peter thought as they continued their search.

'I have it!' Lucia exclaimed and slid open an almost invisible panel showing a console with buttons that had strange characters on them. 'It's Sumeri,' whispered Lucia. She attached the comms device and punched a few buttons. 'It's asking for a code' Lucia sounded frustrated.

Peter saw a panel and pushed it with all his strength, but it wouldn't budge. 'Try your hands, they can burn with fire,' said Lucia urging him on. Peter focused and imagined his hands as flaming tendrils, but nothing happened. 'The sword! Try da sword!' Lucia shouted.

Peter tried to focus on the dimension beyond time and whispered the words. 'Caliburnus, Caliburnus, Caliburnus.' Then louder, he repeated the words.

Nothing.

'The gods do not listen,' he breathed a sigh of resignation. His alter-ego Caius was quiet, and he lost focus.

Then Peter detected a presence behind him. 'We've been found!' They swung around, to see a black fighter craft hovering there, waiting for the kill. Peter swung his PR7; in a split second he loaded a grenade and fired. They covered their faces as the fighter was hit. It shook and wobbled, then lost height, and they saw their opportunity. They jumped onto the top of the fighter, covering their faces against the smoke. The alien craft continued to lose height, then they hit some cloud.

'Let's go!' shouted Lucia as she grabbed Peter and launched herself into the air, transforming once more into the red-eyed demon. Back on the ground, they met up with Vinnie and another vampire, Felix.

'Failure, Total fuck-up!' shouted Peter.

'You didn't get inside mate?' asked Vinnie.

'No. We need access codes,' replied Peter.

Back at the Mojave base, he was on a comms link with General Scott and Professor Picard at Sirius HQ. 'The mission was a complete failure. We need access codes to get onto the ship,' Peter was miserable.

'Couldn't you use your magical powers?' asked General Scott.

'Didn't work this time,' replied Peter, feeling even more unhappy, ignoring the jibe. Lucia touched his arm and smiled.

'The access codes may be embedded in their technology,' said Picard.

'You may be right,' replied Peter, feeling more hopeful.

'For the time being, keep fighting the aliens in LA until we can find a way to get the codes. Scott out.'

Great plan thought Peter.

Vinnie joined them looking unhappy. 'What is it, mate?' asked Peter.

'Bad news: Des, Johnny Two-Times, Fag-Ash Phil.'

'What happened?' asked Peter almost afraid to ask.

'They got ambushed in San Diego. Wiped out. They didn't stand a chance.' They hung their heads in silence for a while, remembering them in happier times. Peter recalled the drunken curry nights in Hereford and the hilarious football matches that always seemed to turn into a rugby scrum.

'I need a drink,' sighed Peter. Lucia followed Peter and Vinnie into the makeshift bar that the various Special Forces soldiers had built. It was empty, apart from one solitary soldier who looked up from his drink. His sullen face cracked as he saw Peter.

'Duke, I haven't seen you since the Saudi gig!' said Peter brightening.

'How are you Pete? Or is Bulletproof Pete these days?' said Duke in his southern drawl.

'Don't feel so Bulletproof at the moment.'

'The Delta and Seal guys call you Superman!' Duke replied. They both laughed.

'Our mission went to rat shit.' Peter was feeling miserable again as Vinnie went behind the bar and poured them three pints of beer. They perched themselves on stools, elbows on the bar, and sipped their drinks. Peter looked at Vinnie, raising his glass. 'Ice cold in Alex.'

'Ice cold in Alex,' Vinnie replied, remembering how Peter saved his life in the Yemeni desert. Peter's first drink hardly hit the sides as it went down. Lucia joined them, sitting on a stool, pulling out a blood bag, sucking on it, like her life depended on it, her eyes sparkling red then back to a bright blue, her teeth showing. They all watched her fascinated, Duke a little shocked.

'Come on boys—time to drink!' said Lucia as Vinnie poured them another pint, followed by a whiskey chaser.

'Nice whiskey, where did you get it?' asked Duke.

'Got the single malt from Sir Nigel at 6. Bottoms up!' said Peter, who walked over to the Jukebox. Celebration Day by Led Zeppelin started to play, the loud music shaking the bottles in the bar. 'Let's party!' shouted Peter. Handsome Mike walked in and downed two pints in quick succession, then joined them as they danced arms on shoulders to the music.

'Eat drink and be merry for tomorrow we may die!' said Vinnie. Then Peter had a waking dream, a future event: he was looking at Duke on the ground, but he wasn't moving. He looked at Lucia, for she read his thoughts. She looked sad but then smiled again.

'Remember that bar in Saudi?' Peter said as he put his arm around Duke.

'Yeah, we nearly got arrested,' replied Duke.

'Sir Nigel got us out of that one!' replied Peter, 'But now I've got a get-out-of-jail-free card!' He got out the card. 'Not much use now is it?' They all laughed, almost falling off their stools. They all raise their glasses.

'Here's to Sir Nigel!' they all cheered.

'Wonder how Sir Nigel's getting on?' burped Vinnie.

'I have a feeling he's okay,' replied Peter.

The military policemen patrolling the complex heard the loud music and looked in on the illegal bar, but Peter, Vinnie, and Duke all pulled faces at them. Lucia showed her claws and fangs. The MP's thought about reporting them, then thought better of it, as Peter finished the last of the whiskey, dropping his head into Lucia's full, firm, soft white breasts.

'I need some milk Lucia,' mumbled Peter as she stroked his head.

'Come, Caius…' as she forced his head against her heaving breasts.

As Peter slept, Lucia lay naked next to him. He dreamed of ancient times. A previous life. He was lying in a soft bed of white linen. It was daytime, and a warm Mediterranean sun was blowing a warm breeze into the room. He could smell the aroma of herbs from the garden outside. On either side of him were two women, both beautiful. One had long black hair and blue eyes—his wife—but he cannot remember her name. The other—his wife's lover—had long brown hair and brown eyes. She was a slave girl but was treated like one of the family. She was from Gaul. Again, she seemed familiar. They both smiled at him as they rested their heads on his chest and ran their hands over his body. He smelled the perfume on the thick hair of the black-haired woman, her eyes full of raw passion as he ran his hands over her round bottom. He would need to satisfy them both before he was allowed to leave the room, as he played with and sucked at their breasts. Then his wife and her lover ran their hands down his body, enticing his manhood, for they were insatiable.

Chapter 26

I Love the Smell of Crispy Fried Aliens

Peter, Vinnie, Handsome Mike, Captain Duke Miller—Peter's old CIA contact—and Lucia, all nursing hangovers of one sort or another, along with three other vampires, are stalking through the ruins of Los Angeles. It is early morning, and the sun shines bright above. Peter wears his sunglasses, military fatigues, and a PR7 slung over his back. Lucia is wearing a hooded cloak to protect her from the blazing sun, a utility belt, two knives strapped to her thighs, and a thin long sword strapped to her back. Before they left that morning Peter, as leader of the team had stressed the need for them to find the alien access codes.

'How?' asked Duke.

'We must find a way,' said Lucia.

'It's in their technology. The Prof…'

Peter stops in his tracks unable to move. Darkness envelops him as he has a waking dream: Flames erupt all around him. He is in a rock cavern, rivers of molten fire flow to his right side, but then he hears something. A deep growl, like an animal, but not an animal, and a dark presence, but he still cannot see it. Then something moves in the darkness, black and foreboding, omnipotent and powerful. He sees nothing as he falls unconscious onto the ground, as Lucia and Vinnie try to wake him.

'Pete, wake up!' shouts Vinnie, pouring water from his canister onto his face. Lucia drags Peter to a nearby building out of sight. Vinnie gives Peter some water, and slowly he comes around.

'There is something worse than aliens out there Lucia.' Lucia then knew the professor was holding something back.

They keep in the shadows as they approach an alien fighter craft. Alien robots, dogs, and four sinister-looking Narzuks surround the craft.

The only sound is the whirring gears of the alien robots as they move around. They hold their breath watching the robots, and halt, as one of the vampires treads on a piece of broken glass. The robots stop and scan the surrounding buildings for movement. They duck behind a wall as thin red laser beams scan the area, looking for signs of humans. Peter motions his team to keep low and quiet.

A rat runs out of the building, and the robots stop scanning, as Peter breathes a sigh of relief. They hear screams; Peter watches as black-uniformed Narzuk SS drag a half-naked woman into a dark corner of a building opposite, her eyes wide with terror. She is shaking as she lies there, and urinates, soaking what's left of her clothes, sobbing, and moaning.

Then the woman goes quiet.

Each alien takes a pill, their eyes glowing an evil black in the dark.

'Are they taking drugs for Christ's sake?' Vinnie mutters.

'These Sumeri filth have no honour,' curses Lucia remembering the **old vendetta**, their ancient war against the aliens.

'That poor woman; let's save her before it's too late!' Peter whispers.

The soldiers aim their PR7 rifles at the robots and fire their grenades. There are huge explosions as the robots stagger; one falls; they fire another volley. One robot explodes, the other's arm falls off. The remaining robot moves towards them and fires from its laser cannon, hitting two vampires and demolishing a wall. Clone troop reinforcements are also closing in.

The acrid smell of burning flesh fills the air.

Peter fires a third volley which sees the robot blow apart and disintegrates.

'These PR7 rifles are the bee's knees!' exclaimed Vinnie taking out a robot.

'What is bees of da knees?' Lucia pouted.

'Means they do the business. They're good,' Vinnie replied.

The Narzuks, now without their robots to protect them, look frightened as they hover over the stricken woman.

Lucia nods and the vampires move at incredible speed.

But Peter is just as quick, as he takes out his titanium hunting knife, and runs at lightning speed and with amazing agility. He cuts a clone with the serrated edge of his knife, then a split second later cuts the throat of an SS Stormtrooper. Lucia raises her sword and slices a dog and an alien clone in half in one movement. Another wounded Narzuk prepares to fire at Peter's back, so to protect him, Lucia slices his arm, and then his head off, making good her promise. Soon, the ground is littered with dead aliens and dogs.

Peter then runs like the wind, remembering the stricken woman, and finds the cowering Narzuks inside the nearby building. The aliens are half-naked, the woman lies whimpering nearby. Before they can recover their laser pistols, Peter has sliced the head off two of them, then stabbed the third.

'It's ok,' Peter says to the woman, gently wiping the green blood from his blade, and putting his jacket around her.

Peter carries the woman to safety, but then spots a group of Narzuks running for cover near a leaking gas main. Peter raises his PR7 with his free hand and fires a grenade which explodes, igniting the invisible gas into a fireball and incinerating the Narzuks into blackened shells. Peter sniffs the air.

'I love the smell of crispy fried aliens first thing in the morning,' he smiles, as he stares at the macabre sight. The woman smiles at him as he puts her down.

At the end of the battle, two vampires are dead and Peter's old CIA buddy, Captain Duke Miller lies critically injured, his clothes torn, and a big gash in his torso, from which he is bleeding copiously. Peter grabs the medical kit from his Bergen and wraps a bandage around Duke's wound in an attempt to stop the bleeding, then injects him with morphine.

Duke nods at him, unable to speak. Peter holds his hand and smiles, looking into his eyes, which are half-open.

Duke is dying. Peter wipes the dirt from his CIA friend's face and smiles.

'Remember Riyadh and that shady drinking den?' Duke smiles and nods weakly.

'Me, you and Vinnie did that drinking game, remember, and we stripped down to our waists. You were with a girl—what was her name?'

'Ratul,' says Duke as he grabs Peter's hand.

'Yes she was nice, you went back to her place didn't you?' Duke nods and smiles; then his eyes go blank, and he just stares, like he was empty. Peter squeezes his hand, then closes Duke's eyelids. Peter shakes his head, remembering him as a good and reliable man, someone you could depend on in a tight spot, like Vinnie.

Peter, Vinnie, and Handsome Mike stand around the body of Duke, cross themselves and say a few words; each to his own.

Felix feeds on a dead human in a frenzy. Lucia's fangs extend, her eyes turn red as she sinks her teeth into another human, an old man, recently dead, draining the body of the precious red fluid. She arches her back in pleasure as she drinks the blood, which drips from her mouth. After feeding, Lucia and Felix look at the bodies of their two dead vampire comrades. 'They fought well,' spoke Lucia wiping the blood from her mouth.

The woman, wearing Peter's jacket, filthy and crying, looks on in terror at the red-eyed vampires feeding nearby, blood dripping from their mouths. She finds a piece of metal and is about to take her own life. Better than being sucked dry of her life force.

'That woman!' exclaims Peter.

Peter runs like a racing leopard to the woman and throws away the metal, and gestures to Handsome Mike who is nearby.

'Oi Handsome put some bandages on this woman, will you, she's injured!'

Mike runs up to the woman. The woman smiles at him as he tends her wounds, and wipes the dirt from her face, removes Peter's jacket and puts a blanket around her.

'What is your name?'

'Angel,' she manages a smile.

'Don't worry Angel, I will look after you.'

Peter and Vinnie sit down and rest, wiping away the sweat, dirt and green blood of the aliens.

'Fuck these Nazi aliens,' Vinnie swears.

'A good alien is a dead alien,' Peter replies, then adds, 'Did you notice these ones are different? They look a bit healthier than the others, and they have red armbands.'

'Yes, like the old Nazi SS,' says Vinnie. 'The ones who committed all the atrocities. They have no compassion; no humanity,'

Peter pauses, then adds, 'Yes, you're right Vinnie, like the Nazis. We've got to find a way!' He punches the air in frustration, remembering the Queen's message to the president. Peter and Vinnie look at the dead Narzuk SS, the weight of responsibility hitting Peter hard.

'Got to find a way to beat them,' Peter whispers.

They are joined by Lucia, who is licking blood from her lips. She moves like an animal on heat, and there is a fire burning in her eyes. Raw passion, like a Spanish gypsy.

'Why do you call him Handsome?' she asks in her husky voice.

Peter was curious. He also had super hearing, but he wasn't a vampire. 'How can you hear from there?'

'You forget I'm a vampire. I can hear da beat of a moth from 500 yards, or a human heartbeat from a mile away. So why do you call him Handsome?'

'Handsome Mike. That's his nickname because the women love him. Vinnie here is "The Terminator" because he's the best sniper in the regiment.'

Vinnie interrupts, 'And he's "Bulletproof Pete" as he has never been shot, and has a reputation as the toughest, hardest, fastest and overall best operator in the regiment. He's got balls of steel.' Peter smiles as Lucia admires his rock-solid body; her blue eyes are wells of desire, as she lets her tongue run seductively over her blood-red lips.

Chapter 27

THE LUST OF LUCIA

Lucia looked at Peter with those soul-searing passionate eyes. Her tongue licked her lips again, her heart beating fast, her chest heaving, showing her nipples through the black leather suit. She still had the bloodlust in her as she locked eyes on him.

'Is everything hard about you, Mr. Peter da Bulletproof?'

Peter's smile widened.

'I think she likes you,' smirked Vinnie as they made their way into a bombed-out building. Peter laughed, she was something, this Lucia. She had such charisma, such animal magnetism, the ancient warrior within him rose as he thought about what he would like to do with her, be alone with her, to taste her. The animal warrior within him wanted her; he also had a sense that he had met her before.

But how? When?

Perhaps in a different life, in a different incarnation, in a different time. The impression was strong, but vague, knowing but not knowing, a warm sun, wearing sandals and robes, the smell of hyssop and lavender.

Then the vision was gone.

Then he thought about his current incarnation, about Jennifer; was she okay? The kids?

Peter smiled at Lucia, 'We make a good team, you and I.'

He lit a cigarette and turned to Lucia.

'Smoke?'

'You know they will kill you, don't you? I can see what the smoke does to your lungs, Peter da Bulletproof,' Lucia reproved him. Peter moved closer to Lucia.

'How long have you been a vampire?'

'Since Roman times,' her eyes pierced him.

Peter had a jolt as he relived the ancient memory.

'I remember something…'

'What do you mean?' asked Lucia.

'A memory,' he muttered. 'A warm sun, wearing robes, the smell of herbs…' Then Vinnie interrupted.

'Would you Adam and Eve it,' Peter beckoned Vinnie to be quiet.

'Excuse my friend Vinnie, he doesn't talk proper English. Lucia, what's it like being a vampire?'

Lucia sounded wistful and melancholic.

'It has its advantages, but I also have regrets. I miss walking in daylight, feeling da warm sun on my face, being with my husband. I miss my family. It's so long ago now…like a forgotten memory.'

'Husband' thought Peter, 'Husband. Why does Lucia seem familiar?'

The beginnings of a tear roll down Lucia's face. Peter didn't think that vampires could not get emotional. He was wrong. Lucia touched his arm and tears fell from her eyes.

'I'm sorry. I miss my family too.' Peter thought about Jennifer.

'Peter, I feel you are concerned for your wife. Do you have a photo?'

Peter handed Lucia a holiday snap he kept in his pocket. Lucia looked at the picture then shut her eyes for a minute or so as if she was searching. She had seen Jennifer before, somewhere, sometime, but she could not place the memory. Lucia handed the photo to Felix, who did the same.

'Peter, your children are safe, but your wife, I cannot see her. She is not in Wales with her children.'

Felix nodded in agreement. Peter sat down open-mouthed in silence; in shock. Vinnie looked at his friend.

'Do you think she's on one of the ships?' asked Peter.

'It's difficult for us to see into da ships, they are shielded.'

Peter stood up and kicked at a dead alien. As he did so, he noticed a Swastika symbol on the uniform. 'Fucking Nazi…'

Peter was in turmoil. He told her to stay in the house. How can she be missing? He must find out for sure. Then he felt a tremendous sense of guilt for leaving his family AGAIN. Then the guilt of being drawn to Lucia *a vampire for fuck's sake! What was he thinking?*

A shell-shocked Peter looked at Vinnie. 'Looks like both our wives have been taken.' Vinnie's eyes watered as he looked at his friend, unable to speak.

Chapter 28

EVERYONE HAS GONE MAD

They walk along the streets of Los Angeles and come to a damaged lunatic asylum. They watched with amusement as a half-naked male patient staggers out of the ruins of the asylum and finds a dead traffic warden. He puts on the dead man's clothes and walks up to a parked alien fighter. Peter laughs as the man puts a bunch of parking tickets on the side of the craft.

'Only in Los Angeles,' whispers Peter as they circle around the asylum, keeping out of sight. A Narzuk comes out of the craft, looks curiously at the man, and then directs his dog to attack. The last thing the mad parking attendant sees is the jaws of the huge alien dog growing larger and larger as it leaps towards him.

They walk around a corner, and a group of Narzuks are cutting up a human. They watch as one slices a man's genitalia, then they eat it, taking turns, their razor teeth slicing through the flesh. Peter and Vinnie cannot quite believe what they are seeing.

'Da filthy aliens are desperate. In their minds, eating a man's penis will make them virile and be able to reproduce,' says Lucia.

'They must be mad,' replies Vinnie.

'Or desperate,' adds Peter.

Chapter 29

ALIEN DICTATOR

Countless millennia ago, there was an elected government on Ergal 5, the home planet of the Sumeri aliens—there was a democracy. Now, the political structure of the Patricians was an imperial military dictatorship; democracy was dead. Disobedience was severely punished, with dissenters taken away to camps for 'indoctrination', and never heard of again.

Their dictator was his Imperial Majesty, Emperor Herg-Zuk.

He explained to his people that, due to the dire situation, emergency measures were now enshrined in law; martial law was in effect. Anyone flouting the permanent curfew was simply shot. Many thought that he was mad, launching into fits of anger if anyone disobeyed his orders. He would hold rallies in which fanatical followers would chant his name and swear oaths of allegiance.

In the Imperial Palace in the capital Sumer, Emperor Herg-Zuk was sitting in the Golden Throne room. Its high ceilings were adorned with murals, and long tapestries hung from the walls. His Golden Throne was made of solid gold and studded with precious jewels. He was reading his favourite book, Mein Kampf, by a certain Adolf Hitler. He liked to read Earth books, especially this one, and like many of the Patrician class, he studied Earth history and culture; it was a fashionable pastime among the Sumeri elite.

The humans had a great literary heritage, for a weak, inferior race, and what a jolly, talented fellow this Shakespeare must have been, most entertaining. He had come across Mein Kampf during one of their occasional raiding parties on Earth. He had heard of this Adolf Hitler and had even tried to abduct some of their Nazi scientists, seeing as they were in such short supply on their home planet, but limited resources had restricted their half-hearted attempts—too many local wars to deal with.

His Imperial Majesty was most impressed by the Nazi movement; strong, ruthless and effective. From the ashes of the Earth World War I they had built a strong military and economy against all the odds. He must find someone on the Earth planet who is sympathetic to their cause, yes he must find someone. He remembered his conversation with his loyal Marshal, Zurg-Uk, his trusted Chief of Staff.

'Our system is failing Marshal. Our DNA is failing, our crops are failing, our financial system is failing, our welfare system is failing, our enemies are eyeing us as weak and frail. This cannot be allowed to continue!'

He banged down his dog-eared copy of Mein Kampf.

Marshal Zurg-Uk breathed in, as he imagined the stupid ideas this book was filling his master's head with. The emperor stood, his eyes alight with passion as he looked at the imposing figure of his marshal, larger and stronger than most Sumeri.

'We shall adopt a new system of strength and national unity, for the common good. I will dissolve the Senate. I am fed up with their incessant meddling. Anyone not of our pure race will be deported or exterminated. We shall expand our territory and take what is rightfully ours.'

'You mean to adopt the Nazi ideology, your Imperial Majesty?'

'Yes, Marshal.'

'But the Nazis lost the war, O great one,' Zurg-Uk gently reminded his emperor, remembering his Earth history.

His Imperial Majesty's face grew a darker shade of green as he looked at his marshal. Zurg-Uk thought his leader's face was going to explode.

'That's because they fought a war on two fronts, they should never have invaded Russia. We will not make the same mistake!' he exclaimed as he banged his fist on the throne.

He was in full flow now, and nothing would stop him,

'That would have given them time to develop their atom bomb, V3 rockets, and their jet fighters. They could have won the war! Zurg-Uk, they could have won!' he repeated clutching his book.

'Yes, your Imperial Majesty. Well, they could have, if they hadn't invaded Russia. And if it wasn't for that professor, what was his name? Ah yes, Alan Turing, who broke the Nazi Enigma machine code. Brilliant fellow,' he mused. Then he looked up at the emperor, and realised he had made a grave error and should have kept his mouth shut. He saw the blood vessels on his emperor's head expand and his face turn even greener.

'Yes, yes if it wasn't for that meddlesome Turing, the Nazis could have won the war.' The emperor sat down indignantly on his golden throne, his golden robes flowing down to the floor, a deep frown on his face.

'You shall address me as Your Imperial Majesty Emperor Herr Herg-Zuk Marshal, is that clear?'

'Yes, your Imperial Majesty,' The Marshal bowed low, wishing to ingratiate himself, once again, with his master even if he was quite mad.

'I will issue new orders,' he stood letting his golden robes flow about him.

'With immediate effect, all dissenters, political activists, and troublemakers will be executed. All our slave clones will be put to work in our military facilities. They can work sixteen hours per day. We can always manufacture more if they wear out. This important work is being overseen by Lord Grim-Uk.'

'Yes, Your Imperial Majesty,' the Marshal bowed again.

'All disabled, mentally ill and infirm will be put through our processing facilities. We no longer have the resources to look after them. They must be sacrificed for the greater good.'

The marshal hesitated.

He knew what that "processing" meant; he had a sister who was disabled.

He coughed politely.

'Herr, my sister…'

'Ah yes, I remember you telling me. Don't worry Marshal,' the emperor smiled, 'as a loyal member of our elite, one of the Patricians, I will give you special dispensation. To my loyal followers, we shall form a party of national unity, and we shall adopt a new salute. The Narzuk Salute.'

The emperor stuck his hand out, in a salute.

'Henceforth, you shall be called Narzuks, the Sumeri military elite. You shall wear a black uniform like the great Nazi Gestapo.'

Marshal Zurg-Uk thought he was quite mad but kept quiet. He just had to follow orders and bide his time. He still remembered that difficult conversation twenty years ago. Now he was standing before the emperor once again; much water had gone under the bridge. He liked that human saying.

They were joined in the resplendent Golden Throne room by a black-uniformed Sumeri general, who shifted nervously on his feet, as he saluted. He looked up at the awe-inspiring Great Golden Throne, and the emperor, who was looking down at him with disdain. The general was wearing all his shiny medals, hoping to impress his emperor.

'Ah General Kurk-Ik, thank you for joining us.' The general looked at his superior, Zurg-Uk, for reassurance.

The emperor gazed levelly at Zurg-Uk and the general. They both looked impressive in their gold, braided black Narzuk uniforms, decorated with medals, the emperor recalling their deeds against their own people and military expeditions to other planets. Good loyal Narzuks.

Zurg-Uk remembered receiving his 'Order of the Eagle' for his campaign of intimidation of clones and Plebeians on home planet Ergal 5 and the wars against neighbouring planets, desperate for their resources. He had tried to mitigate the worst excesses of some of the more fanatical Narzuk troops; he still had some principles after all. He was tired of war, but he wore his medals with pride.

But former allies were now enemies. Desperate times.

They both bowed before their master. Two clone servants stood by his side, heads bowed. Imperial guards dressed in red stood either side as they approached the throne.

'Your Imperial Majesty,' they both bowed low.

Herr Herg-Zuk raised his hand for them to stand. He pressed a button on his throne, and a holographic image of Earth appeared.

'Gentlemen,' he smiled. They smiled back and waited in silence.

Chapter 30

THE MOMENT HAS COME

'The moment has come. You know I have been considering the full-scale invasion of Earth for some time. Our agents there have located a political party sympathetic to our cause. They call it the Nazi party, it is an underground movement now, but at its head we have our man, our traitor in their midst General Grimbald. He is a powerful man in their military. Our agents have contacted him. He has promised us their nuclear codes and fighter defence codes. He has given us strategic information that is vital to the success of our invasion.' Marshal Zurg-Uk stepped forward.

'What does the traitor want in return, Imperial Majesty?'

'Oh, he wants to rule a city—New York, I think its name was. Would you like to meet him?' Out of an anteroom, a skinny, rat-faced looking human stepped forward. He was wearing an Earth US General's military uniform. He nodded to a slave who helped Grimbald turn on his translator.

'Gentlemen, I want you to welcome General Grimbald.' The emperor got out of his chair and clapped Grimbald on the back. Grimbald and the Marshal looked at each other.

'It is Earth custom to shake hands,' said Grimbald as he held out his hand to the marshal. Strange custom, thought the marshal, as he shook Grimbald's hand. It felt weak and clammy, his smile was weak and his dark eyes were shifty. He had the feeling that this Grimbald traitor was untrustworthy; weak, with no backbone.

He didn't like him.

'Greetings General Grimbald,' the marshal smiled, 'We shall conquer Earth together, and you shall be made king of…excuse me what was the name?'

'New York,' replied Grimbald.

'Excellent, excellent. You know General Grimbald is related by blood to Adolf Hitler?' smiled the emperor, his eyes alight.

'Really?' Zurg-Uk feigned interest.

'Yes, his grandmother was Hitler's sister. He is the great nephew of Hitler himself. That great blood runs through his veins.'

May the Great Gods help us, thought Marshal Zurg-Uk. The emperor was all smiles. All his plans were finally coming to fruition. He could use this Grimbald puppet to conquer Earth, consume all its resources, and build a new race. He would be a hero, and go down in Sumeri history, as the emperor who saved his people.

'I shall save the Sumeri people. We shall be saved,' spoke the emperor regally.

'Yes, Imperial Majesty Emperor Herr Herg-Zuk,' the Marshal bowed, but he had grave reservations about this Nazi ideology.

'How is the training going for our Narzuk troops, Marshal?'

'Going very well my Emperor, their training is almost complete.'

The emperor turned to Grimbald.

'We are also building elite Narzuk troops, we call them the Narzuk SS, after Hitler's Nazi Waffen-SS; they shall be invincible. They are being trained by Lord Grim-Uk. They will be utterly ruthless. Nothing will stand in their path! They will wear a special red swastika on their arm to mark their special status.'

The Marshal looked at his own white swastika on his armband, a small difference but a huge gulf in their philosophy. He had some principles, but these Narzuk SS had none at all. And they got better rations than his own men; it wasn't fair. He then recalled the history of the Nazi SS on Planet Earth. Even for a cold-hearted Sumeri war veteran it chilled his bones, as he recalled the passage from the Imperial library, which held the combined knowledge of the Sumeri people, as well as many other planets which had been conquered in the name of his Imperial Majesty.

"The 36th Waffen-Grenadier Division of the SS was a military unit of the Waffen-SS during World War II and was led by Oskar Dirlewanger. It was formed for anti-partisan actions against the Polish resistance. The SS unit saw action in Hungary, Slovakia and against the Soviet Red Army towards the end of the war. During its operations, it engaged in the mass murder, rape, and pillage of civilians.

During the SS unit's campaign time in Russia, Dirlewanger burned women and children while they were still alive and then let starved packs of dogs feed on them. He rounded up hundreds of Jews and injected them with strychnine. His worst crime was the destruction of Warsaw, during the Warsaw Uprising, and the massacre of 100,000 of the city's population."

'Step forward Grim-Uk,' shouted the emperor. Out of the shadows stepped a figure all in black, wearing a thin smile, haughty and empty-eyed, like he had no soul. He was wiry, thin and had an evil glint in his red-tainted eyes. He wore a red armband with a black swastika-like symbol and a black carved figurine around his neck, which he played with.

'Marshal, let me introduce Lord Grim-Uk,' the emperor said enthusiastically. 'He will now lead our crack Narzuk SS Stormtroopers to allow you to focus on the military aspects of the Earth invasion. You will be in charge of the main Narzuk force and clone armies, Marshal. Grim-Uk will implement the breeding program—our plan to create the hybrid humans and save our race. He will also lead the special operations unit, to keep the human population in check. He reports directly to me.' The emperor leaned forward in his throne.

'Is that clear, Marshal?'

'Yes, your Imperial Majesty,' he replied, pretending to be pleased.

Grim-Uk stepped forward popping a pill into his mouth. 'Marshal, I am a disciple of Doctor Vlad-Uk. He taught me everything he knows. I have prepared detailed plans for our breeding program which our illustrious emperor has approved. We have already harvested some human females from Planet Earth; our experiments and breeding programme are going to plan. We have already bred some hybrids. Himm-Uk, my brother, will be my deputy.'

The Marshal looked at Grim-Uk. He had spent too long in the torture dungeons of the Doctor with his thin, unsmiling face, his empty, black eyes, devoid of compassion, or any feeling, and the red veins which stood out, *a sure sign of booster drug addiction.* The behaviour of these addicts was unpredictable, he would need to be careful. And there were rumours that he worshipped an unholy god deep below in the caverns beneath the Royal Palace—some secret Narzuk SS sect. Grim-Uk continued.

'With my Special Operations unit, I will squash the human race into submission, squeeze them and crush them. I shall set up work camps and use them as slaves. Any un-pure humans will be processed in our facilities,' Himm-Uk enthused. The emperor held up his hand.

'Yes, Lord Grim-Uk. Good, good. I have great confidence in you. Now an important matter: our spies have heard a rumour of a book. Tell me more,' the emperor's eyes came alive as he leaned forward in his throne. The veins in Grim-Uk's eyes stood out red, as he spoke.

'Great and illustrious Emperor, if I may. It has come to my attention that our arch enemies, the Night-Crawlers have come into possession of an ancient book of magic. It holds great power.' Grim-Uk paused for emphasis, the red veins standing out in his eyes.

'Go on, go on!' urged the emperor, leaning forward on his Golden Throne.

'It is called the Book of Borossus. It is written in an ancient dialect of their Greek language—difficult to translate, but I am learning the language, for the time when it comes into my possession—which it will, by the will of Bael, the great and holy one.'

'We must have it - we must have it!' shouted the emperor, banging his fist on the throne.

'I shall make it a top priority, O great and illustrious leader.' Grim-Uk bowed low.

'And if you get a chance to kill the leader of the Night-Crawlers, that cursed Count Cassian, do it. He has caused us too much trouble over the centuries. ***The ancient vendetta still lives!*** The emperor banged his fist on the arm of his throne again. 'I want him dead. Dead you understand!'

'It will be my pleasure O Great One,' Grim-Uk bowed low again. Then he coughed politely.

'Imperial Majesty, the matter we discussed…' Grim-Uk glanced at the Marshal.

The emperor leaned forward on his throne. 'Marshal, we will be carrying some special cargo in the mothership. Lord Grim-Uk here will be responsible for its transportation and security.' The emperor looked at Grim-Uk who nodded.

'It's my ship, may I ask what we will be carrying?' asked the marshal, taken aback.

'No, you may not,' replied Grim-Uk. 'It falls under Narzuk SS Special Operations Command. Remember, I report to his Imperial Majesty.' Grim-Uk bowed low again to the emperor, who smiled.

Then he turned his back on the marshal to look at Grimbald, walked up to him and awkwardly shook his hand. 'Did I do it correctly?' asked Grim-Uk.

'Yes,' replied Grimbald smiling.

'I understand you have royal blood—you are related to Adolf Hitler himself. Fascinating, tell me more.'

'Yes, Hitler was my great uncle, Lord Grim-Uk,' Grimbald enthused. 'Have you read Mein Kampf?' he added, his dark eyes widening.

'Yes, many times, many times. It is required reading for my Narzuk SS!' enthused Grim-Uk. They walked to an alcove and sat down. Grim-Uk and Grimbald talked and whispered in a huddle while the emperor secretly listened in on the conversation on his hidden earpiece for a while smiling and nodding.

Marshall Zurg-Uk sighed heavily, at the thought of their race adopting this Nazi ideology. But he kept his silence, for he knew the consequences of speaking out, as he glanced at Lord Grim-Uk in a huddle with the earth traitor Grimbald.

Chapter 31

PRICE OF FAILURE

The emperor turned a stern face towards his uncomfortable-looking marshal, who shifted awkwardly in his boots. The marshal felt affronted over Grim-Uk's snub, but his thoughts were interrupted by his master's matter-of-fact voice.

'Marshal, how are the military preparations for the invasion proceeding?'

The marshal shifted in his black boots, looked at the general beside him, and his eyes lowered. General Kurk-Ik stuttered as he spoke. Grim-Uk now stood by the emperor, a hand on the throne, red eyes glinting.

'The…er, mothership is almost…nearly ready, but repairs have taken longer than anticipated…' General Kurk-Ik looked at the marshal, for reassurance, then again at his master.

'The mothership… it is thousands of years old. Our engineers have told us it is structurally unsound. It is not safe.' The Marshal gritted his teeth, knowing His Imperial Majesty would not like this, and they were both afraid of his violent temper.

Herr Herg-Zuk's face slowly went a dark shade of green, and he slammed his fist onto the arm of his throne. His blood vessels bloated on his forehead, and a piece of skin fell off his brow. A slave clone stepped forward to put some medication on the Emperors' forehead, but the Emperor pushed him away, like a stray dog.

'There cannot…cannot be any delay!' he shouted, raising his diseased hand and pointed fingers at them. His hand was shaking with rage.

'We do not have the resources to build another ship. We do not have the time. We cannot wait another hundred years to build another ship, it will be too late then. Are you committed to the cause?' His Imperial Majesty stood up, his eyebrows raised.

'Well?'

The marshal and general drooped their heads and bowed low. They nodded their heads. The emperor focused his attention on General Kurk-Ik as he walked closer.

'General Kurk-Ik, I gave you personal responsibility for building the mothership, and you have failed.'

The emperor walked forward looking directly into the general's ashen face.

'I do not tolerate failure!' He shouted.

'Well, are you loyal? Are you committed? Because if not, I can always find replacements.' They got on their knees and pleaded for mercy, the general shaking.

'That's better then, stand up gentlemen,' the emperor's demeanour changed as he smiled at them. 'We cannot wait for conditions to be perfect before we begin our invasion.' He moved closer and put his hands on their bowed heads.

Grimbald looked on bemused.

'We shall build a race of half-human half-Sumeri, a supreme race with all the best qualities of Sumeri and humans. We shall conquer the earth, we shall have dominion over it, and all its peoples. They will be our slaves, doing our bidding and working in our factories. We shall rebuild our people until we are great again. We will create an empire that will last a thousand years.'

'Yes, Herr Herg-Zuk, Your Great Imperial Majesty,' they cowed.

'Now, I want that mothership ready within one year, or heads will roll. Dismissed.' Herr Herg-Zuk looked at his marshal, who knew what he must do.

The booted footsteps of Marshal Zurg-Uk and General Kurk-Ik echoed in the tall, stone ceiling of the Great Imperial Hall as they left their master. They were silent as they walked out of the Golden Throne room and into the high vaulted ceiling of the Great Imperial Hall, with huge hanging portraits of beautifully dressed past emperors, and murals of better times.

'One year; we will have to take shortcuts,' the general looked up at a huge mural on the high ceiling, trying to remember the painter, trying to forget his apprehension.

'General,' the marshal smiled at his colleague.

'I have a special reward for you. These gentlemen will escort you.' Two booted Narzuk SS officers from the Special Operations unit stood impassively before the general.

The general stopped in his tracks, and his eyes widened in fear. He knew the stories, his heart skipped a beat, as he looked at the marshal. The marshal saluted him. It would be the last time he would see him.

General Kirk-Uk knew what was in store, good grief, he had organised countless disappearances himself, so he knew what to expect. He felt in his pocket for a suicide pill, looking for a way out.

The marshal knew he would not be seeing see him again. As the two Narzuk SS officers took one arm each of the general, his head slumped.

Zurg-Uk felt sorry for him. 'Let him say goodbye to his family first, we owe him that much. There's a terminal here.' Marshal Zurg-Uk led his condemned colleague to a video terminal, then pressed a few buttons and a picture of his wife appeared. They heard loud booted footsteps behind them. It was Grim-Uk, wearing a thin smile. He popped a pill into his mouth.

'General Kirk-Uk, please follow me. Your wife cannot help you now. Myself and my mentor, the good Doctor, have devised a new torture regime, and we are very keen to test it out before the invasion. This way if you please.' Zurg-Uk managed to whisper in Kirk-Uk's ear, 'I will look after your family.' Then the general was bundled into an elevator as he was escorted off to the lower levels of the Imperial Palace, the secret home of the torture chambers of Dr. Vlad-Uk.

The marshal felt a shiver go down his spine. He did not like this Grim-Uk and his Narzuk SS. They had no honour, and they had dark secrets. At that moment he felt lonely.

Deep down in the dungeons below the Royal Palace, Grim-Uk escorted Kirk-Uk to the lower levels, the darkest and most remote caves; *he had something special planned for the general.* The lighting was dim as Kirk-Uk thought he could hear something in the silence of the caves, something unnatural. He stopped and shivered, but the fit-looking SS guards pushed him on. Then he heard a deep growl, distant and indistinct which echoed through the dungeons. The guards looked nervous as they approached a containment facility. The unnatural growls echoed throughout the complex of caves and tunnels. The nose of the general started to bleed as they heard a deep guttural roar, the atmosphere changed and the temperature dropped to freezing. The general shivered as he turned around looking wild-eyed and terrified at Grim-Uk.

'Kirk-Uk, my pet is hungry, it hungers for your flesh!' he said as he played with the black macabre carved figurine around his neck.

Kirk-Uk coughed as an awful stench hit him, his heart pounding as he was shoved through a thick steel door and slowly looked up at the terrible entity before him.

Chapter 32

NINE WIVES

Grimbald appeared from the Imperial Hall, his thin features wearing a smile. The Marshal studied Grimbald, trying to gauge him; get the measure of him—this human, this Earth traitor, with shifty dark eyes.

'The emperor wants me to join you, to see the mothership.'

'As you please,' he nodded. He had never particularly liked humans, they had too much spirit for his liking, still, soon they would be his slaves—including this Grimbald upstart. But he had to be careful, the Imperial Emperor thought highly of him. It must be the Nazi blood of Adolf Hitler running through his veins—his physical demeanour did not impress him.

They left the Imperial Hall and walked through the tall corridors of the Imperial Palace. Tapestries and paintings of past military leaders and great battles adorned the walls. Solid gold vases lined the corridor every fifty paces. Grey-uniformed clones bowed as they passed until they entered a shuttle bay and walked into the marshal's personal shuttle, where his pilot was waiting.

'To the ship works,' barked the Marshal.

As they left the opulence of the palace and lavish houses of the ruling Patricians and Narzuks, in the foothills of the Great Mountain, the shuttle glided silently over a barren, desert-like plain. Where there were once lush green pastures, was now dirt and rubbish from the factories. As they looked down, they could see a few Plebeians dressed in rags scavenging in the garbage, looking for scraps of food, and things to sell, to buy food for their families.

The marshal remembered one particular dinner party held by the Emperor. It was attended by many gaudily-dressed Patrician politicians and Narzuk military in their stiff uniforms. The marshal bowed to his Emperor, 'The people are starving Great Emperor.' The emperor, who was conversant with human history, and also a little drunk, joked 'Let them eat cake!' Everyone laughed nervously.

That's how revolutions start, thought the marshal, as he adjusted his uniform and began to relax a little.

He looked at Grimbald, who smiled, brushing his greasy hair and staring with his black eyes. Marshal Zurg-Uk, who knew his Earth history also knew that Hitler was a raving lunatic, who ruled by fear, a great dictator yes, but a man who made many foolish decisions. Could he trust Hitler's great-nephew, this Grimbald fellow?

He smiled back at him.

In the distance, they could see the ship works, and as they came nearer to them, it took Grimbald's breath away. Marshal Zurg-Uk had not been there for over a year, leaving the details to his soon-to-be demised general. But his mouth almost dropped at the sheer scale of the ship works complex. Soon, it began to fill the horizon. It was one hundred miles wide and ten miles high, reaching up into the polluted atmosphere of the planet. General Grimbald looked astonished at the sheer scale of the construction works, as his mind tried to compute it.

The marshal shook himself out of his stupor and barked to his assistant. 'I want to see the chief engineer in his office—in one hour!'

The shuttle arrived at the docking bay, and they disembarked. They were escorted by a nervous aide to a VIP carriage on the internal train system. Zurg-Uk turned to the Earth-traitor in feigned interest. 'The spaceship works are so large that they need their own transportation system.' Grimbald nodded.

'You must use a seatbelt, sir,' the aide insisted.

The marshal waved him away as they set off at an incredible speed. Zurg-Uk felt the G-force hit his ribcage and stomach as they rounded a bend and he put his seatbelt on. He looked on in disgust as Grimbald threw up, an assistant rushing to clear the mess on his Earth-General's uniform. When they arrived, they went straight to a meeting room where an impatient Marshal Zurg-Uk tapped the table waiting for the chief engineer.

The Chief Engineer, Oluk walked confidently into the meeting room. He hadn't much time for military men—or politicians for that matter.

'Well?' queried Zurg-Uk.

'Well, what?' Chief Engineer Oluk replied.

'Why is the mothership construction so behind schedule?'

'There are unanticipated delays due to the age of this ship. It is thousands of years old, Marshal, we are doing the best we can. Major structural works are necessary before she can launch in five years.'

'Forget five years, she launches in one year, and that comes directly from His Imperial Majesty Emperor Herr Herg-Zuk.'

Oluk felt weak at the knees. His scientific mind could not compute such nonsense.

'One year—but that's impossible!'

'We must launch in one year—throw more men at it if you need to.'

'Marshal Zurg-Uk, with all due respect, it's not just a matter of throwing more men at it. We only have a few engineers who are qualified to work on a project of this magnitude. As you know, everything, including manpower, is in short supply.' The Marshal knew this, and he also knew that without Oluk they didn't stand a chance of rebuilding the mothership. His tone softened.

'That's why we must launch in one year—while we can. Our race is dying, Oluk, so this is our only chance. In five years, we may not have enough engineers, pilots, and soldiers still alive to make this expedition.' The Marshal stared hard at Oluk to emphasise the point.

'I understand. We will have to take shortcuts,' Oluk advised.

'Take shortcuts.' The Marshal replied and walked out.

Oluk's mind raced. For a chief engineer, taking shortcuts was anathema, in a complex engineering project, each stage built on the previous one. How could he take shortcuts? In his research on Earth engineers he had encountered a maxim that perfectly captured the situation – *"Even if you have nine wives you can't make a baby in one month, it still takes nine months."* That is what he felt like saying to the Marshal. But he knew it was useless. It would fall apart at the first solar flare it passed, and then you would have wished you'd listened to me, Marshal! He was glad there were no black holes in the vicinity else the ship would be doomed.

The mothership was his baby, and now it would set sail as a cobbled-together flying wreck, and ah yes, he had also studied Earth culture, like all good fashionable Patricians, *which he found fascinating. Tied together with bits of string and Sellotape.*

'Very fitting' he pondered, then laughed, 'shortcuts it is then.' He recalled the pictures of their destination, Earth in his mind. Shame to destroy such a beautiful planet though. It was the most beautiful planet he had ever seen, rich green forests, snow-capped mountains, white sandy beaches and tropical islands, majestic rivers—surely it was made by a heavenly intelligence. A higher power—what forces would they be up against?

Chapter 33

BUYERS REMORSE

The huge, ugly, black mothership, a hundred miles wide, is orbiting Earth. The massive bulk is clearly visible from Earth. Hundreds of smaller craft dock with it, offloading their human cargo, as well as food, water, and mineral deposits.

On the bridge, General Grimbald is agitated as he looks across at the imposing figure of Marshal Zurg-Uk, waiting for a lull in the frenetic issuing of orders on the huge bridge. Zurg-Uk has not shouted any orders for five minutes to the nervous deck officers and is being attended to by his attractive skin doctor, a perfectly formed half-human, half-Sumeri hybrid. She is bald with blue sparkling eyes as she smiles and massages his skin and whispers in his ear.

'This is the time' Grimbald thinks, clearing his throat.

'Marshal Zurg-Uk, I have heard reports of our troops eating the genitalia of humans, even when they are still alive. This is barbaric!'

'Grimbald, it is an old custom of ours, dating back centuries. Our troops believe if they eat the genitals of the conquered inhabitants it will make them fertile again—that we can reverse our decline.'

'Yes, but it is barbaric Marshal, we must stop this practice at once.' Grimbald's last vestiges of humanity were rising to the surface.

'Anything that will give our troops hope for the future and improve morale is a good thing, even if it is misguided. Request denied.' the Marshal says with an air of authority as he turns his attention back to his attractive skin doctor.

Grimbald falls into a sullen silence, brushing his greasy black hair, beginning to regret his decision to betray his fellow humans. But he had made his bed, and now he has to live in it.

Buyer's remorse.

Chapter 34

SAFER THAN FORT KNOX

SIRIUS COMMAND BUNKER - VIRGINIA

Deep down in the bowels of the top secret Sirius headquarters in the Virginia Mountains, vampire elder Cassian, Generals Scott, and Schmitt and President Wilson are engrossed in conversation. They feel safe surrounded by hundreds of feet of solid rock, and twelve-foot-thick solid steel doors. President Wilson staggers slightly and sits down, helped by General Scott, and takes a pill from his pocket.

'Maybe it is time to hand-over' thinks the president.

They are joined by Professor Picard. 'Do you think the aliens can detect this place?'

'Safer than Fort Knox,' replies General Scott.

As they discuss their next counter-attack against the alien menace, they hear a far-away booming sound, faint at first, like the distant sound of an artillery gun. Then silence. The table seems to move ever so slightly.

President Wilson stops talking.

They all looked at him. General Scott has that nervous feeling in his stomach, the result of many years' military experience, which tells him trouble was afoot.

The room vibrates, and there is a booming sound. They are rooted to the spot as they look at a glass of water vibrating on the table, spilling water.

Ten seconds later, a louder boom. The room vibrates again. They look around wide-eyed. An aide runs breathless into the conference room.

'Mr. President, sir! Our outer defences have been breached—we're under attack!'

'Those doors are 12 feet thick, for Christ's sake!' General Schmitt exclaims.

'Hurry! We must evacuate to the train! They have found us!' shouts General Scott. Schmitt beckons to Scott.

'Bill, we need to initiate the auto-destruct sequence. I'm hoping we can take as many of them out as possible. Cassian, get your people onto the train!'

Cassian, eyes turning red, disappears in a flash to the caves below where hundreds of vampires are preparing for war.

Generals Scott and Schmitt go to a panel with large red buttons. They both insert plastic keys.

'Commence audio verification. Schmitt M A8JK999 verify.'

'Audio verification. Scott B Z1FL777 verify.'

'Commence auto-destruct sequence 15-minute countdown.' Schmitt looks at Scott. 'Get the president out. I need to finish here.' Scott has a sinking feeling that he won't be seeing his old colleague again as he reaches out and shakes his hand.

The panel flashes red and counts down from 15 minutes.

15:00.

14:59.

Soldiers and staff are running everywhere; there is chaos. There is another deep boom, louder this time.

'Everyone get on the train! MOVE! RUN!' shouts Scott.

'Where is my son?' President Wilson looks around the chaotic room, bewildered, but he is nowhere to be seen.

Alien robots are outside the complex, blasting the 12-foot-thick steel doors with their laser cannons. The door is slowly melting and starts to glow red hot, then white hot. At last, a large hole appears. The robots clear an entry. Clone aliens and Narzuks, their commanders, alien dogs and robots enter the Sirius Headquarters. The robots retract their heads inside their bodies to get through the rock entrance ceiling.

There is an eerie silence as the alien army fans out, exploring the complex. All is quiet as they enter the main command center, chairs and tables have been knocked over indicating that people have left in a hurry. The huge main viewing screen shows alien spaceships and desolated cities. Computer monitors still flash data as a Narzuk officer moves towards a flashing red panel. The alien stops at the panel, then realising what it is, frantically gestures for a nearby robot to destroy it, but it is counting down in a soft female voice.

'Three.'

'Two.'

'One.'

The wide-eyed Narzuk announces the order too late, as the whole complex explodes. Most of the alien troops are trapped inside the inferno. No-one survives, except one Narzuk, who crawls out of the hole in the steel door, uniform singed and smoking, his face black from the smoke, he coughs as he talks into his wrist communicator.

'Marshal Zurg-Uk, the human president and the Night-Crawlers...'

The alien has a fit of coughing, then continues.

'...have escaped, we were wiped out.' The Narzuk collapses and does not move again. Flames erupt from the 12-foot blast doors, incinerating a group of clone soldiers and robots standing outside.

Deep below the mountain, a sleek, silver Sirius bullet train slowly pulls away from the command bunker lower level platform and disappears into a tunnel. Three surviving robots appear on the track behind the train ready to fire as the train accelerates.

General Schmitt appears on the platform, badly injured, exhausted and uniform ripped to shreds, he limps forward and staggers, as he gets down on one knee, levels his PR7 rifle, checks the sight, takes a deep breath, and fires a grenade at the tunnel ceiling. Flames and a huge explosion erupt from above the robots, and they are crushed by rocks and debris. As the dust settles, there is silence.

The rocks from the explosion have sealed the tunnel, as the train moves away at an incredible speed, their rear blocked by large boulders.

General Schmitt manages a small smile of satisfaction, before he collapses to the ground, succumbing to his injuries. From his pocket he retrieves a photo of his wife and two daughters, clinging onto life. He holds his belly in pain and then his eyes close, still clutching the photo.

Inside the train, there is equipment from floor to ceiling, and dishevelled-looking soldiers and aides. General Scott is panting. President Wilson is bent over in pain and is very pale. The general looks at his friend.

'Jesus Christ - that was a close shave. Are you okay Frank? You look white as a sheet.'

'No. My pills - left pocket.'

General Scott takes the pills and gives one to his friend. He finds some water and gives it to him. The president is shaking as he looks at his friend.

'Call the Executive Committee…in the conference room. Help me walk, Bill. And find my son!'

The general puts his arm around the weak president as they make their way to the conference room. Professor Picard walks past carrying a box. 'Sacre bleu – un rasage proche!'

Seated is a frail Wilson, as well as General Scott, CIA Director Smith and a few presidential aides. Professor Picard joins them, as does a silent Cassian.

'Gentlemen, I find myself in a position where I cannot continue my duties as president for health reasons. The whereabouts of the vice president are unknown, Fraser is still missing, most of the joint chiefs are missing. Schmitt's missing. It's just us now. Therefore, I have decided to appoint General Scott as acting president for the time being. From now on, you will take orders from him.'

The president looks each person in the eye.

'Mr. President, you always have my support,' says a languid CIA Director Smith. Everyone else nods and looks at Bill Scott, wondering if this man can get them out of trouble. But is he made of the 'right stuff?'

'I want you to give Bill Scott your full support. Now, find my doctor, somebody,' says the weak president as he collapses onto the floor.

Chapter 35

ESCAPE FROM HELL

STREETS OF SANTA MONICA

Peter and Vinnie, exhausted, found themselves on the streets of Santa Monica. Peter was awash with emotion. Failure to get on the spaceship and find a way to defeat the bastard aliens, failure to find out where his wife is, guilt for leaving his family defenceless. Sadness at losing Des, Johnny, and Phil. He was going to make these alien bastards pay. And pay dearly. He seemed to be looking through a haze as he staggered and looked around.

Lucia was flying above them in demon mode, black wings flapping, keeping a lookout. They were covered in grime and dirt, and coughing on the dust from demolished buildings. The streets were littered with the bodies of Sumeri aliens and soldiers. Peter and Vinnie stood back-to-back, firing in all directions. Peter grabbed another magazine from his webbing and stuffed it into the PR7 rifle, but the reading on his magno battery was low.

His own energy was waning. There was a wild look in his eyes.

But the battle blood was in him, in the ancient warrior Caius, as he fired three rounds and took out a group of Narzuks, in a blaze of smoke and fire.

'Bastard Nazi aliens,' he muttered under his breath, his eyes wild with battle fever. He staggered, head spinning, as he fired a grenade; a robot took a hit and fell over, then there was silence. The immediate danger was over, but as he looked around, he saw the nameplate of a building, which triggered something in his mind. He was angry, frustrated and belligerent.

Peter was shocked, 'Christ, it's the Readers Digest building.'

'I've been doing their competitions for years. I've never won a fucking penny.'

Pete was frantic, his mind swimming with anger and frustration.

'Now let's blow this building!' Peter ordered, staggering as if drunk.

'Don't waste yer ammo!' Vinnie replied.

Peter ignored him, fitting a grenade to his PR7 rifle and firing.

'Fire in the hole!'

The building exploded into a thousand pieces; concrete, glass, and dust flying in all directions.

'When the revolution comes…never mind Vinnie,' said Peter, looking deranged, laughing and crying.

'I fink it's already started mate,' Vinnie shouted, shaking his head, worried by what he saw. His best friend seemed unhinged.

'Where's my wife you bastard aliens?' Tears rolled down Peter's face as he staggered around, 'Why don't you fuck off back to your own planet!'

Then Peter turned to Vinnie.

'Vinnie; Who the fuck am I? Who am I?'

Vinnie held Peter in his arms as Peter sobbed and looked at his friend.

'Am I a freak? What the fuck am I?'

'You're "Bulletproof Pete" – my best mate.'

'You're also Caius, the warrior…you must find a way to combine the two, for both our sakes, else it will eat you up!'

They both sat down. Peter laughed; so did Vinnie.

'I need a beer,' said Vinnie.

'Yeah, Ice Cold in Alex,' replied Peter. They both laughed, then looked up as they saw Lucia approaching.

'If you two boys have stopped da playing, we need to move,' Lucia scolded them as if they were two naughty children. Vinnie grinned, but then Peter's sixth sense kicked in; they were in danger.

'Let's move, they've found our position—RUN!' shouted Peter, but he no longer had the energy of ten men his energy was waning.

It was dusk. Peter, Vinnie, and Lucia were running in escape and evasion mode, trying to avoid the oncoming alien craft and ground troops, homing in on their position. Peter thought he saw an escape route down a street.

'Down here!'

They ran down the dark alleyway, but Peter had made an error, there was no exit, it was a dead-end. Tall buildings rose on either side.

But no exits.

His heart beat like a drum, as he heard the sound of an alien craft approaching, and the unholy barks of alien dogs echoing through the night.

'Fuck!' he shouted, looking desperately this way and that. Their instincts told them to check their PR7 ammo. No bullets, just two grenades. Vinnie shook his head. Peter was also out. Was this the endgame, thought Peter?

Chapter 36

FLYING DEMON

Slowly they both turned around and looked at Lucia, in the semi-darkness of dusk, the witching hour between this world and the next, when the veil that separates the Earthly world from the supernatural world is at its thinnest.

Lucia was transforming, her eyes turning red, her body growing larger, and leathery wings started sprouting from her back. Her arms extend growing longer, and more muscular. She walked towards the two friends. Vinnie backed away.

'It's okay mate,' said Peter quietly, for he knew her intentions. Lucia, now transformed into a demon, grabbed Peter and Vinnie, and leapt into the air, her large, black, leathery wings beating up and down, as they rose into the night air. A few more beats and they were soaring over the darkened streets of Los Angeles, observing the remains of what was once a great city: fires burning, smoke rising. Alien patrol craft hovered in the distance, looking for their next human victim.

Lucia's red eyes scanned the streets below for alien ground troops, then they heard the whirring and grinding noise of a fighter, which was gaining on them, but as Lucia focused her attention on the craft, two Narzuk sharpshooters fired from a street below, the orange laser fire hitting her full in the chest. She screamed in anger and pain, as she saw the burn marks on her chest, her mouth opened revealing her fangs, her eyes a wild red colour. She stopped flapping her black leathery wings, and they lost height.

'Lucia!' shouted Peter hanging on in desperation, as they lost height again. Suddenly they were in freefall. The ground was only fifty feet away. Vinnie lost his grip, but Peter grabbed his arm, his other arm hanging onto Lucia.

A few seconds from death.

Somehow Lucia managed to flap her wings, and they slowed, but her energy was depleted, her red eyes dull and lifeless. She looked at Peter.

'Sorry…'

When they were ten feet from the ground, Lucia collapsed onto the hard concrete, and they all fell into a crumpled heap. Peter picked himself up and looked at Lucia, who was unconscious. Vinnie slowly picked himself up, limping. 'Fuck,' muttered Vinnie, as he rubbed his ankle. Lucia did not move. Peter looked at Lucia in horror, noticing the bloody wound on her stomach. It seemed to be healing, but very slowly. He noticed before that vampires have remarkable powers of recovery and self-healing, but he wasn't sure if she was alive or dead.

'Lucia!'

Peter looked around him desperately and tried to rouse her limp body. Vinnie hobbled towards him and grabbed his arm.

'We've got to move now!'

'I'm out of ammo!'

'Me too!

He looked around him and could see two objects approaching fast. Luckily the alien craft had veered off, presumably on another mission, but he could also see a black mass moving towards them, in the darkness, and he wasn't sure if it was a flock of birds, or something else.

He looked again at Lucia, his heart sad. She was becoming important to him. Her black leathery wings wrapped around her like a cocoon, protecting her, shielding her naked, vulnerable body. He could not leave her, nor could he leave Vinnie, his best friend.

His mind raced for a solution.

Caius, Caius, his alter-ego.

Quick as a flash, he picked up both of them, one in each arm. He ran slowly at first, then picked up speed, as he ran down the street. He called silently to his Caius alter-ego, gaining strength. He felt the sinews and muscles, in his body growing stronger. He felt strong as an ox as he leaped forward.

He looked behind him, the two objects in the distance were getting closer. He could see the black mass coming towards them. Birds? Maybe, it was difficult to tell in the darkness.

They were being hunted by two aliens, on what appear to be hovercycles; evil-looking Narzuks. Grinning; intent on their prey. Peter ran faster. He had to protect his friends and find sanctuary.

The black mass was getting closer. Peter looked again. No, not birds, but bats, big bats, and they were closing in on the two Narzuks on the hovercycle. He could feel his heart pounding in his chest as he ran through the darkened streets.

Then something told him to stop.

He looked around, as the two outriders were swamped by the swarm of huge bats. The night creatures enveloped them, biting and attacking them, as they fell to the ground, screaming.

They were not out of the woods yet; Peter could hear the sound of robots not far behind, and the unholy barks of alien dogs in the distance, hunting them down, sniffing around debris and buildings, picking up their scent.

They were being hunted.

The pursuit was relentless. *Someone wanted them dead.*

Peter raced through the streets; out of the corner of his eye he could see another alien fighter closing in. But behind the fighter there was a black swarm, they had left the hovercycle riders, and were now converging on the alien ship. The bats surrounded the ship, and it started to wobble this way and that, as if blind, then some bats were sucked into an intake. Flames and bits of cooked bat spewed from the fighter, which now plummeted towards the ground, smoking and flaming—directly towards Peter.

Seconds to live. He put Vinnie down.

'In here!' shouted Peter to Vinnie.

But his Caius alter-ego was leaving him, and Peter now felt weak, vulnerable. He staggered under the dead weight of Lucia.

Chapter 37

WE ARE LADIES

'For fuck's sake Pete, are you window shopping or somefin!'

'I've got an idea. Get inside the shop.'

They all tumbled into an abandoned shop. He lay Lucia down. They looked around them; it was a dress shop, dark and dirty. Perter's mind was racing; their situation was desperate. He assessed their situation: No ammo. Just two grenades. Vinnie was injured. He felt desperately weak after his exertions carrying Lucia and Vinnie who were both deadweights. Caius had deserted him. Lucia was still unconscious, but alive he sensed.

The sword, summon the sword. No, he felt too weak. The effort of summoning that holy sword last time nearly killed him. No, he would need to think on his feet. If they were found, they were done for.

He sensed they were looking for him—the aliens were hunting him! They were hunting Caius. It looked like his reputation had preceded him.

But now he felt as if all the energy had gone from his body as he tried to figure out how they could disguise themselves. Vinnie dragged a cocooned Lucia into the store backroom as Peter looked at the dresses in the shop.

His superpowers had failed him.

His patron angel had deserted him.

Then he had it.

'Vinnie, put a dress on mate—quick, before they come.' Vinnie looked at him as if he was mad.

'Are you fucking mad? Are you raving bonkers? You know it might just work!' as Vinnie realised what Peter was up to.

A party of aliens approached, dogs growling, with saliva dripping from their jaws. Robots started scanning the surrounding buildings that were still standing. They stopped after scanning the dress shop. There was an eerie silence. Aliens walked towards the door of the dress shop. A withered, diseased hand opened the door.

The red-eyed Narzuk SS officer had a look of shock as he saw Peter and Vinnie dressed up as women, copious amounts of makeup on their faces, put on in a hurry. Peter was wearing a blonde wig, and Vinnie was a brunette. Vinnie grinned sweetly and showed his crooked teeth, as Peter pouted his lips.

'We are ladies, do you like my dress?' he said in a deep, lady-like, but squeaky voice.

The first alien was joined by another. Vinnie smiled again, while adjusting his underwear, and talked under his breath.

'I hope they don't fancy me, or else we're in big trouble.'

Peter smiled, in a ladylike fashion, and under his breath whispered.

'Well, I certainly wouldn't fancy you, you ugly bastard. Let's hope they reject us.' He smiled again.

The two Narzuks look on in puzzled silence, They ran a scanner over them, which beeped red. They shook their heads, muttered something in alien language between them, turned up their diseased alien noses and walked out. Vinnie and Peter collapsed in relief.

'How did you know we wouldn't be taken?' asked Vinnie.

'I noticed they don't take the ugly ones mate, and you're an ugly bastard,' said Peter.

'Brilliant plan,' replied Vinnie.

'I think they want white, pretty, women. No diseases, no defects. Good breeding stock. Part of their Nazi Aryan plan for world domination, no doubt. Evil bastards. By the way, where did you put the PR7 grenades?'

'They're in my Alan Whickers,' replied Vinnie. Pete was puzzled for a moment then laughed. Knickers.

'Make sure those bastards have gone, will you? Get a brew on, and I will check on Lucia,' ordered Peter, still laughing.

'Sounds like a plan to me.'

After Vinnie had double-checked that the coast was clear, they changed out of their women's outfits and wiped away the makeup. They joined a sleeping Lucia in the storeroom, relaxed, and ate in silence from a mess tin. Peter smiled at Vinnie as he slurped his tea. They had shown their resourcefulness in a difficult situation, thinking on their feet, SAS style. It would make a good story to tell. He could imagine Des and the boys laughing their heads off, as he told the story—if they were still alive.

Peter was thoughtful as he looked at a still and quiet Lucia. She was no longer in demon mode, her face pale and beautiful, red lips and long black hair, she looked like any other human woman. Why did he feel this attraction for her? It was not just because she was beautiful—Goodness knows he had spent enough time on missions abroad to miss female company, but there was something different about her, something that was familiar and lingered in the memory.

It was the eyes! The eyes are the window to the soul. He had known those eyes before—looked into those eyes. Soulful eyes, like those of a wild Spanish gypsy, deep and passionate. Time seemed to stop, as old memories rose to the surface. It was evening, he was walking on a hill outside of a walled city. It was warm. He was holding the hand of a woman with long black hair and blue eyes— his wife, his heart thumped as he remembered their lovemaking that afternoon. They had been joined by their new servant girl, a beautiful girl with brown hair and sparkling blue eyes. Strange, but he knew them both. It was an earlier life when he was a Roman, well-to-do, with a comfortable villa atop a hill. But as he looked at his wife on that warm night outside ancient Rome, a light came out of the sky, a blinding light, and a being approached, who tried to take his wife. He struggled with the being, then he felt a stabbing in his heart, and he fell. He could smell herbs as he lay on the grass, dying; the woman with blue eyes crying, trying to comfort him.

Then he came out of his vision.

They eventually nodded off, exhausted, but grateful for their narrow escape.
Caius was a fickle ego—still, it was early days.

Chapter 38

MESSAGE FROM JENNIFER

Peter is dreaming, trying to process the day's events in his mind. Is he doing the right thing? Is Jennifer safe? His kids? Peter is lying in a cave, it is dark, and he can feel the sand underneath his body. His fingers touch the sand, which is damp. He can smell the salty odour of the sea and the sound of waves crashing gently on a seashore, somewhere outside the cave. He feels at peace with the world.

Still, in his dream, he wakes up and walks out of the cave into bright sunshine. The sun feels warm and pleasant on his skin as he stands there. He looks at the gentle waves of the sea in front of him. The place seems timeless; as if time didn't matter here, it just is. Seagulls fly above him as he stands on the beach, the warm seawater lapping over his bare feet, the cool breeze from the sea brushing his face. In the distance, he can see someone further down the beach. As they get closer, he can see it's a woman, and she seems familiar. As the woman gets nearer to him in the hazy golden light, he can see it's Jennifer, her long brown hair flowing over her shoulders as she walks towards him smiling, graceful as a swan, like a goddess; then she holds his hand. Her brown eyes sparkle as she kisses him.

'I love you,' she smiles. They both look up the sandy beach to the dwellings near the shore. Under the warm blue sky sits a temple of blue crystal with white pillars, a gold dome adorning its top. It radiates a beautiful light which transfixes Peter. It is the same light that radiates from his patron, the Archangel Michael. He cannot take his eyes from it. They seem to stand there on the beach for what seems like an eternity, then Jennifer looks at him pleading.

'Help me!'

Peter wakes up from his dream, heart pounding, knowing Jennifer needs his help, and he knows he cannot find his wife without Lucia's help. Jennifer and Lucia were in his dreams. There was a connection, but he couldn't quite put his finger on it.

He stares at Lucia, not quite believing what he is seeing. Somehow, a group of bats has covered Lucia's lifeless body, how they got in the room, he wasn't sure. The bats caress and protect her with their black leathery wings, making soothing sounds from their bodies. One of the bats bites another and drips the red blood into Lucia's mouth. She stirs, then her eyes open, and she sits up straight, the bats moving away into a corner.

'Lucia! I need to talk to you!' says Peter.

She smiles, stretches her arms, all signs of injury gone, apart from the burn marks on her black leather suit. He helps her up, and they stand to look at one another in silence, as if they had known each other for centuries, timeless and profound. Lucia moves towards him, pressing her body against his, moving her lips towards his. He tries to resist but is caught in her spell and is unable to turn away as her lips meet his. He tastes her sweet blood red lips.

'Thank you. Thank you for saving me Peter da Bulletproof,' she says in her deep East European, earthy accent, kissing him again.

'I thought I had lost you too…Caius,' Lucia smiled.

He is lost in the moment. Then he pulls away, her eyes smiling at him, he had known those eyes before, in a life long ago. The eyes are the window to the soul. But his love for his wife overcomes his passion for Lucia. 'I had a vision. Jennifer needs our help. I'm convinced the aliens have her, we must find out where she is!'

'I will help you, Peter,' Lucia says softly, 'I know how important she is to you, and in some strange way she is important to me too.'

At that point, Vinnie stirs, farts and then burps loudly, breaking the tension. 'I have to live with this guy. God help me!'

Chapter 39

THE SIGIL OF PRINCE MICHAEL

Peter's sharp hearing alerts him to movement in another room. They draw their weapons, adrenaline rushing. Peter kicks the door down. It is dark, so he turns on the torch on his PR7. Peter sees two sets of frightened eyes and is surprised to see two men huddled in the corner of the room, shivering under blankets. Vinnie has his PR1 aimed at the two men.

'Do not hurt us, please, we do not have any food!'

'Stand down Vinnie. We are not here to take your food. What are you doing here?'

One of the men with a beard speaks up.

'We are hiding from the infidel aliens. May Allah curse them. Do you have any water?' says the bearded man.

Peter passes him his water bottle which he grabs, gulps down and passes to his friend. The bearded man looks up at Peter.

'Thank you. Come sit with us.' Peter and Vinnie join them. Peter has some Mars bars in his kit which he shares out.

'I am Ahmed, and I am a Muslim,' says the man with a long black beard.

A Jewish man, wearing a Judenhut cap, shakes Peter's hand.

'I am Abraham, and I am a Jew. We have been sharing what food and water we have, sharing stories. We are worried about our families—our children...what is to become of us? Our faith is the only thing that keeps us going.'

'Though we have lived in the same apartment block for years, this is the first time we have ever spoken to each other. We found that we have much in common,' says Ahmed.

Ahmed and Abraham smile at one another. 'In the midst of adversity we have found a common bond,' adds Abraham.

'This is my daughter,' says Ahmed, his face sad, as he holds a photograph of a young girl. 'I took her to school three weeks ago. Now I don't know what's happened to her.'

'I shall pray for her,' says Abraham, touching his friend's arm.

Peter, although not religious, can see that they have become close, even though they are of different faiths. They have put their differences aside in the common struggle. He thinks it strange how adversity brings people together. Peter remembers his father telling him about the Blitz in London, when he was a boy, and how everyone went to the underground, sharing food and singing songs to keep their spirits up.

Wartime spirit.

'The enemy of my enemy is my friend,' says Ahmed, looking at Abraham.

'Wise words,' he replies.

'Let us hold hands and pray.' The two men, from different faiths, now hold hands. Ahmed hesitates at first, but then smiles and holds the hand of Abraham.

'Join us,' says Abraham. Peter sits down and joins them, holding hands. As he sits down, Abraham says, 'Every day of freedom is an act of faith,' they all nod and pray, each to their own.

'I'm going to get a brew on,' says Vinnie feeling awkward. Lucia leaves them and goes outside to keep a lookout, keeping the door open to let some light in. Peter prays with his two unlikely companions, his thoughts turning to Jennifer and his family, hoping they will be together again, praying he will find a way to rescue Jennifer and return safely back to Wales.

They sit and pray in silence, each one to their own god. Peter is touched by his new-found companions and smiles; just for a moment, he forgets about the war and his wife. Peter looks at the two men; different clothes, different religions, different beliefs, and wonders what has changed. Up until recently, he has been fighting a war on terror, but now everything has changed. The terror is now the alien menace—a common enemy. Former enemies are now forging alliances, holding hands together.

This would have been unthinkable before.

Maybe something good will come out of all this, he thinks. This catharsis has shocked him, yet it has made him realise that after all is said and done, we, as inhabitants of Planet Earth, are all one family under God.

He is humbled by this thought.

Peter's thoughts turn to his patron—the entity surrounded by blue light. It is definitely a supernatural being, the Archangel Michael. He has never been much of a churchgoer, but now things are different, everything had changed. He becomes silent within and prays to Michael. In his mind's eye, can see a being surrounded by a brilliant blue light, holding a silver sword, smiling benevolently at him. Peter feels like he has contacted a friend, and although the being speaks no words, he feels comforted and reassured, that in the end, all will be well.

Also, that miracles can happen.

Vinnie has two cookers going, and Peter joins him.

'Never seen a Jew and a Muslim praying together – that's something,' says Vinnie as he nursed the pot.

'We'll share the food – what we have, Vinnie – it's the right thing to do.'

'Ahmed, Abraham. Come, join us around the fire.'

They all sit around the cookers, warming their hands. Vinnie makes some tea and passes it around. 'Only got two mugs, sorry,' says Vinnie. 'But it's British tea, best in the world.'

Pete's new companions beam with pleasure as they sipped the warm liquid, their mood much improved. Their eyes nearly burst out of their sockets when Vinnie ladles out some steaming beef stew and dumplings into a mess tin. As it is passed around, they nod their thanks. It is the best food they have tasted in weeks.

Peter gives Ahmed his fire-stick and shows him how to use it.

'Get some tinder… dry tinder and get a spark. Then put on twigs or paper on it. You have plenty of old paper here,' he nods at the rubbish in the corner of the basement. 'Then put some wood on top. I saw some broken furniture down the corridor, you can use that. Make sure you open the door.'

Ahmed nods and pays studious attention. 'Thank you,' says Ahmed. 'You are a true man of God. What is your name?'

'Peter. I am also Caius.'

Ahmed hugged Peter.

'There is something about him,' says Abraham. They all nod and agree. Abraham takes both of Peter's hands and thinks he is looking into his soul. Abraham looks at Ahmed. They know Peter is different. He has given them hope for the future.

'We should rest,' says Peter; feeling hot he rolls up his sleeve. There on his forearm is a symbol in black – clear as day. He has never seen it before; he is shocked, and marvelled by it.

Ahmed and Abraham's eyes nearly pop out of their heads when they see it. Abraham, being a scholar, puts on his glasses and holds Peters muscled forearm up, so he can look closer.

'I have studied ancient Jewish texts, including the "Testament of Solomon." This, my friend, is the sigil of the Holy Archangel Michael. Peter knows intuitively what this is. It is the indelible mark of the Angel Michael.

'You have been marked by Mikail,' says Ahmed in a hushed whisper, also recognising the symbol.

'It is one of the few things that Jews and Muslims agree on. We both acknowledge the Angel Michael,' added Abraham.

'Don't forget the Prophet Abraham,' says Ahmed. They both smile.

'I have been in his presence in my Caius alter-ego,' says Peter. 'He protects and guides me. When I am with him, I have a feeling of infinite love and joy; infinite power, and a feeling that everything will be all right. I am a different person then; I am Caius.'

Ahmed and Abraham nod enthusiastically.

'I have been called to help mankind in its war against the alien menace. I use Michael's flaming sword to cut down the unholy.'

Ahmed and Abraham stand around Peter looking at him in awe. Lucia overhears the conversation and is shocked by the mark on Peter's arm.

'It is da mark of da Archangel Michael!' Lucia turns a whiter shade of pale. 'Da One who stands before God's throne. God put him in charge of all da angels, Prince Michael, chief of God's Heavenly Army. He cast the demons out of heaven in da Holy War. I am a demon. We are afraid of him. He terrifies us to the bone.'

She bows down before him and kisses his hand. Lucia now realises she is bound to Peter, their fates intertwined, past and future. Maybe he can help her win salvation—*one day.*

Peter looks at her, lifts her head and looks deep into her eyes. He knows this woman, this vampire, they have been together before but where?

When?

'Lucia, there are good demons as well as bad. You are a good demon. There is hope for you. There is also love.'

Abraham recognises Lucia for what she is a demon vampire, and backs away, crossing himself. 'Golem,' he mutters.

'I must inform Cassian,' Lucia touches Peter's arm, looks into his eyes, then goes outside and keeps lookout again, casting her mind into the ether, into the darkness, to her master Cassian. Their minds meet as one.

"Cassian, he has da mark of Da Lord of Hosts. Da one who terrifies us, da one who cast us out. It is da prophesy. He is the one from da book of prophecy. He is da warrior that we seek."

"Lucia, our fates are now intertwined. You must protect him at all costs. He is our only hope, for da humans, and for us, Lucia."

The others sleep and snore on whatever piece of concrete floor is least uncomfortable. Lucia looks at them sleeping, all except Peter, who is meditating. He does not need much sleep. This Peter, he is special, he has powers on a par with her own, if not greater. Their meeting, their coming together, was no accident.

It was fated.

Yet there is something familiar about him, deep in her memory, yet it escapes her somehow, just below the surface of her psyche.

Chapter 40

LUCIA'S BLOOD-THIRST

Lucia wandered outside into the fresh night air. She was hungry; she needed blood, human blood. She sniffed the air for the smell of humans. Any human, dead or alive, it did not matter. Not for her the taste of alien blood, for it was poison. She was a demon now and her eyes glowed red as she hunted for prey. She sniffed again she looked right. Her eagle eyes and super senses detected something 500 yards up the bombed-out street.

There was a body.

Within the space of five seconds, she descended on the quarry, an old man, weary and frightened. She did not have pity as she sunk her fangs into his neck, his jugular, and drained the old man of blood. There was a look of gratitude in his eyes as he closed them for the final time and lay motionless.

'I did you a favour old man,' said Lucia, thinking the old man wouldn't have lasted much longer anyway. She looked around her as she heard a sound, then saw a rat scurrying across the street. Her senses absorbed all around her in a flash. She stood still as a statue. There was an alien patrol approaching 1000 yards from the east. In a flash, she was back in the basement. She licked her lips from the blood and kept a watch until the early hours, occasionally looking at Peter, the superhuman with superpowers on a par with her own. His rock-hard muscles and deep god-like voice - *she wanted him.*

Peter, unable to sleep, came out of his meditation and joined her looking into her eyes, alive and wild. He could read her mind, and she smiled, wickedly. Memories swept through his mind—old memories—as he looked at Lucia; warm nights under cloudless skies, the smell of lavender and rosemary; a walled garden where children played. And another woman, with brown eyes, a beautiful slave girl there was a connection between the three of them. A vision of a white linen bed where the three would lie, laughing, and kissing each other with a tender passion.

They looked up at the night sky, there was a full moon. She held his hand, and as they kissed he could taste blood on her lips, but it did not repulse him.

'I will keep lookout Lucia. Get some sleep.'

As Peter woke up with a jolt, he saw the dawn light shining through a gap in the door into the basement, and Lucia was staring at him. She wore a cloak to protect her from the warm sun outside.

'We should get moving. I have been monitoring da alien patrols. They come every half hour and da last one was two minutes ago.'

Peter thought about asking if his new companions wanted to come with them and discussed it with Vinnie, who looked daggers at him.

'Peter there is a church near here, but we have been too frightened to leave this place. Take us there. Come with us,' pleaded Abraham.

'We could do with somewhere to rest up,' said Vinnie.

'The aliens do not like it,' said Ahmed. Peter calculated the risk. It was not far, so they would not slow them down, and be a burden.

'Okay we go to the church; see how safe it is,' replied Peter.

Peter and Vinnie stood outside the dress shop, taking in the morning air, this time in military gear. Lucia emerged from the shop in a black cloak and looked at Peter who was staring at a flower, growing out of the rubble. Amid the destruction stood a beautiful pink flower. Peter stared at it in a trance.

'Even in the midst of hell, there is a glimpse of heaven.'

'Didn't know you were a poet,' grunted Vinnie.

A column of bedraggled and exhausted refugees shuffled slowly past, heading towards a large white church in the distance.

Another hooded figure moved towards the shop.

'Felix, old friend, we are well met!' said Lucia, glad to see her vampire friend again.

Peter walked over to the hooded vampires.

'Lucia we are heading towards the church, with Ahmed and Abraham.'

'I will stay here with Felix and rest. Come back at dusk.'

'Don't seem to be any aliens around here,' said Peter, curious.

'There's a good reason for that, Captain Peter da Bulletproof,' Lucia teased him.

Felix spoke. 'Like us, it seems the aliens will not go near a church. This is a new development.'

'Why is that?' asked Peter.

'Because, like us, God has turned his back on da aliens—the Sumeri race,' answered Lucia.

Vinnie was curious. 'Why is that?'

Lucia looked at him.

'Probably because of their diabolical experiments on other races. Humans were not the first to suffer at the hands of the Sumeri aliens.'

'So, we're safe inside the church?' asked Peter.

'Yes, not even their alien ships will go near it. But I will not go inside,' Lucia hesitated a sad look in her eyes. 'I am ashamed. We will wait here.'

'You could have told us this before Lucia!' said Peter annoyed.

Peter nodded and turned to Vinnie.

'Useful intel. Let's head to the church then and rest up for a bit.'

All around, there was devastation; buildings were lying in ruins. In the midst of the rubble stood a huge, white, gothic church with gargoyles carved in stone looking down at them. Refugees limped into the church carrying what worldly possessions they had left and collapsed, exhausted, into any space they could find.

For once they found peace.

Chapter 41

A New Hope

Peter and Vinnie, with Ahmed and Abraham, tired and filthy, follow the refugees into the cool, white stone church. Peter feels a sense of peace and silence.

'For here the Angels dwell,' he mutters.

They collapse into a pew and drink some water. The congregation is singing the last verses of 'Morning has Broken.' The church's high stone ceiling echoes the voices of the congregation as sunlight streams in through the stained-glass windows depicting the twelve stations of the cross. In the pulpit, a bearded, long-haired and scruffy-looking priest is offering the holy sacrament to worshippers. He looks 'lived-in,' but there is an aura of goodness about him, a man of God. He is wearing a loose-fitting crumpled white habit with a red cross, and around his neck, he wears a long crucifix.

Peter takes all this in as he patiently joins the queue. As the priest puts the wafer into his mouth, their eyes meet for a second, and there is a moment of recognition. Back in the pew, Peter wonders about the priest.

'There's something about that priest.'

'Now you come to mention it,' said Vinnie half asleep.

Peter finds the singing soothing, and it relaxes him. He thinks about Jennifer, in their house in Brecon, and the dream of the cave and the beach where they met briefly, as he dozes off.

Peter is dreaming. He sees Jennifer walking in the Brecon hills. The sun is shining, and the birds are singing. The grass is green, all is tranquil. Then he sees Jennifer rooted to the spot as an alien ship lands. Peter shouts and screams.

'Run Jennifer, run!'

But she does not move. The aliens stream out of the ship, and she is captured, struggling and shouting. Peter is running towards her, but she is taken inside the ship, and it takes off. He feels sad and helpless as he shakes his fist at the fading ship.

'It's all my fault. I should have stayed with her, then everything would have been all right!' Peter can feel someone shaking him. He opens his eyes. It's Vinnie. 'You were shouting in your sleep mate.'

The priest finishes his sermon and crosses himself.

'Go in peace and may God be with you. In the name of the Father, Son, and Holy Spirit. Any who wish to, are welcome to stay. I have a little food in the kitchen.'

Most of the congregation stays in the pews praying for salvation, some wander towards the kitchen and help themselves to pasta, tuna, and tinned tomatoes. Afterwards, they came to the priest, and thank him, as he is handing out blankets. Many people are sleeping in the pews. A few nervous individuals peek outside the church, wondering if it is safe to travel. They are startled as two young Narzuks wander towards the church, shields switched off, tentatively looking inside, and scream as they enter. Peter and Vinnie jolt awake as the aliens writhe in agony on the floor.

'Christ, did you see that?' Vinnie looked at the aliens. The congregation stands around the two aliens in disbelief.

'Looks like they have a weak spot. Slot 'em,' ordered Peter.

Vinnie shoots them through the head, and then searches them for any devices or useful intel, but there is nothing. They have black uniforms and a red armband with a black swastika on their arms—*the worst kind of alien.* As Peter looks closer, he notices a strange black carved figurine around their necks. It looks like an animal, but not an animal. Something diabolical. As he touches it he feels weak and unsteady. He can see fire and flames and a mountain—and something else. All he can see is flames all around him, then Peter staggers, and Vinnie catches him, 'Are you all right mate?' asks a concerned Vinnie.

'There are worse things than aliens in this world Vinnie.' Did he just see his nemesis? He thinks as he recovers himself.

The bearded priest looks at the two dead aliens, then at Peter and Vinnie, and walks towards them. The rough-looking priest's eyes light up. There is a look of recognition in his eye.

'Is that Peter Morgan?' he says in an earthy Geordie accent.

Chapter 42

REUNION

'Yes, how did you know?' It suddenly dawned on him as he recognised his old friend. 'It's Sebastian!'

'Christ, knock me down wiv' a feather, it's Sebastian Harris from A Squadron!' said a surprised Vinnie.

'Sebastian, we all wondered what happened to you!' Peter exclaimed as he shook the priest's hand. 'By the way, it's Captain Peter Morgan now if you don't mind!'

'Captain, eh, fancy that! How about a brew?'

'Sure.'

They followed Sebastian into his small office at the back of the church, full of pictures of saints including Pope John Paul. They all sit down for a cup of tea, Vinnie helping himself to some pasta and tuna.

'Didn't recognise you with the beard, Sebastian,' joked Peter.

'It's great to see you again, Sebastian,' Vinnie added.

They all laughed and begin to relax a little.

'It's been a long time. What a mess, eh?' Sebastian said, relaxing in his leather chair.

'Yeah, it's a mess alright. What made you become a priest?' asked Peter.

'After Yemen, I just couldn't do it anymore—the killing, the fighting—I couldn't detach myself from it. Too much stress…I had a nervous breakdown. I lost six months of my life.' Sebastian drank his tea looking at his old comrades.

'Remember Yemen?' Peter and Vinnie nodded remembering the chaos.

'We were lucky to get out alive. If it wasn't for that Bedouin…' reminisced Peter.

They all nodded remembering the thin, wiry Bedouin man who saved their lives. 'Then after that, I decided to become a priest, doing something for God, somewhere far away from England. Somewhere new. And here I am. What are you two doing here?'

'We're on secondment to an organisation called Sirius, set up to fight the aliens. Got some awesome weapons but to be honest we're fighting a losing battle,' Peter is downbeat.

'There's always hope, I have learned that. Trust in God and all will eventually work out. You know, it's strange, but we don't see these aliens near the church. They keep away from it.'

Peter reflected on the recent event with the aliens outside the church.

'They have a weakness; they cannot enter a church.'

'What, like vampires?' asked Vinnie.

'It is a House of God,' the priest was serious.

'I think I see a plan coming together. Sebastian, do you fancy joining us?' Peter felt hopeful as Sebastian scratched his beard, looking thoughtful.

'I don't like to leave my flock, they need me. But meeting you again, I think this is His work, and he has chosen me for this.' Sebastian rubbed his bearded chin, then looked up. 'Yes, I will join you.'

'You know, for the first time, I'm beginning to feel some hope,' Peter brightened.

'Do you need weapons and ammunition?' Sebastian looked at Peter.

'Yes, we're out.'

'Follow me.'

They followed Sebastian through an old wooden door, well hidden behind a stone pillar. They walked down some steep stone steps, their footsteps echoing as they entered a crypt carved out of stone; cool and dark. There were tombs and strange statues. Vinnie coughed on the dust and switched on his torch.

'Give me a hand,' Sebastian gestured to Vinnie.

They helped Sebastian move the stone lid of a tomb. Inside were automatic weapons, ammunition, grenades and a Gatling gun. Vinnie picked up the Gatling. He has a big smile on his face.

'Nice. Now that's what I'm talking about.'

'Suits you,' grinned Sebastian.

'Do they still call you The Terminator?'

Vinnie grinned and nodded.

'Are you still Bulletproof Pete?' he glanced at Peter. 'The one endowed with…shall I say special powers?' Sebastian looked at him as if he were looking at the devil.

'Yes, I…have been going through something of a transformation lately. My Caius ego seems to be getting more dominant.' Sebastian looked at him like he had seen a demon and crossed himself, then Peter changed the subject.

'It's not Sirius-compatible ammo, so we'll leave our kit here, and use these weapons instead. This is great Sebastian, but why are there guns in a church of all places?' Peter was curious.

'One night I was sleeping in my office at the back of the church, I heard a disturbance. I don't sleep too well—old habits. I saw some gang members creeping down to the crypt. I asked them what they were doing, and they owned up. They thought it would be a great hiding place. So they agreed to give up their guns, and in return, I would help them find a job. Part of the deal was they had to come to church every Sunday and commit to God, instead of crime. Amazingly it worked. Most of them have proper jobs now.'

'Nice story,' Peter smiled scratching his stubble.

'God works in mysterious ways,' said Sebastian as he led them back up to the church.

They went back to Sebastian's office where Peter spelled out their mission. 'Our objective will be the local Sirius Command Bunker in the Mojave. From there, we can travel to Sirius HQ and update them on our discoveries.'

They walked back into the church. Sebastian looked at Peter for a moment as if searching for something.

Chapter 43

CONFESSIONAL

'Peter, your heart is heavy. Will you take confession with me and cleanse your soul?' Peter looked at Sebastian, unsure. 'Don't worry about me. I will just pray.' Vinnie sits in a pew and fell asleep, snoring.

Peter is reticent. 'I can't remember the last time—I think I'm beyond redemption, Sebastian, old friend.'

'This way into the confessional, Peter.'

Sebastian gave him a card then they sat in the confessional. Peter read from the card.

'In the name of the Father, and of the Son, and of the Holy Spirit. Amen. Er, what do I do now?'

'May the Lord be in your heart and help you to confess your sins with true sorrow. Speak from your heart, Peter my son, God will help you.'

'I feel guilty; guilty for leaving my wife and family again. I am never at home. I have not been a good father.'

'Go on, my son.' Peter opened his heart to Sebastian.

'I have killed men, sons, and fathers. Lord, forgive me.'

'Go on my son.'

'I have lusted after other women. It is a lonely job being a soldier.'

'You have many sins, my son. You must spend time with your family you must be faithful. Now repent.'

'Lord Jesus, Son of God, have mercy on me, a sinner.'

'God, the Father of mercies, through the death and resurrection of his Son, has reconciled the world to Himself and sent the Holy Spirit among us for the forgiveness of sins. Through the ministry of the Church, may God give you pardon and peace, and I absolve you from your sins in the name of the Father, and of the Son, and of the Holy Spirit.'

'Amen.'

'May the Passion of our Lord, Jesus Christ, the intercession of the Blessed Virgin Mary and of all the saints, whatever good you do and suffering you endure, heal your sins, help you to grow in holiness, and reward you with eternal life. Now go in peace and sin no more.'

Peter is tearful now. 'I want my family. I want my wife - forgive me, Jennifer, for leaving you. I'm so sorry!'

Sebastian came out of the confessional cubicle. They went to a secluded area where he held Peter in his arms; Peter cried great heaving sobs, cleansing his soul. He felt like his heart was breaking as he rested his head on Sebastian's shoulders.

'Let us go into my office,' prompted Sebastian.

'What is this transformation, Peter?' asked Sebastian as they sat drinking tea again in his office. 'You know you are not natural, don't you?'

'There is a wood near my home in Wales. It is a special place, a holy place, a place of great peace and beauty. Also, in the Desert in Yemen.'

'Go on my son.' Sebastian poured some tea.

'There I had a vision. I met an old priest. He told me my name is Caius, an ancient warrior. It all fits; my middle name is Cai, meaning Caius, in Latin. You know my reputation, Sebastian, I can run faster than anyone else, I can fight longer than anyone else, I can stay awake longer than anyone else, I have the strength of ten men. There is also a holy sword, and only I can summon it. The priest told me it is one of the seven holy swords of Prince Michael.'

'Michael appeared to me in the desert. He spoke to me, and gave me the sword,' said Peter. Sebastian dropped his cup on the floor, spilling his tea.

'The Archangel Michael!' Sebastian sat open-mouthed, 'The One who is like God, the Lord of all Angels.' He crossed himself and looked heavenward.

'He told me it was my soul mission to fight the aliens. It was my destiny. He told me about the sword. I can only call the sword, in times of great need. It takes great effort I can tell you - the last time it nearly killed me, but it has a power of its own, Sebastian, I am not sure if I am controlling it, or it is controlling me.'

'God works in mysterious ways,' whispered Sebastian in awe.

'The sword is called Caliburnus, though it has been called by other names; Excalibur was one of its names. It is a very old sword, as old as the Archangel Michael himself. The sword gives me power, strength, and courage. I have visions of battles, fighting, ancient wars. Maybe that's the edge we need to fight these alien bastards.'

Peter rolled up his sleeve, as Sebastian retrieved the glasses from his pocket.

'Holy Mother of Christ, Peter. Do you know what this is?' asked Sebastian.

'Yes. It is the Sigil of Michael.'

'He has marked you, Peter!' Sebastian crossed himself again and looked heavenward, whispering a silent prayer. Then he looked at Peter, a mixture of awe and pity on his face.

'Your abilities are not natural…they are supernatural. The sword that you summon, it is a supernatural weapon. You are the incarnation of this ancient warrior, come now in time of mankind's greatest need, to fight for us, for that is your duty.'

'It is a heavy burden to carry, Sebastian.'

The priest put his hand on Peter's shoulder. 'It is your destiny, but I will help you Peter—or should I call you Caius?' he said, as he put a crucifix around his neck.

Chapter 44

UNHOLY ALLIANCE

Peter, Vinnie, and Sebastian carry new guns as they step out of the church into the daylight. Sebastian gives Peter and Vinnie a crucifix each from his rucksack and anoints their foreheads with holy water. There are no aliens, or alien craft to be seen anywhere. Vinnie carries the Gatling and Peter two M16 203s, fitted with grenade launchers. Peter feels invigorated, back to his old self. He feels like he could conquer the world, his blue eyes shine like the sun.

Sebastian wears a dog collar and crucifix under his old military uniform. There is silence as people follow the soldiers outside the church and gaze up to the heavens; a new hope beckons. The sun rises in the east to a brilliant dawn, A white dove flies up to greet the sun. To the west, clouds part, and a beautiful rainbow appears.

Peter, Vinnie, and Sebastian stand in silence for a while, in awe at the spectacle.

Peter leads Vinnie and Sebastian back to the dress shop. Felix and Lucia are inside, but back away when they see the priest, like cats confronting a dog, hissing and showing their teeth, their eyes blazing red. Sebastian, open-mouthed crosses himself when he sees the vampires.

Lucia is dismayed, 'you would bring a priest?'

'What is this?' exclaimed Felix. Peter tried to explain.

'This is Sebastian, our friend.'

'These are vampires. I know a demon when I see one!'

Sebastian retrieves a silver crucifix from his pocket and thrusts his crucifix near the two vampires. They scream and back away eyes burning red, talons extended, like a tiger that is cornered.

"In the Name of the Father, and of the Son, and of the Holy Ghost. Amen. Most glorious Prince of the Heavenly Armies, Saint Michael the Archangel, defend us in our battle against principalities and powers..."

Peter and Vinnie intervene and stand between the Priest and the vampires. Peter turns to face Sebastian.

'Sebastian, back off! These are our friends!'

'You keep strange friends!' screams Lucia as she looks at Sebastian's crucifix. Peter puts a hand on Sebastian's shoulder.

'Sebastian, calm down. There are some things you need to know. The vampires have joined us in our battle against the aliens!'

'You would befriend demons?'

'As you say, God works in mysterious ways,' Peter stared at the priest who, perplexed, sighs a deep breath, scratching his beard.

'He certainly does.'

Lucia is staring daggers at Sebastian, her eyes still glaring red. 'Put away your crucifix, priest!' she warns in a deep guttural voice, 'before I tear your throat out!'

'Best do what she says,' says Peter, as he hides his crucifix inside his jacket, nodding to Vinnie to do the same.

'I am sorry, please forgive me. What are your names?' asked Sebastian, trying to come to terms with his new accomplices.

'I'm Lucia, this is Felix. Please, understand we are trying to help you,' replies Lucia resuming her normal appearance.

Lucia and Felix stand apart from Sebastian. Lucia touches Peter's arm. 'What's da plan then, Peter?' she asks, trusting her friend, and lover.

'Travelling by day is too dangerous, there are too many patrols. So we rest by day and travel by night. Besides, you don't like the sunlight.'

Peter laid out a map on a table of their location, near the church, and where they were heading.

'Lucia, update Cassian telepathically on the new information about the aliens' fear of entering churches. Okay?' Lucia nods. 'We need to make our way out of Los Angeles and back to the Sirius base in The Mojave Desert. I don't want to fuck about anymore in LA.'

'Suits me,' says Lucia, pouting her lips at Peter. They rest up for the day, but Peter can't sleep, he has too many things going through his mind. He fingers the crucifix Sebastian has given him; his thoughts turn to Jennifer, and his children, as he says a silent prayer to Michael, to protect them. Then at dusk, they venture out to the streets of Los Angeles. The soldiers and vampires creep from building to building, trying to avoid detection.

Out of nowhere, three Hispanic men appear wearing basketball singlets and tracksuit bottoms and approach Sebastian.

'Hey Father, are you a soldier now? That's cool.'

Out of the corner of his eye, Peter can see movement, as an alien patrol comes around the corner. 'Bogies!' shouted Peter.

'Quick, in here man!' shouts another gang member.

They all dive into a derelict building and fall over one another onto the floor. Two Narzuk aliens are in there holding a woman prisoner. They stand up in surprise and scream in anguish as they see Sebastian and his crucifix. One of the aliens touches a device on his wrist, activating his force field, and within a split-second Vinnie shoots him, but the bullets bounce off, ricocheting around the room.

Quick as a flash Peter punches the alien, piercing his shield, sending him flying against the wall, and killing him. Lucia, with lightning speed, spears the other alien with her sword, piercing his shield. Their hearts leap as they heard the unholy grunting barks of alien dogs and the mechanical whirring of robots approaching nearby.

'They know where we are!' Peter's adrenaline is rushing through his body as the storm gets closer. His plan to stay hidden and escape quietly from LA is already screwed as he gives Vinnie that look before a battle.

Chapter 45

LAST STAND

'I'm fed up with running,' shouted Peter, 'Fuck it. Let's fight! We will take on the robots. Lucia, Felix—dogs and aliens! We only have thirty seconds before the robots fire, then we need to get out. STANDBY, STANDBY, GO!'

The gang members joined in. 'We will fight too!'

In true SAS fashion, the three soldiers leaped out of the building. Vinnie let rip with his Gatling gun, bullets sprayed like fireworks, spitting fire, stopping one of the robots, sparks flying everywhere. Vinnie screamed.

'I am the Terminator!'

The gang members and Sebastian fired with pistols and machine guns. Peter screamed, 'I am Caius!' He carried an MI6 in each hand, firing grenades from both launchers, scoring a direct hit on the other robot. One of its legs dropped off, and it fell down with a heavy crash. Vinnie could see smoke pouring from his aging Gatling.

'Oi Bulletproof, my gun's overheating. We don't have much time!'

Lucia and Felix, moving quicker than the eye could follow, jumped over the clones, then turned around and sliced them in two. A dog jumped on Lucia. She ripped its head off. Felix jumped on another dog's back and strangled it. Smoke and flames poured from Vinnie's Gatling gun, and then it stopped firing.

The robot's primary weapon sparked and hummed louder, glowing orange, ready to fire, as an alien fighter craft came round the corner. Peter, wide-eyed, shouted at his comrades.

'Run! Back to the building!'

But he did not run with them, for he was now Caius, Eternal Warrior incarnate.

Time seemed to stop as Vinnie screamed at him to move, but Caius smiled at his friend, as he grew in stature, seeming to grow taller.

'I am Caius, and I will not run.'

They sprinted back to the building as the robot's weapon fired and blasted all around them. They collapsed on the floor out of breath. Rubble and dust fell around them.

The aliens backed away in fear from Caius, unsure of what to do against this human, this holy being, with a crucifix around his neck, but the robots advanced, their programming not able to compute the enemy which now confronted them.

The robots now stood 50 feet away, Caius picked up a piece of steel pipe and then moved like a bolt of lightning. The aliens stood rooted to the spot open-mouthed, as Caius advanced towards the robots, running quick as a cheetah. He jumped on the back of a robot, smashed its eyes with the steel pipe, then with both hands ripped its head off. Another robot fired, hitting the other robot in the back, pushing it forward, as it toppled on top of Caius, appearing to crush him.

There was silence all around, as Narzuks and clones walked slowly towards him, thinking this human was finally defeated.

But he was not.

The downed one-ton robot moved as Caius pushed it off, stood up, grabbed both M16s, loaded both with grenades and fired at the remaining robot. It looked shocked as it looked through the flames, staggering back. Caius kept firing from both M16s, the bullets spraying off the white robot in all directions. He focused his fire at the robot's neck, which appeared to be a weak point. The head dropped forward, and it stopped moving. Then he jumped onto it, grabbed its head with both his hands, and started to turn the head clockwise, until its red eyes flickered and blinked out.

The robot stopped moving. The remaining aliens scattered, not wishing to suffer the same fate. Caius looked around him, for he was alone. He went back to the derelict building looking for his friends. Caius was diminishing now, and he felt like himself again, just plain old "Bulletproof Pete."

Vinnie poked his head around the corner, witnessing the devastation and smoking robots. Peter walked into the room with the others and grabbed Vinnie's arm in friendship, smiling at him.

'We can beat these aliens, Vinnie, I'm sure we can.'

Lucia stepped forward. 'I admire your optimism, Peter da Bulletproof.'

'I saw you, Peter, fight those robots. You are more than human, I think you are this warrior,' said Sebastian in hushed tones.

'I am Caius,' he replied. They all smiled, feeling reassured they had a champion on their side. 'Now I must rest a while,' said Caius who was returning to his alter-ego, Peter.

'The effort of being Caius has drained me.' They looked on in sympathy at their champion, who sank to the floor, and put his head in his hands, which shook as he took deep breaths, putting himself into a meditative state.

'Give me five,' said Peter quietly. Lucia put her hand on his head, stroking his hair, willing his fast recovery; they could not do without him.

The woman who was present in the room sobbed.

'Please help me!'

Sebastian comforted her; put a blanket around her shoulders and looked around the room. 'Is there a back way out?' he asked her smiling gently.

'Looks blocked off to me, Sebastian,' replied Vinnie as he coughed on the dust.

'Is there a basement? Vinnie, go and have a look, will you?' asked Sebastian as he put a water bottle to the woman's lips.

Vinnie searched the rooms, wading through old newspapers and rubbish until he came across a door marked "B." Outside in the street, they could hear the whirring and grinding of approaching fighters, and the barks and growls of the vicious alien canines.

Peter's eyes popped open from his self-induced meditative state. 'Quick, we don't have much time!' He knew they only had seconds before they would be overrun.

Vinnie shouted, 'Over here!' He kicked the door, but it didn't budge. Then he fired a few shots and it released. He switched on his M16 rifle light as they all struggled down the stairs, Sebastian carrying the woman. Vinnie fixed the door shut behind them.

'Not sure how long that will hold.'

The woman, wearing a black dress, muttered something in Spanish, thanking Sebastian and crossing herself. They surveyed the basement, looking for another exit. Sebastian looked at Peter, a worried look on his face.

'This could be a death trap. One way in but no way out.'

'What's behind that rubbish over there?' Peter asked.

They clear the rubbish to reveal a brick wall, Peter shines his flashlight and runs his hands over the wall.

'The bricks look newer here. I wonder…what's on the other side?' Peter looked at the woman, who nodded.

'Si, I work here senor. There is a sewer—other side.' She pointed.

'Bulletproof, let's blast it. I have some C4,' Vinnie offered.

'Do it,' ordered Peter, still feeling weak.

Vinnie made a shaped charge about four feet high, and 18 inches wide as Peter gestured to the team to move.

'Hide in that corner. Five-second delay. MOVE IT!' shouted Vinnie.

As the wall was blown down they were covered in dust, which hung in the air. They walked coughing through the rubble to the dark tunnel on the other side.

They all looked up as there was a pounding on the basement door behind them. The Hispanics and rescued woman looked frightened, looking to Peter for reassurance as Sebastian looked behind.

'Lord Protect us, they found the basement!'

Chapter 46

BATTLE IN THE SEWER

They walked into a dark, wet and slimy tunnel. The smell was awful. Sebastian retched and coughed.

'Which way?' asked Vinnie, looking back into the basement putting a scarf around his face to mask the smell.

Peter looked at his compass under torchlight.

'We head east—that way. Quick, they're not far behind us!'

Vinnie grinned at Peter.

Peter knew that grin.

'I left a present for them.'

An alien robot blasted the basement door, which flew off its hinges. It hovered down into the basement as it scanned the area and saw the hole. Peter gestured for the group to be quiet as he saw the red laser scans of the robot on the far side of the tunnel. The robot moved towards the hole, unaware of what awaited it. As it reached the hole in the tunnel wall, there was a big explosion, the basement collapses around the robot, covering the surprised robot under a 5-foot-thick pile of bricks and concrete.

Vinnie grinned again.

'How do you like that, tin-man?' Vinnie laughed.

'Good job, Vinnie, you bought us some time,' Peter clapped him on the back.

Lucia asked, 'How long?'

'Maybe five minutes.'

They hurried down the sewer, looking behind them. Sebastian half-carried the woman who was struggling.

Peter was impatient. 'We need more speed.'

There was a noise behind them—movement, the sound of bricks falling on the tunnel floor, along with angry sounding whirring, and grinding noises. As they looked back, they could see the robot hovering into the tunnel, looking annoyed, its lasers glowing orange as Peter looked back.

'That robot looks pissed off. Don't think he liked your present, Vinnie, me old mate. Let's take out the sewer roof.'

They fitted their last grenades into their M16 launchers and switched on the MI6 torches to light the target area.

'After three. One, two, three, FIRE IN THE HOLE!

Peter and Vinnie scored direct hits on the roof of the tunnel above the robot, the sewer collapsed, covering most of the tunnel behind them.

'Now he's really pissed off.' Peter urged them forward. 'Let's pick up the pace.'

Vinnie wiped his nose. 'It don't half pen and ink down 'ere.'

'What is pen and da ink, Mr. Vinnie?' asked Lucia.

'Yeah, what's pen and ink mean?' asked one of the Hispanic men.

'He means it stinks down here Lucia,' Peter smiled as he looked at Vinnie, his Terminator friend. The Hispanics looked at Vinnie, confused at his cockney banter.

'Pen and ink—rhymes with stink,' explained Vinnie as the Hispanics smiled and clapped him on the back.

'We like you man—you're cool.'

They all reached for scarves or whatever was to hand, to mask the smell. They travelled on for several more hours in silence, trying not to stumble in the darkness. Peter looked at Lucia, curiously.

'Lucia, why don't you use a gun? It would be a lot easier.'

'I know the value of each death. I look them in da eye as I kill them.' Sebastian looked at Peter.

'She has a point, Peter. Do we know what we take when we shoot someone from a distance?'

Lucia continued, 'In humans after I take their blood I can see their souls depart, and replaced by something unholy, a demon. They then become vampires like me—it is better for them if they are already dead. Not sure if these aliens have souls, though, I see nothing after I end their miserable lives—especially da ones with the red armbands. The Narzuks.'

Sebastian looked at Lucia and crossed himself.

'Lucia, you are the devil.'

'It takes one to know one, priest,' Lucia barked in a deep guttural voice. Peter stepped in between them before a fight broke out, and gave Lucia a stern look. She shrugged her shoulders innocently.

They walked in silence, deep in thought. Peter was wondering if they were ever going to get out of this shit hole; he glanced at Lucia who had stopped.

'I can see some light at the end of da tunnel.'

'I can't see any light, are you speaking metaphorically?' asked Vinnie.

'That's a big word for you, Vinnie,' joked Peter.

'I know a lot of big words, ain't it,' Vinnie replied keeping the banter going. Sebastian interrupted his two friends.

'Will you two stop arguing? Lucia is trying to tell us something.'

'We vampires are very sensitive to da light, we shun sunlight, it is our curse, but there is definitely light ahead, though you may not see it yet.'

A minute later, they could see light at the top of the tunnel. They were standing underneath an old rusty iron ladder leading upwards to the street above. Peter climbed it, moved the manhole cover and stuck his head out. His eyes blinked at the brightness of the morning LA sun—they had travelled through the night.

'Come on up, I can't see anyone.'

Chapter 47

PERSISTENT ROBOT

Lucia and Felix put on their hooded cloaks before they climbed out. The others stood around on lookout duty as Peter looked at his map and blinked, covering his eyes from the sun.

'Sebastian, we need to get the Mojave base undetected. I'm sure the aliens are hunting me.' Lucia nods, every alien in LA seemed to be hunting them.

Their backs were turned to the manhole as the robot silently poked its head above the cover, but it could not get through the hole, it was too small. Its servos ground and whirred as it tried to get through.

Vinnie saw the robot and grinned.

'Well, would you Adam and Eve it, that stupid robot got its head stuck. Now I'm getting seriously pissed off with you. I've already blown you up twice, but you don't give up, do you? Now, my name's Vinnie "The Terminator" and you, my son, are due to be terminated.'

Vinnie placed some C4 around the robot's head and gestured for the party to move off. As they moved away, the robot's head exploded, Just a square box remained where the head was.

'That's why they call him "The Terminator,"' smiled Peter.

Sebastian looked heavenward, 'Amen to that.' Peter now looked impatient.

'Vinnie, if you have quite finished playing with that robot, we need to cover some distance to reach base.' Then he saw something.

He wandered over to look at the remains of the robot's head—a square silver metal box, made of a similar-looking metal to titanium. It had circuits and small red and green lights running around it. The lights blinked on and off several times a second. Vinnie removed the flashing box, as if holding a bomb, not taking his eyes off it.

'Quite heavy,' said Vinnie.

'Vinnie, remember Star Trek? Data the android—looks a bit like his brain.'

'I remember—should hold some useful intel.'

'Exactly—wrap it carefully Vinnie. We will take it back to base.'

Peter looked at his map and then at Vinnie.

'Find a vehicle, will you?'

One of the gang members put up his hand.

'We'll get a ride, we know this area.' Five minutes later, they had hot-wired a large Chevrolet 4x4 which even had petrol. Peter was pleased and impressed with their new recruits.

'Thanks, guys, good job, let's get moving.' They all crowded into the jeep keeping their eyes peeled for enemy patrols. Vinnie drove off, Peter gazing into the distance, his super eyesight scanning the horizon.

'Thank you, we owe you our lives man,' said a gang member. Peter nodded; the other gang members were staring at Lucia, who was sitting next to Peter. Lucia playfully bared her fangs.

'If you're wondering, I'm a vampire.'

'That's cool man—I dig it.'

On the outskirts of the city, they stopped at a deserted gas station. They walked through the run-down store looking at the empty shelves searching for food.

'They must have a storage area,' hoped Peter as they followed him down a narrow dark corridor with a sturdy-looking steel door barring their way. But it was locked. Sebastian and the gang members tried to force it, but it wouldn't budge. Peter stepped forward and demolished it with one small kick. Inside were containers of water and shelves packed with food. They helped themselves to packets of crisps, biscuits, tins of tuna, crispbreads and went back to the jeep.

Peter gulped down a litre of water, forgetting how thirsty he was in the dry Californian heat.

It was dusk when they drove off again, Vinnie at the wheel, eating as they went. They drove through the night, the stars in the desert sky shining bright, windows open to let in the cool night air after the hot LA sun.

'Sebastian, take over mate,' said Peter as he nudged Vinnie, who was nodding off. They stepped out and stretched their legs, while Sebastian took the driving seat. Peter looked up at the desert sky, his eagle eyes looking for anything unusual as a streak of light crossed the sky. Was it a meteor? Then he saw an object moving at right angles against the sky. 'Too high up,' thought Peter as he climbed back in. Immediately Vinnie was seated, he dropped off to sleep, his loud snoring filling the vehicle.

'I hope these aliens don't have snoring detectors else we're in trouble,' joked Peter. Even Lucia smiled at the joke. They all fell asleep one by one except Peter, who could not sleep. He leaned forward to Sebastian, his hands clamped on the steering wheel.

'Sebastian, remember Yemen. The Bedouin man—Abd Al-Wali?'

'How could I forget, he saved my life, God bless him.'

'And mine,' replied Peter.

'Wonder how's he getting on?' wondered Sebastian.

'I have a feeling he is surviving; he's too wily for these aliens,' smiled Peter.

'Yes, too clever,' Sebastian agreed.

Peter's mind went back to Yemen and the desert—the beginning of his spiritual and warrior awakening. It was his worst, and his best experience—the making of him.

In the distance, his eagle eyes could make out alien fighters patrolling, and heading their way, black dots in the blue sky. Getting bigger.

His sixth sense told him they were looking for him.

Caius.

Chapter 48

TO STEAL A PLANE

MOJAVE DESERT

Tired, tanned, hot and dirty, Peter approaches a rocky outcrop in the desert and places his hand on a patch of flat rock. A panel opens, and a retina scanner scans his face as Vinnie watches the sky for any incoming.

He enters the correct return code, and the rock opens enough to reveal a steel door.

'Now speak your id code,' instructs a friendly female voice.

'Fuck, what's my code?' mutters Peter in frustration.

'I do not recognise that code,' returns the annoying female voice. Peter racks his brains as Vinnie gazes out into the desert. A black dot in the distance, growing larger— coming their way.

'Pete, hurry the fuck up will you!' urges Vinnie.

'Morgan, Peter. Sirius ID A777ZA. Confirm.'

'I do not recognise that code,' returns the annoying female voice. 'You have one more attempt,' it intones, like a school mistress.

The black dot gets larger. 'Pete for Christ's sake!' shouted Vinnie.

'Morgan, Peter. Sirius ID A0777ZA. Confirm.'

'ID confirmed,' comes the reply. The steel door slides open to reveal a cave, and they go down some rocky steps.

'Hurry. The door will shut in thirty seconds,' shouts Peter.

They now stand in a dimly lit cave-like structure. They face a steel door. The door slowly opens, as he is greeted by General Scott.

'General, I thought you were at HQ in Virginia?' says Peter in surprise.

'A lot's happened since I last saw you, Captain Morgan.'

'Sir, we thought we saw some incoming alien craft.'

'There has been a lot of activity around here the last few days. We think they're trying to find this base.'

'Maybe they're looking for me. I've stirred up a hornet's nest,' coughs Peter, then adds, 'we have some important new information about the aliens.'

'That's great news Captain. Get some chow, and we will meet again at 1300.'

'General grumpy is being nice for a change,' thinks Peter. An aide interrupts the general.

'Apologies, Captain. Excuse me.'

There are personnel running around, moving equipment and shouting orders. An aide gestures to Peter and his party.

'Captain Morgan, this way, please. The mess is the fourth room on the right. Medical bay, 2nd left.'

'I know.'

'The general will see you at 1300.'

Peter walks past the medical bay and is surprised to see President Wilson in bed. Peter likes the president—a decent, honourable and wise man but is worried by his pale pallor. He smiles warmly as he sits by his bed.

'Mr. President, how are you?' Wilson is weak as he looks at Peter.

'Not so good son, the aliens didn't get me…I'm afraid that cancer did.' The president coughs, and Peter can see there are tears in his eyes.

'Help me up, son.' Peter helps him to sit up in bed.

'Captain—Peter, I have heard rumours of your powers, and your deeds in battle. It is time for you to become the hero, my son.' He grips Peter's arm—'for if you do not, we are lost…lost.' The president coughs and takes some breaths, then recovers himself.

'This country…this world needs you. I'm relying on you to save the day. General Scott is running things now. Excuse me, I need to rest.'

Peter is contemplative as he leaves the medical bay. For all his superpowers he cannot help the president beat cancer, but he is right—he must become the hero, however reluctant he is about it.

For him and Vinnie.

For Jennifer and Gill.

For the world.

As he walks down the corridor, head down, carrying the world's burdens on his shoulders, he smiles as he bumps into Colonel Wight.

'How are you, son?'

'Lot on my mind Colonel. But we got back alive—and we got some intel. Alien intel—so overall pretty good.' He shakes the colonel's hand warmly; the colonel holds onto it.

'Good to have you back, son. Keep this to yourself, but our attrition rate is 80%, and that's Special Forces. We seem to be fighting a losing battle.' He looks Peter in the eye, still holding his hand.

'We need good men like you, Captain,' speaks the grizzly silver-haired colonel. 'We…we are all relying on you now, son. We have heard the stories of you fighting the aliens—bringing down their ships.'

'Thanks, Colonel, I'll see you later.' Peter walks, then stops and turns.

'We can beat them, Colonel—we just need to find their weakness.'

'That's the spirit!' then the Colonel walks off.

Peter takes Vinnie aside. 'There is something we need to do—it cannot wait!'

'What's that?' asks Vinnie registering Peter's tone.

'We need to steal an X-37D.'

Chapter 49

AN UNEXPECTED JOURNEY

It is midnight. Peter, Vinnie, and Kojak are whispering in the semi-darkness of the X-37D launch bay.

'Vinnie, I cannot force you to come with me, it's probably a court martial if we go.'

'Pete, I'm not letting you go on your own, court-martial, or no court-martial. We're in this together.'

'Vinnie, I need to know Jennifer and the kids are ok,' replied Peter.

'Didn't Lucia say Jennifer is not there?'

'I need to see for myself. I need to know Vinnie!'

Peter, now turns to Kojak, asking the silent question.

'Aye laddy, in for a penny, in for a pound,' replies Kojak in his inimitable Scottish accent.

'Thanks, Kojak. It's decided then—we go. We take minimal kit,' replies Peter.

'If we get court-martialed you could always break us out of jail with your superhuman powers,' smiled Kojak.

They all laugh. 'That's the least of my worries,' replies Peter as they file into the X-37D.

'Where do you think you are going Mr. Peter da Bulletproof?' says Lucia as she joins them on the X-37D. Peter smiles, then hears shouts from outside. 'I will deal with it,' says Peter striding outside onto the concrete launch bay to be greeted by two military policemen, pistols out, who regard him with fear in their eyes.

'Gentlemen, let me explain.' With lightning speed, he grabs both their pistols and cracks them over the head, and they fall to the ground unconscious.

Alarms sound as Peter rushes back on board. He talks to Kojak in the cockpit.

'Operating launch bay doors!' shouts Kojak; Peter watches as the launch bay doors open at a snail's pace.

Kojak fires up the engines, 'Pete get seated, it's going to be a rough ride!' Vinnie secures the fuselage door, as they hurriedly put their seat belts on. Peter can see the launch bay door from his seat through the open cockpit door. There is an agonising wait as the launch bay door leaves just enough room for the X-37D to launch.

'Gun it!' shouts Peter, as Kojak pushes the thruster forward. They are pinned to their seats by the g-force as they are propelled forward into the desert night, launching into the clear dark desert sky, the stars shining above them.

'Engaging shields,' Kojak's voice comes over the tannoy. 'ETA Wales about one-and-a-half hours.' He enters the coordinates for the Brecon Beacons as Peter watches the LED speed display increase from 1000mph to 3000mph. Lucia leans toward Peter and rests her head on his shoulder.

Vinnie leans forward in the seat behind them.

'What is it, Vinnie?' asks Peter.

'I was finking.'

'Yes…' Peter waits patiently, Vinnie is hesitant, which is unusual for him.

'I was finking we could do a detour…'

'To where exactly?'

'We can pick up my father and Ron before we go to Wales,' says Vinnie.

'Vinnie, our mission is dangerous enough as it is. Western Britain has little alien activity, whereas London will be like alien Piccadilly Circus mate!' Then adds, 'do you know where they are?'

'In situations like this—a war, we have a safe-house outside London, in the country. That's where they will be. If they're still alive.'

'Let's go see Kojak,' says Peter, annoyed that their plan might change. They walk into the cockpit, where Kojak is tracking alien activity.

'Slight detour, we're picking up Vinnie's family North of London, Kojak,' says Peter, awaiting a fiery response from the Scottish pilot—he is not disappointed.

'Away an boil yer head laddy, t'will be difficult enough as it is!'

'Kojak do it, please. Vinnie, give Kojak your coordinates and keep him topped up with coffee and sandwiches from the galley.'

'Thanks, Pete,' Vinnie smiles.

'Ok laddy, accelerating to Mach 7. Hang on.'

Kojak shakes his head muttering, as Peter goes back to Lucia.

'Slight diversion,' says Pete as he touches her shoulder.

'I heard,' replied Lucia.

'I need to visit my family, I miss them terribly,' there is a tremble in Peter's voice as Lucia holds his hand.

'I am jealous of your family Peter, you are lucky. I had a family once.' Lucia thinks back to her husband Caxus, killed by the alien filth, then looks at Caius, and rests her head on his shoulder again. Caius would make a good husband, she thinks, but he is already married. She would have to make do with being his lover. Her mind drifts back again to Roman times—her husband Caxus, her two children, and the beautiful slave girl, with long brown hair, and brown eyes. Beautiful. She loved her too; her eyes lit up when she smiled. She treated her like one of the family, and they soon became lovers, spending many happy afternoons in the bedroom, laughing and playing like children.

Then her husband Caxus would join them—it seemed normal. Caxus, tall, strong and clever, charismatic, an ex-soldier—much like Caius really—then the thought hits her like a sledgehammer. Are they one and the same? Her heart pounds as she looks at Caius again.

CAXUS? CAIUS?

It seemed the winds of fate are dictating events now.

After crossing the Atlantic in record time, the X-37D is flying at 100 feet above the choppy waters of the Bristol Channel, throwing up spray behind them. Peter joins Vinnie and Kojak in the cockpit, as they cross south to Somerset, then to Wiltshire. Kojak points to a screen.

'Vinnie, keep your eyes glued to that screen for alien activity, laddy. Destination Broxbourne, Hertfordshire—activity will increase as we get nearer London. ETA ten minutes. Vinnie, have we lost the last contact?' asks Kojak.

'Yeah, I fink so, it's not on the screen anymore - I fink we outran them.'

Chapter 50

REG AND RON

Five minutes later they piled out of the X-37D and stood in a cold, muddy field. The dawn was breaking over the horizon. There was silence as they looked around; no outward signs of an alien invasion, and 400 yards away stood a lone, dark, uninviting house. No lights.

'That way,' said Vinnie. They jogged off leaving Kojak to mind their transport. They carried PR1 hand pistols, and Peter had a PR7 rifle with a grenade loaded into the grenade launcher, just in case they had a contact. They stopped as an owl screeched nearby and flew above them. Lucia drew her sword and sniffed the air. 'There is an alien foot patrol one mile distant—we must hurry!'

The house was in darkness as they approached; no sign of activity. Vinnie went to an outhouse nearby and eased the old wooden door open, moving some boxes to reveal a wooden trap door. Vinnie lifted the creaking door. He was met by two sets of eyes and the smell of stale beer and cigarettes.

'Dad?' a voice replied.

'Vinnie—it's you, God be praised!' Reg, wearing a white shirt and cardigan went up the steps, followed by his brother Ron carrying shotguns and a satchel. Vinnie and Reg hugged one another tightly, and then he shook Ron's hand. Reg turned to Peter.

'Hello Peter, hope you're looking after my boy, Vinnie.'

'Yes, Reg. Now we must get going—there's an alien foot patrol nearby. Silence until we reach the plane. Vinnie, you take the rear, I will take point. Go!' They ran as fast as they could back to the waiting X-37D, it's engines ticking over. They ran up the steps to hear Kojak shouting over the tannoy.

'We've got incoming! Move yer arses!' They scrambled to get a seat and get belted as the X-37D lifted and hovered for a few seconds, before shooting off at speed on a westerly heading. Ron banged his head on the fuselage as he struggled to get his seat belt on in time. Vinnie helped Ron and Reg to get comfortable, before stowing their shotguns away.

Reg produced a flask and handed it to Ron, before passing to Vinnie. Vinnie gulped some whiskey looking at his father, delighted to be reunited. Reg stank of sweat and beer, but he was alive, thank God. 'Mum?' asked Vinnie? Reg shook his head silently, unable to look Vinnie in the eye.

'Vinnie, I am sorry, Gill was taken from us, in the Blind Beggar. There was nothing we could do,' Reg looked at his son trying to find the right words to comfort him. Vinnie nodded, recalling the scenes as he witnessed Gill's kidnap by the alien filth.

'How did you get to the safe-house Dad?' Vinnie asked quietly.

'We made our way north in the dead of night when the patrols are quietest. To the Lea. We found a boat and made our way up the canal and river, then hid during the day, then made our way to the safe house.'

A thought flashed through Peter's mind as he overheard the conversation. What if Jennifer had been taken too? Then he dismissed it. Lucia looked away, not meeting his eyes. They were pinned to their seats as the X-37D accelerated to full speed. 'ETA Brecon 20 minutes Pete,' Kojak's voice came over the tannoy.

Peter had a swig of the whiskey and faced Vinnie, Reg, and Ron. 'You did well to get to the safe-house, Reg.' Peter took another gulp, feeling the warm liquid in his chest and stomach.

'This war is a guerrilla war; guile and stealth are what's needed.' Peter finished the whiskey. Ron got a bottle of Glenmorangie from his satchel and shared it around. Peter smiled—single malt—and filled his plastic cup.

'Myself and Vinnie have been fighting aliens since day one. They are unholy bastards, but I think I'm starting to get the measure of them. In the next couple of days, there's going to be a big offensive.' He looked at Ron and Reg, 'We aim to strike a blow against these alien bastards.'

'Good luck son,' replied Reg. 'What about London, Pete, it's overrun with the alien bastards.'

'When were done in the US we're coming back to London—that's a promise,' replied Peter, looking Reg and Ron in the eye.

'Where are we going now?' asked Reg.

'We're going to visit my family in the Brecons. I need to know they're okay.' Lucia looked away lost in her own thoughts, afraid to tell Peter of her fears.

Kojak gently landed the plane in a clearing in the woods in the hidden valley where Peter's home was. The world's would-be-saviour got out, stretched his legs, and took a deep breath of the fresh Welsh air, filling his lungs—nothing like it. The sun was rising higher now, and there was a mist on the ground. A deer wandered out of the wood into the clearing, looked at them, then scampered off. Vinnie looked at Peter, knowing what was running through his mind.

'Let's go,' said Peter, the stress etched on his face, as he led the way down a grassy path through the woods. As he walked up his garden path, his stomach was in turmoil. The house was in darkness. A million thoughts ran through his mind as he knocked on the solid oak door.

Silence.

Then he knocked again.

'Who is it?' said a whisper.

'It's Peter, who is that?'

'It's Ruth, your sister!' The door opened, and a tearful Ruth stood there in a dressing gown, holding a torch, then wrapped her arms around her brother as she hugged him tightly, tears rolling down her eyes. 'I thought we would never see you again!' she cried. Peter held her at arm's length.

'Where is Jennifer, where is she?' Peter's blue eyes blazed.

'Come inside—all of you.' Ruth's crying eyes could not meet her brother's.' They all sat around the kitchen table while Ruth boiled a kettle on the Aga stove.

'Where are the kids?'

'Asleep.'

'Jennifer?' Peter pressed. Ruth avoided his gaze as she made some tea, then she turned and looked at her brother.

'She—she went for a walk and never came back. I'm sorry Peter, I really am,' she sobbed into his arms again.

They heard footsteps down the wooden stairs; Sally and Robert ran to Peter. He knelt down and hugged them, tears in his eyes.

'Daddy's here!'

'Auntie Ruth—Daddy's back!' Then Peter looked at Lucia, handing her a framed photo of him and Jennifer.

'Lucia, is Jennifer in the vicinity?' Lucia looked at the photograph—at her brown eyes and hair; *she seemed familiar somehow.* Her eyes rolled back as she went into a trance and her body stiffened. Sally and Robert hugged Peter.

'Who is that lady?' asked a frightened Robert.

'Lucia—she's a good friend, but she's a bit different.'

At last, Lucia came out of her self-induced trance. 'She is not in da Brecon Beacons. She is not in Wales or England. I cannot find her anywhere. I am sorry Peter.' Peter fell silent, then looked at Ruth.

'Ruth we cannot stay. I have to get back.'

'But you only just got here!'

'I need to find Jennifer!' Then Peter hugged his kids. 'I promise I will find mummy. Promise. Now give me a big kiss.' Reg came forward. 'Me and Ron will stay here and look after the kids. We will guard them with our lives.'

'Thanks, Reg,' said Peter shaking his hand.

'Look after Vinnie, will you?' said Reg. Peter nodded. Lucia looked at Ruth and the two East End gangsters.

'I will ask Lady Vesilia for help, you will have visitors like me. Do not be afraid,' said Lucia.

'You will be well guarded,' said Peter. 'Vinnie, leave a radio here and show Reg how to use it.'

'Can I come with you?' asked Robert, his big blue eyes gazing up at his father.

'It's dangerous son. You stay here with Auntie Ruth and Reg and Ron.

'Call me uncle Reg,' said Reg as his face cracked with a smile.

'Do you know any card games, Uncle Reg?' asked Robert. Reg's face cracked as he smiled. 'Yes, son.'

Peter felt hollow as they made their way back to the waiting X-37D. He was downcast as he slumped down in his seat, a feeling of hopelessness filling his soul. Vinnie didn't know what to say to his old friend, but *he knew what he was going through.* Vinnie went to the cockpit to find Kojak snoring, he nudged him awake and went to the galley to make him a coffee, then came back as Kojak readied the X-37D for take-off.

'Any luck?' asked Kojak.

'No Jennifer's been taken,' replied Vinnie - he avoided Peter's gaze as he came into the cockpit. 'Let's get back to base and face the music,' ordered Peter, looking grim, his worst fears now confirmed.

Chapter 51

COURT MARTIAL

An hour-and-a-half later Kojak docked the X-37D into the landing bay in the Sirius base in the Mojave Desert. They strolled out of the plane onto the concrete launch bay to be met by four nervous-looking military policemen.

'Give me your weapon. You must follow me,' said a poker-faced MP, but Peter ignored him and followed the MPs out of the launch bay and down a long corridor.

'He's here,' spoke Poker Face into his radio, glancing at the warrior. Lucia walked next to Peter as passing soldiers gave Peter a suspicious glance.

'Everyone knows,' said Peter. Lucia nodded, her eyes blazed a little red, her nails extended and fangs showed—*ready to kill anyone who harmed her lover*. The MPs looked at her nervously as Peter bumped into Handsome Mike in the corridor, and they stopped.

'Pete, I would have done the same. Don't worry.' Mike patted him on the back. How did everyone know? Well, he had hardly kept quiet about it in the mess. All soldiers talked about their families, whether they were still alive, or not.

Was it worth the trip?

Yes. He had seen his children and now they had extra protection. Now he knew he had to look for Jennifer.

That was his focus now. 'Keep moving,' said poker-face.

'Go fuck yourself,' replied Peter, his countenance changed.

They stopped outside a large room. He could hear the agitated voice of General Scott inside. No change there then. Poker Face grabbed Peter's arm and felt his iron hard muscles. 'Captain Morgan, you come inside, the rest of you wait outside.' Peter looked at him fiercely, and Poker Face loosened his grip, fear in his eyes, as a trickle of blood oozed out of his nose.

Inside the room were Scott and Colonel Wight and another —a panel, seated at a table. They looked stiff-lipped, crusty and very formal, like an old school headmaster about to punish a pupil for a foolish prank. Poker Face was joined by two MPs who grabbed the warrior by the arm and marched him in. Peter felt a little annoyed at this, the ancient battle blood stirred, as he surveyed the panel in front of him. General Scott looked at Peter as if he had just stepped on a dog turd.

'Captain Morgan, you stole an X-37D without permission on some fool errand of your own. It is in direct contravention of standing orders and a court-martial offense. Well, what do you have to say for yourself?' Scott's neck turned red as he barked. Peter yawned as he remembered a panel job interview at the local council, as a teenager. He had hated it.

Bureaucrats.

'I needed to check on my family, General.' Peter stood there trying to remain calm as he thought the veins on Scott's neck would burst as he stood up to face him.

'Needed to check on your family? Good God man, that's a luxury we cannot afford. Handcuff him, Sergeant!'

'No handcuffs can hold me,' Peter's voice deepened, and the blood rose as his eyes radiated a silver blue. He was no longer nonchalant, nor patient, as he was handcuffed by a hesitant MP. He seemed to grow larger. Dark shadows flickered in the corner of the room. The MPs moved away from him, eyeing him nervously; *fear in their eyes.*

'Captain Morgan, the X-37D you took is one of only three in the United States. You have jeopardised our military capability. Under the emergency powers given to me, I order you to be held in solitary confinement until further notice.'

'No cell can hold me!' The lights flickered, and the table shook, as Caius's deep voice boomed around the room. The MPs loosened their grip.

'We will hold a formal Court Martial at our convenience.'

'This is bullshit!' Caius's deep voice cried as the Eternal Warrior incarnate rose to the surface, the room now shaking.

Then the room went dark.

Pitch black.

And silent.

When the lights came back on again, Lucia was standing next to him, her eyes turning a deeper shade of red. The temperature in the room plunged. The water froze in General Scott's cup. Scott's breath was a mist as Caius's demeanour changed—his blue eyes blazed.

'You cannot confine me. I am Caius the Eternal Warrior!'

The room shook at his words. A dribble of blood dropped from General Scott's nose, he dabbed the blood with his handkerchief as he shivered in the freezing cold and observed the warrior standing in front of him. He felt fear as Caius held up his hands, which turned to flames—red, orange, yellow flames erupted from his hands, and melted the handcuffs, dripping molten metal onto the floor, and the metal table.

'It is the prophecy,' spoke Lucia solemnly. Caius's deep voice boomed, shaking the room once more.

'I am Caius, General Scott, come to deliver mankind from the clutches of the alien filth. My patron is the Holy Angel Michael himself; *he has marked me. See.*' Caius held up his muscled and sinewed arm showing the black sigil, the signature of Michael himself. General Scott sat open-mouthed, in a cold sweat.

'Unless you want me to bring down the powers of Heaven…'

'…and Hell,' added Lucia,

'…down upon you, you will let us go. I am Caius, I have spoken.'

Caius now grew taller, his head touching the ceiling, and shone with a blue light—all around him was a blue light. The MPs ran from the room terrified, as Lucia's red eyes blazed and showed her fangs. General Scott clutched at his neck, as if being choked, his nose pouring blood as Lucia locked eyes on him.

'Caius…Captain Morgan,' he gasped, 'I, I was mistaken. I am sorry. We need your help. Do not hurt us!' cried General Scott as he hid under the table. Colonel Wight sat impassively and looked at Caius in wonder. Caius slowly transformed back to Peter again, as General Scott whimpered.

As Peter and Lucia walked down the corridor, he turned to her.

'Let's get some sleep, Lucia.'

'Of course, my love,' then she held his hand and kissed him. The powers of Heaven and Hell had brought them together in a common purpose— God's purpose. Peter then knew that a greater power than him was pulling the strings of fate—'for who knows what plans he holds for us?'

Chapter 52

PREPARE FOR BATTLE

In a conference room, situated deep within the Sirius Mojave command bunker, are seated General Scott, Cassian, CIA Chief Smith, Professor Picard, Colonel Wight, and a few senior officers. Vinnie, Sebastian, Lucia, and Felix are also around the table. Around the periphery are a few Special Forces soldiers, who look as if they have been to hell and back, which in fact they have.

Scott is about to start the proceedings when Peter walks into the room. As he looks around the room, everyone stands up, including the senior staff, and stare at him. Scott looks nervously at him as one of the Delta Force soldiers goes up and shakes Peter's hand.

He shares a few jokes with his comrades in arms before General Scott gestures everyone to sit down.

'Thank you, gentlemen,' gestures Scott, dismissing the soldiers who leave the room. Peter takes his place at the table next to Vinnie.

'Everyone, just to bring you up to date: We thought that our Sirius HQ command bunker in Virginia was undetectable, but we were over-run two days ago; we narrowly escaped.' He looks at Sebastian, 'Thank God. We are still getting ourselves organised here. In many ways, this command bunker is better hidden than the HQ, so we hope to remain undetected.'

'We were very careful not to be followed.' Peter assures the general, forgetting the court-martial incident. He could have killed him of course, but he is an excellent general—*even if he is an arsehole.*

'Okay Captain, please update us with this new information you have,' there is fear in his voice as he looks at Peter President Wilson, supported by medical staff, walks into the room. He sits down next to his general, who is concerned. 'Mr. President, you should be resting.'

'It's okay. I want to hear the latest news. Where is Schmitt?' Scott is silent for a moment, then speaks.

'He didn't make it. Stayed at his post until the last minute. Made sure we got away.'

'Can they follow us here—down the tunnel?' asks the president.

'The railway tunnel was destroyed, so hopefully not,' replies Scott.

'Captain Morgan was about to update us with important information.' A weak President Wilson smiles at Peter.

'Go on, son.'

'Yes sir, the aliens are not as invincible as we thought they were. Like vampires, they cannot enter a church.' Scott looks annoyed at Cassian.

'Cassian, why didn't you tell us this?'

'This is a new development. Please realise that we haven't seen these Sumeri for many years. It seems, like us, God has turned his back on them.'

'This might be the edge we need,' says Scott, hopeful.

Peter stands up and looks at Sebastian. 'Let me introduce an old friend of mine, Father Sebastian Harris. He used to be in our regiment but left to become a priest. We bumped into him by accident.'

'Serendipity, maybe,' Wilson ventures.

Sebastian walks to the table, while Cassian and Lucia back away.

'Mr. President, I run an old church on the edge of Los Angeles. I noticed that even though they were attacking buildings and people, they wouldn't go anywhere near my church. It just so happens that a couple of stray aliens were outside. The ones in black, the ones with the red armbands.'

'Narzuk SS,' says Lucia. 'That's what they're called.'

'How do you know?' asked Peter.

'I heard the other Narzuks talking.'

'The rank and file?'

'Yes,' replies Lucia.

'The ones with the white armbands?' asks Peter.

'Yes. The Narzuk SS are hated by everyone it seems.'

'Including their own troops,' adds Peter.

'The Narzuks were complaining about rations and how they are treated so badly by their SS counterparts,' adds Lucia.

'What happened to the aliens—the Narzuk SS who entered the church?' asks Scott.

'I think they were on drugs or something—they strolled in and collapsed in agony,' replies Peter.

'We can use that,' Scott smiles for the first time in weeks. Sebastian continues.

'General, there are many homeless refugees and survivors wandering around, here and there. We need to tell them that churches, indeed mosques, and temples, any place of worship, are now places of sanctuary from the alien invasion.'

'Sebastian, I will make sure that information is disseminated. This is useful, but we still need to find a way to attack the aliens, attack the ships. Our fighters are no good; artillery doesn't work. I'm open to any suggestions. Anyone?' ventures General Scott, a look of desperation on his face.

'I noticed the aliens are wary of a crucifix when I wore it. And maybe we could use holy water against them,' says Sebastian hopefully. 'Yes holy water would probably work, but you would have to be very close up.'

'No replacement for a PR7 bullet then,' replies Peter. 'No, I would say not,' replied Sebastian.

'Keep your crucifixes and holy water away from us please, else you can find yourself some new allies!' screeched an unhappy Cassian, his eyes turning red, the talons on his hands now getting bigger.

'Sebastian has a sackful of crucifixes and holy water, but we must keep them well hidden when near a vampire,' Peter suggests trying to keep the peace. 'Or maybe it's more trouble than it's worth,' he sighs. Vinnie, having acquired a taste for coffee, is busy drinking cupfuls and stuffing biscuits into his face. A large biscuit drops into his coffee, spilling some of it onto the floor. He looks embarrassed, but then Peter takes the robot's head from a rucksack eager to change the subject. 'General Scott, Vinnie retrieved this from a robot.' Peter puts the metal box on the table in front of General Scott. 'Thank you, Corporal. Professor, will you have a look at this please?'

'Oui. It looks like a CPU of some kind.' The professor smiles in admiration at Peter and Vinnie, as does President Wilson.

Cassian speaks up while looking warily at the priest. 'General, each vampire can carry one or two soldiers up to the spaceships. We will be undetected, and they will not be expecting it. We will have to do it at night.'

'Cassian, Captain Morgan failed in that mission before, what makes you think he can succeed now?' asks Scott as a veil of silence hits the room. Peter's eyes flash blue and seemed to grow larger - malevolent.

Chapter 53

PETER THE INDEFATIGABLE

'General,' interrupts Peter, ignoring the jibe. 'With the professor's help we may be able to access their codes, from the robot's head—to get into the ship.'

'Okay, I like that idea. We can plant a small nuclear device on each ship,' a smile creeps back across the general's face.

'We don't want too much collateral damage,' replies President Wilson, 'There may be prisoners on board; we want to give them a chance to escape.'

'A small briefcase nuclear device should suffice Mr. President—powerful enough to cripple the ship, but not enough to create too much collateral damage,' replies Scott. Wilson smiles, then looks at Cassian.

'That would work. Will you help us Cassian?' He is eager to bring the vampires back on board.

'Yes, just keep your abominable instruments away from us!' Cassian's eyes flares red.

Peter is concerned.

'What about the captured women on board?' he asks, thinking about Jennifer.

'We could rescue those as well,' says Cassian.

Peter speaks up again.

'Mine and Vinnie's wives are on board one of those ships, somewhere in the world. My wife!' Peter and Vinnie exchange glances as the room shook a little as his voice reverberated around the room.

General Scott looks aloof.

'I understand, but you must not lose sight of the objective,' says the general in a monotone voice, eyebrows raised. Peter thinks about taking Scott's head off with a punch. Peter and Vinnie stand up, looking at the general. Wilson can feel the tension in the room.

'Don't worry son, we will do everything we can,' says President Wilson, then adds, 'we appreciate the efforts you and Peter are making in this war,' looking at Vinnie this time.

General Scott is abrupt.

'That's all, gentlemen. The senior staff will remain behind. There will be a final briefing at 15:00.' The president gestures to Peter.

'Can you help me back to my room, son?'

'Of course, sir.' The president puts his arm around Peter as they walk down the corridor to his quarters.

'You must understand, General Scott has a tough job to do. He can be uncompromising at times.'

'I understand Mister President,' Peter replies. As Peter walks, his thoughts go to his father. He died when Peter was young, so he didn't know him that well, but he remembers going fishing for salmon with him, hiking in the glorious Brecon hills and his father reading travel books to him at bedtime. 'The world is full of adventure,' he used to tell Peter.

He liked this President Wilson. He was a wise and compassionate man. Not like that arsehole General Scott. 'But I suppose he has a job to do.'

More Special Forces troops are assembled for the 15.00 briefing. As they walk down the corridor, they bump into Handsome Mike again. Peter notices a woman with him, the one they rescued. Peter smiles at the Latino woman, who smiles back at them.

'This is Angel,' says Mike.

'Obrigado,' says Angel to Peter in a Portuguese accent, her dark eyes shining.

'Terminator, good to see you and Bulletproof again!' says Mike.

Peter joins in. 'Handsome, you're still alive. God must have a sense of humour.'

Vinnie teases him. 'Hey, Handsome Mike. You're still alive, those aliens must fancy you!'

'We heard you kicked some alien ass…' smiles Mike.

'Yep me and my best mate Vinnie,' Peter grins.

Also assembled are vampires from around the world. They all look like they belonged to separate clans, but they all defer to Cassian, who is their leader. A small group of vampires approach Cassian, bow and introduce themselves.

'Count Cassian, we were sent by Lord Aswerne to help you fight the alien filth. He sends his greetings.' A vampire dressed all in black approaches Cassian and speaks in a clipped English accent. 'We remember the old alliance. The Lady Vesilia has sent us to fight by your side. Command us,' he says, giving a Roman salute. Cassian is moved by their loyalty, there is a hint of a smile on his face as he speaks.

'I thank you, comrades, you are most welcome, join us.'

General Scott addresses the mix of Special Forces soldiers—Navy Seals, Rangers, and a few others. Peter even recognises a couple of them from his SIS missions in the Middle East, 'the cream of the crop' and he feels proud to be in their company. The room is filling up fast. Something is being planned.

At last.

Chapter 54

THIS IS NOT WHAT WE SIGNED UP FOR

'Attention please,' General Scott cleared his throat and drank some water. 'Phase One saw our ground war against the alien invasion. Our losses are around 80%, even with the help of our vampire friends here. On the positive side, we have seen alien ground patrols drastically reduced. Alien air patrols have, however, increased. Every time we kill an alien, that's one they cannot replace. I know I keep saying that, but it is worth remembering. We kill enough, and they will retreat. New information has come to light of the aliens' weaknesses which we can take advantage of. Basically, they have the same weaknesses as vampires—they cannot go into churches.'

The newly-arrived vampires looked up in surprise.

'Now we enter Phase Two of our operation. It will be in two parts. Conventional forces will team up with vampires for another ground offensive. Remaining troops are ordered to go to the nearest church, mosque, synagogue or temple—any holy ground, as safe havens. This information will be broadcasted worldwide on the EBS, radio and in Morse code. Simultaneously, Phase Two will see Special Forces, that's you guys, team up with our vampire friends who will transport you to designated alien spaceships around the United States mainland. There, your primary objective is to plant small nuclear devices to cripple each ship. The secondary objective is to rescue any women you find on the ship. This 'two-pronged offensive' will start in 33 hours precisely, at midnight tomorrow. We will coordinate simultaneous attacks in multiple cities throughout the US and other countries in a worldwide counteroffensive.'

'Why aren't we attacking the mothership?' asked Peter.

'It is still in Earth orbit, Captain. Too difficult to attack,' replied Scott. 'We will focus on the Earth-bound ships for the time being.'

'Fair enough' thought Peter.

'How do we get on to the alien Earth ships?' A soldier asked. Cassian stood up.

'We will carry two soldiers each and fly onto the ship. We can fly up to a height of about a mile, two at most, and that's about our limit.'

'Yes, but how do we get on the ships? Do we need codes?' asked the soldier again.

'Our Professor Picard is accessing this information as we speak. You will each be given codes before the mission,' replied Scott. Peter thought he sounded optimistic but prayed the professor could access the codes in the robot's brain. Scott continued.

'Once on board, the priority is to plant a nuclear device to cripple the ship. If you are detected, fight your way out, killing as many aliens and infected women you can find.'

'Assuming we survive, we can glide down to Earth,' added Cassian.

Handsome Mike stood up and protested.

'Killing women is not what we signed up for, sir!'

General Scott's face went red.

'You will carry out your orders, soldier, period! Same for the rest of you. Sometimes your best is not good enough. Sometimes you have to do what's required.'

'Now he's quoting Churchill,' thought Peter. Logic says that he's right, of course *but is it the human thing to do?*

Cassian, who was sitting beside the general, looked at him.

'Thank you, General. We cannot allow infected women to live. Otherwise, our planet will be overtaken by this new hybrid alien race. Humankind will become just a memory!'

Peter stood up. 'It seems the aliens have been very clever, holding our women as hostages.' A moral dilemma indeed he thought.

Handsome Mike persisted.

'How do we know if they're infected, sir?'

Cassian continued.

'General, perhaps I can help here. When a human woman has been fertilised with alien sperm, they look sickly and turn a pale shade of green. The incubation period is the same as humans, around nine months. The hybrid babies are born with an egg sack around them. Unfortunately, the stress on the human mothers is usually too much for them.'

The general's face is less red now.

'If you see an infected female, do not hesitate to shoot, is that clear? From what I've heard, you will be doing them a favour.'

The Soldiers look at each other in horror and disgust. There were loud mutterings and complaints as several soldiers stood up and protested. These were battle-hardened, highly skilled soldiers, but there was an ethical limit to what they would do, and what they would not do. Many of them had wives and girlfriends who were also missing. They had also been kidnapped by the aliens. Peter and Vinnie were not alone in their plight. Peter could not hold back any longer. He stood up to face the general, his blood hot with anger. His countenance changed, he grew taller, the soldiers looked at him, one muttering, *Maybe the rumours are true.*'

'General, Mike is right, many of us have wives and girlfriends who have been kidnapped by these bastards, so what about women who are not infected, can we save those?'

The general looked frustrated and irritated, he was used to people following orders, but these soldiers were the cream of the crop and used to debating strategy and tactics. He gave the insolent Peter a dirty look. He didn't like soldiers who questioned his orders. In any other circumstances he would get a reprimand, or worse. But after the sham court-martial, he thought better of it - *his Caius alter-ego had put the fear of God in him. This Caius was only partially human — he was a demi-God.*

'Okay, so save any uncontaminated women, but mission parameters are to kill as many aliens as possible. There will be one eight-man team for each ship. Four soldiers and four vampires. There is no backup. There are three ships we need to target in California. Other targets will be allocated shortly. One more thing, Sebastian, stand up please.'

Chapter 55

ANGRY VAMPIRES

Sebastian turned to face the soldiers and vampires, who were staring daggers at him, and hissing, showing their fangs. 'The alien race is damned, they cannot go near churches, that's why they are designated places of sanctuary. The aliens are afraid of priests and holy objects, so after the briefing I will issue you with holy water and crucifixes…' There was uproar as the vampires all stood up, red eyes blazing, fangs now extended, ready to tear the priest apart.

Cassian addressed his vampires, trying to calm them, 'Brothers and sisters, we have been assured these objects will remain hidden whilst in the presence of vampires.' Then he turned to look at the soldiers. 'Please remember this, or we will rip your throats out and you can fight the aliens on your own. *Is that understood?*' The bemused soldiers nodded.

'Thank you, Cassian and remember what he told you. This may give us a small edge if you get close enough,' said Scott.

Peter stood up. 'I think these holy weapons will only work on the Narzuk SS—the evil bastards with the red armbands—the ones kidnapping the women and running the concentration camps. Remember the church, Sebastian?' The priest nodded, then Peter recalled the terrible vision he had when he touched the black figurine around the Narzuk's neck; *he saw something terrible and powerful.*

He pushed the memory back into his mind, but he knew one day he must face it, whatever it was. 'I don't think it will work on the rank and file Narzuks, and certainly not the clones,' Peter added, 'But these Narzuk SS are unholy.'

'Thank you, Captain Morgan. One more thing: remember to use your PR7s on full automatic to disable their shields,' said Scott.

'No shit Sherlock,' said one disgruntled ranger.

'You will be given specific orders on targets after this briefing. Good luck. Dismissed,' ordered General Scott.

'I'm beginning to think these holy weapons are more trouble than they're worth!' sighed Peter to Vinnie as they joined Sebastian who was handing out crucifixes. 'Keep them hidden,' Peter reminded Handsome Mike as he lined up.

Scott walked back to the command and control centre, which was filled with computer screens, charts and technicians who were dashing back and forth. Other military technicians were glued to their screens, knowing their decisions could make the difference between life and death. Scott turned to an unshaven, haggard-looking technician, shirt unbuttoned to the waist, who looked as if he had not slept for three days, coffee cups covering his desk. He was Sergeant Chief Control Officer Ryan, and he was Scott's right-hand man in the control centre.

'Any sign of the mothership?'

'Still in Earth orbit sir,' replied Ryan.

'New York?'

'Sir, our Special Forces are trapped there. It's that massive wall they erected around the city, General. They are hemmed in!'

'How many Sirius bases do we have left?' Scott grunted, hoping for some good news, anything.

Sergeant Ryan looked at a screen—the Sirius base geographical map, dotted with the locations of their bases, on a huge 20-foot screen.

'In the continental United States, the New York, Virginia, and Washington bases are gone, and Texas is under attack. Only we and Chicago are left and they're confined to base, due to radiation.'

Scott nodded. 'Get some chow and shut-eye Ryan, that's an order.'

His men were the best—his soldiers were the best. Alien ground patrols were down, but they were still losing. He hoped this insubordinate Captain Morgan fellow, "Bulletproof Pete," aka Caius, was their silver bullet against these alien bastards. He now regretted his confrontation with Captain Morgan. He now realised that he was not dealing with a mere mortal, there were supernatural forces at work here.

God knows, they needed a saviour.

Chapter 56

THE COUNTEROFFENSIVE BEGINS

Around the world, refugees are flowing into churches, mosques, and temples and praying for salvation. In a Hindu temple in New Delhi, Indian and Pakistani foot soldiers, once mortal enemies, help each other treat injured comrades. They share their meagre rations with each other and with the refugees inside the peaceful quiet of the temple. Pakistani and Indian refugees and soldiers join in solemn prayer as the rays of the sun shine through the skylight. A soldier watches as three doves fly up into the dome of the temple. Afterward, they share bread and water, joined in common purpose.

NEW YORK

Meanwhile, at the Statue of Liberty, New York, conventional forces are trapped and being fired upon by Narzuk troops and robots. Ben and Oliver of the 69th Infantry Regiment are cornered. They look out from the top of the statue down on the alien force. Robots are priming their laser cannons, then firing at the statue, large chunks of metal and concrete fly everywhere as the statue shudders and starts to lean at an angle. Regular clone troops far outweigh the crack

Narzuk shock troops of Marshal Zurg-Uk, and fan out, taking up positions. A Narzuk sniper takes aim, and Ben takes a direct hit from a laser rifle. Oliver looks at his friend with a hole in his chest, lying motionless beside him.

'You alien bastards!'

Oliver fires a rocket launcher at the robots, but it takes ten rockets to take down one robot. Meanwhile the Statue shakes violently. He doesn't have much time.

Red-eyed vampires swoop down from the statue and attack yellow-eyed dogs and Narzuks. The vampires grab the black-uniformed soldiers and drooling dogs with their talons then fly up again, dropping them from a great height, as they fall screaming to the ground.

The last of the Special Forces sent to New York, low on ammunition, exhausted, cold and hungry are trapped at the top of the Empire State Building. They desperately defend the top two floors and are hemmed in by clone soldiers and robots on all sides, both sides desperate to hold ground.

Alien fighters circle the top of the building, as vampires and giant bats swoop and land on the craft, making them crash into the building.

LONDON

Two alien fighters hover firing over the Tower of London. Irish guards and vampires are fighting the Narzuk and clone troops in hand–to-hand combat. One detachment of guards run out of the Tower, but are confronted by alien robots, and are trapped. The troops are massacred by laser blasts from the robots. Bodies litter the courtyard. One female soldier fights hand to hand with a Narzuk.

'You alien bastard! I'd rather die than be taken by you!'

As she struggles, another Narzuk SS uses a device to inject her, and she falls unconscious. The Narzuk SS officer gestures for her to be taken on board a nearby ship, for transportation. A group of ravens, eyes blazing with anger, peck at the legs of the alien troops, who shout in pain and annoyance.

Vampires, who have been hiding in the nooks and crannies of the Tower of London, now appear, their red eyes blazing, fangs showing and hissing at the aliens. The regular, grey-uniformed clone alien troops look up in terror but are told to stand firm by their black-uniformed Narzuk superiors.

'Night-Crawlers!' screamed the crack Narzuk troops, aiming their laser rifles.

The angry vampires swoop down, their leathery wings carrying them, attacking the clones and Narzuks alike, in revenge for their fallen human comrades. But the robots appear and fire deadly laser blasts, and most of the vampires are killed.

A team of heavily-armed Narzuk SS is breaking into the secure part of the Tower. They look at the royal collection of The Crown Jewels in wonder; they have never seen anything so beautiful and majestic. They smash the security glass and carefully put the jewels into containers, first the Sovereigns Sceptre with Cross with the Great Star of Africa at the top, then the Imperial State Crown. They carry out heavy boxes and put them on an alien transporter ship. 'Argtuk ook ik New York,' barks an officer.

In the city of London, a huge, black, ugly alien spaceship hovers over the NatWest Tower, one of the few remaining skyscrapers, putting it into the shade, occasionally making grinding noises as it slowly rotates. At the top of the building, having cleared the top floors of stubborn Narzuks, vampires and British Special Forces silently wait. They are tense as they wait until the alien patrol has passed, checking their watches. They watch in anticipation as a black patrol craft slowly passes, scanning the building. They hide in the shadows until it has passed, the soldiers blackening their faces, and checking their weapons. An SAS trooper, Artie, all in black, checks his watch, and gestures to his human and vampire comrades. 'Wait till we have the codes. We attack on my signal. Synchronise watches – I have 11.16.'

He remembers his fallen comrade, and friend, Des, killed by the bastard aliens, somewhere in California. He remembers Des, his old-fashioned ways, their discussions on life, putting the world to rights, his terrible jokes and their drunken curry nights after a mission, with Pete and Vinnie. He remembers Johnny Two-Times and Fag-Ash Phil. Johnny who said everything twice, 'Givus a fag, Phil. Givus a fag.' Phil, who smoked like a chimney but was as fit as a fiddle. He could eat, talk and smoke at the same time. Vinnie, who always made him laugh, and BulletProof Pete, he hoped and prayed he was the saviour everyone hoped he was. Comrades in arms. Brothers, one and all.

Now it was time for payback.

Chapter 57

THE PROFESSOR'S LAB

MOJAVE BASE

Peter, Vinnie, and Lucia walk into the laboratory the professor has set up. He is engrossed in his experiments, hooking the robot's head to a strange-looking computer. The robot's head is flashing red and green lights.

'Ah oui, Captain. I have managed to bypass the security protocols in the robot's head. I am now downloading the information. There are a million terabytes of data stored here…fascinating, fascinating.' The professor grins as he looks at the flashing images on his computer screen. Peter has a vision of Data in Star Trek being hooked up to the 'Borg Collective' and realises the massive amount of information the professor's computer must process.

'Professor what about the codes?'

'Didn't you hear what I said young Peter?' the professor says sharply. 'A million terabytes of data…it will take me a while to sort through, and it's in Sumeri, the alien language.'

'I will stay with you, uncle,' says Lucia remembering what her uncle professor had taught her about being a human computer, to compute all pathways, all branches of logic, and come up with an answer.

'Thank you, Lucia,' smiles Picard, remembering that she was an expert in Sumeri, the alien language. He has taught her, after all. He smiles again, as she kisses him on the cheek.

'The robot is connected to a central computer. I'm amazed there are so few security protocols—no firewalls…' adds the professor.

'Looks like they took shortcuts,' said Peter.

'Let's get some kip,' says Vinnie yawning, looking at Peter.

The next morning Peter returns to the lab praying for good news. The lab is littered with empty coffee cups and printouts. He is greeted by a grinning but tired-looking Professor. 'Ah Peter, we now have access codes for all the Earth-bound ships, downloaded from their central computer. These are the codes for the Los Angeles ship. I will give them to Lucia. The rest I will give to the general.'

'Thank you, Professor only you could have done this!' says Peter shaking the professor's hand. 'My young assistant was most helpful,' the professor teases, and Lucia smiles. Peter looks at the strange-looking computer again. 'What is that computer? I have never seen one like that before.'

'It is a quantum computer my boy, I built it myself. But it has a lot of bugs. Even though I have an IQ of 350, I'm still not clever enough to write code that is completely bug-free.'

Peter nods fascinated. 'When we have more time Professor, tell me how it works.' He has a vision of alternate realities, all existing at the same time, himself, Vinnie and Lucia, different versions of people and things, co-existing, at the same time. In one reality he has hair, and Lucia has green eyes, not blue. Jennifer is a blonde and the alien ships look a bit different; the alien's skin is a darker green. He nods as he begins to understand. Alternate realities; parallel universes.

The professor looks at Peter wondering if his mind could comprehend the multi-dimensional complexity of quantum mechanics. The concept of not binary states of true or false, but a multitude of possibilities all existing at the same time. Multiple universes.

Then Picard gets on the phone. 'General, I am sending you the ship codes now. The attack must be coordinated. Do not give the alien filth time to get organised.'

'Thank you, Professor, out.'

Lucia and the professor look intently at Peter. 'You can do it, my boy, you can do it!' The professor claps him on the shoulder.

'You are Caius, it is da prophecy,' says Lucia, her blue eyes ablaze with hope.

'These alien bastards are going to get the shock of their life,' smiles Peter vindictively.

Chapter 58

MIDNIGHT ATTACK

DOWNTOWN LOS ANGELES

It is close to midnight. Peter is leading an eight-man team including Vinnie, Handsome Mike, Sebastian, Lucia, Felix and two other vampires, Abel and Arnoldo. A massive black alien ship glistens above them in the darkness, slowly turning and emitting unnerving grinding noises. Vinnie looks up.

'I wonder if Gill is up there.'

'Unlikely. I suppose if anything, she would be on board the London ship, but then again, who knows?' Peter is double-checking their equipment, including the cumbersome nuclear device.

'Have you got the alien comms device?'

'Strapped into my rucksack,' replies Vinnie.

Lucia is tense and focused.

'Prepare yourselves. Peter, I will carry you, and Felix will take Vinnie seeing as you have so much equipment.'

Pete turns to Vinnie. 'Just got a coded message from Artie. He's on top of the NatWest tower ready to strike the London ship. I wished him good luck from both of us.' Then Peter thinks about Des and the boys.

Peter marshals his team together and looks at his watch again, knowing that precise timing and coordination are critical to success. He reminds his team that they must retain the element of surprise, as around the world, other Special Forces are launching their operations simultaneously. They check their watches. 11:59pm.

Midnight is zero hour.

Everyone is tense, ready for the off.

'One minute to go. Stand by…' Peter gets into the zone, his adrenaline pumping through his body.

Suddenly, two men come out of the darkness, Gregg, and Fred. Fred gingerly approaches Peter as Vinnie levels his PR1 pistol at them.

'Who the fuck, are you?' asked Peter.

'Excuse me, we think our women are on that ship.'

'Are you kidding? We're starting an operation! Thirty seconds stand by…' shouts Peter, annoyed.

Vinnie holsters his PR1.

'Pete, these guys are looking for their women, just like us. Let's cut them some slack, eh?'

'What makes you think we can help you?' asks Peter looking at his watch.

'You're going to the ship, aren't you? asks Fred.

'Is nothing a secret? Jesus. Lucia, can you find a vampire to carry these two? We go in ten seconds!' shouts Peter, furious that his operation has been interrupted.

Gregg and Fred pick up some parachutes and are strapped to Abel and Arnoldo. As Peter looks at Gregg and Fred he mutters under his breath, 'This mission is fucked up already,' unhappy that their mission may be compromised. But deep down, he knows that he would have done the same. Fred looks up at the ship.

'How are we going to get to the ship?'

Peter looks at his watch. Midnight.

'No talking. Go. It's a GO!' Peter orders.

The vampires transform, and large leathery wings appear. They carry them all up to the ship in the inky blackness. Fred and Gregg are terrified as they see a red-eyed demon smiling at them. Gregg screams out loud.

Peter is furious, 'Shut the fuck up, or I will shoot you myself!'

After five minutes, they land on the ledge of the massive black ship. Fred and Gregg shiver against the wind and cold. Vinnie retrieves the comms device and hands it to Lucia. Peter is examining the black panels on the outside of the ship.

'I'm hoping there is an interface lock here.'

Using his head torch, Peter searches for an interface. He finds one and gestures to Lucia. Vinnie shivers.

'Hurry up, I'm freezing my bollocks off here.'

Lucia slides back the panel and fits the device. It lights up, and some alien characters appear. She studies the strange language.

'Let me see now, the professor gave me these codes. The alien language is not so different from Sumeri...that's it.'

Lucia presses some buttons and a bay door opens into the spaceship. Peter holds up his hand.

'Quick! Move it.' They all move in except the two new recruits. Peter shoves Gregg and Fred through the opening as they stumble onto the floor of the ship. Vinnie and Handsome Mike keep a lookout while Peter orders Sebastian to take personal responsibility for Fred and Gregg. Sebastian grabs them both by the scruff of the neck and barks at them in his earthy Geordie accent.

'You two. I may be a priest, but I'm ex-SAS, and I love these boys as my brothers so if you give us any more trouble I will shoot you. Understood?' They nod nervously.

The air is musty and stale; the corridors are dimly light and dirty, with cables and wires sticking out everywhere. Vinnie coughs on the air as he keeps lookout. 'Whoever built this ship had a bad day at the office,' mutters Vinnie, coughing again.

Peter and Lucia are engrossed in the computer terminal in front of them. 'Lucia, do you know the layout of these spaceships?' asks Peter.

'No. I do not. I shall login and view the schematics. The rest is instinct. I can smell these aliens…'

Lucia uses the device again at the terminal tapping some keys to view the ship's layout. A diagram pops up which Lucia studies, figuring out their current location and the location of the centre of the ship, translating the Sumeri language in her head.

'Do you know where the women are being held?' whispers Fred. Lucia nodded, looking annoyed at the interlopers.

They are taken by surprise, as a robot turns into a corridor towards them. They dive for cover into a storage room. The robot stops at the open bay door, presses some buttons, and the door slides shut. Then it returns to its duties. The team ventures back out to the corridor. Lucia looks at the schematics again.

'Lucia, any ideas?'

'Peter, follow me. Stay silent.'

A terrified Fred looks at Lucia.

'Who, what are you?'

'My name is Lucia, I am a vampire, our ancient enemy is da aliens da humans seek to destroy. Humans and vampires have now united.'

'The enemy of my enemy is my friend,' quips Peter.

'Well put, Mr. da Bulletproof.'

'I'm looking for my wife,' Fred whispers.

'I will help you. As they say, look for friends in unlikely places,' says Lucia.

'Can we crack on!' says Peter, impatient and still furious.

'Shall we begin our business, gentlemen?' says Lucia.

A frightened Gregg looks nervously at Lucia.

'Whatever you are, I am grateful for your help. I'm scared.'

'So am I,' says Fred. Peter is annoyed but sympathetic.

'I get scared sometimes. It's natural—shows you're alive,' replies Peter scanning the area for alien activity.

Lucia is trying to focus.

'Silence, please!'

They walk down dark, poorly-lit corridors, some of which seem to be falling apart, either due to lack of maintenance or poor construction. The smell is awful.

'I think they built these ships in a hurry,' whispers Peter.

'Pen and inks as well,' coughs Vinnie through the stale air.

Chapter 59

THE MISSION IS COMPROMISED

The team moved into a cleaner, more open, and well-lit part of the ship. It appeared to be a holding area where the women were being held. They were all attractive and aged between eighteen and thirty-five. Some were female executives in business suits, some looked like dancers, others housewives. But most looked dishevelled, terrified; some looked angry and stony-faced.

They crouched low and tried to hide. Peter was saving himself for the inevitable battle which would come, there was no point in inviting trouble. Peter and Vinnie looked in vain for their wives.

'Our wives aren't here, are they?' whispered Vinnie.

'Doesn't look like it. Slim chance they were,' replied Peter.

Gregg's face then lit up like a Christmas tree as he saw his girlfriend.

'I can see Ann there, look!' shouted Gregg as he stood up. Peter yanked him down, nearly pulling his arm off. 'Shut the fuck up, you will get us all killed!'

The women were being herded by clones into another area, built of a white plastic metal alloy, which looks like a medical facility. The medical apparatus appeared more like instruments of torture than instruments of healing. They saw Ann being taken to an area where there were beds, soft lights, and weird alien music.

Fred was elated as he saw his wife.

'There's my wife, Susan!'

Two aliens, Narzuk doctors, clean-looking, wearing white coats over black Narzuk SS uniforms, walked in and smiled, and gestured Fred's attractive wife to lie on the bed. They fitted translators so she could understand them. She was wearing a transparent tunic and a green armband. She bared her teeth at them. The alien doctors' smile disappeared as they gestured again to Fred's wife, but she was reluctant.

'Lie down.' The alien doctors spoke through translators as they were preparing needles to put into her arm. Their black eyes were reddish as the veins stood out. They took another pill.

Susan was indignant.

'Don't you grunt at me, you alien creep. Take me back home right now. You don't scare me one jot. Now listen here, don't think for one moment you can have your way with me—oh no, my lazy husband thinks he can have his way with me, but he can't, and you're not either!'

Vinnie whispered to Peter under his breath.

'Looks like she's giving them a hard time.'

'Fred, are you sure you want her rescued?' Gregg asked as Peter and Vinnie looked hard at Gregg.

The aliens look at each other and hold their heads as if they have a headache and take a pill. Then as they wave a rod-like device, Susan blinks and opens her mouth, but she cannot speak; *she is paralyzed.*

Fred whistles in admiration. 'I've got to get me one of those.'

'Quiet,' said Peter.

Gregg is desperate.

'Are you going to help me?'

Peter made a decision. He was angry at Fred and Gregg's behaviour, and angry that his mission was compromised, but he had to help them. It was the right thing to do.

'Lucia and Gregg, you come with me to get Gregg's girl and Vinnie, you go with Felix and Mike to get Fred's wife. We must not be seen, we still have a mission to execute for Christ's sake!'

Lucia and Peter crept past a medical bay. The aliens were using a device to heal a woman's chest wounds. When they were not looking, Peter put one of the devices in his rucksack as they sneaked into the same bay as Ann and hid. They waited until she was alone.

'Ann, we're here to rescue you, quiet now,' Peter whispered.

Ann put her arms around Gregg. On the other side, Vinnie and Felix got into Fred's wife's cubicle. Then, Fred crept in. It seemed like the paralysis effects had worn off.

'It's about time you turned up. Do you know how long I have been here?'

'For once in your life, shut up woman. I'm here to rescue you!'

As soon as Vinnie and Mike stepped back out into the common area, they were spotted.

Chapter 60

FIREFIGHT

A Narzuk doctor pressed an alarm button, then ran and hid, and a strange sounding alarm went off. There was a fierce firefight as clones rushed into the medical area, lasers ready. There was a deafening sound as Peter fired a grenade, destroying half the medical facility.

Peter transformed into Caius, the Eternal Warrior, battle blood now flowing in his veins, blue eyes blazing. He now held a PR7 rifle in each hand and fired on automatic, creating devastation. Explosions rippled through the common area and part of the medical facility, demolishing it, and killing most of the clones. Alien limbs and body parts littered the floor, while Vinnie herded the party through another exit from the medical area. Caius emptied both magazines and dropped them to the floor, as Lucia gave him a sword. Caius was in his element now.

No fear. Just bloodlust.

'I am Caius!'

Fast as lightning Caius reached a group of cowering aliens, and sliced them in half, in one movement. A robot rolled into the area, priming its weapon, glowing orange Peter he only had a few seconds before it fired.

'Caliburnus, Caliburnus, Caliburnus' he shouted, with all his heart. But there was no contact with the higher dimensions. The magical sword did not appear in his hands. It did not answer him.

The Gods were silent.

He paused at his failure to summon the sword. What was he doing wrong? Was it his annoyance and impatience with Fred and Gregg? He simply was not in the zone.

This was one fucked-up mission!

He calculated he had five seconds before the robot fired. Quick as a flash he leaped onto the robot, grabbed its head and twisted it, round and round, until, smoke and flames erupted from its neck, and it died. All the other aliens were dead, but staring at him, though, was another kind of alien.

It was different to the black-uniformed Narzuks, not the Narzuk SS, nor the rank-and-file Narzuks with white armband swastikas.

They didn't have the skin lesions and evil look about them that the Narzuks had. They were clear-skinned and wore grey uniforms, these seemed to be the regular soldiers, and slaves of the Narzuks. These aliens were very pale green and had dark grey eyes, not black. But they had a blank look about them, like robots. These were the clones.

They all scattered, except one, who stared at Caius. Caius stared him in the eye, but couldn't kill him.

'Go,' said Caius.

The clone alien understood and scurried out. Caius had to think quickly.

'Mike, Lucia, get these women out of here! Lucia, I will meet you back at the landing bay in ten minutes, we have a job to do.'

Lucia was concerned about the remaining women in the facility, who looked frightened and were trying to hide from the battle. 'What about the other women?'

'Rescue as many as you can!' shouted Peter, knowing it was the right thing to do.

Fuck the orders.

Lucia found four women crying and in distress.

'Follow me if you want to live!'

The women did their best to keep up with Mike and Lucia as they ran through the ship until they reached the ledge. They all clung to Lucia as she spread her wings and carried them, gliding downwards towards the earth, and safety. Lucia dropped them into the street below and flew back up again; the women waved in gratitude.

Aliens, both Narzuks and the grey-uniformed clone troops avoided the crucifix-wearing priest. Sebastian looked worried, in two minds, his moral compass conflicted. 'What if they're infected?' Peter's alter-ego Caius shrugged his shoulders. Sebastian crossed himself, he looked at Peter and was shocked by the change in appearance, as if he had aged, and grown larger and stronger, but it was wearing off now, and he staggered, as if tired. He looked weakly at Sebastian.

'Go help Lucia rescue the women. Me and Vinnie have our mission.'

'No, Peter - I'm going to watch your back.'

He was Peter again, but weaker, his Caius alter-ego seemed to drain his personality. He smiled weakly at Vinnie, regaining some strength. Peter rested for a minute, taking deep breaths, then he and Vinnie raced off to the centre of the ship to find the best place to put the small nuclear device that Peter was carrying. Peter felt the weight as he ran—it wouldn't normally bother him. Vinnie put a grenade into a robot and mowed down a few aliens with his PR7 on full auto.

They turned a corner and saw what looked like a huge power plant room.

'Perfect. Vinnie—in there!'

As Peter turned, time seemed to slow down as he took a deflected blast from a robot and another from an alien's pistol. He fell to the ground, shaking, his arm and chest bleeding. The aliens crept closer, ready for the kill.

Peter looked at his friend and smiled weakly.

'Finish the job, Vinnie!' holding his chest. 'I'm okay. Remember, I'm "Bulletproof" Pete.'

Chapter 61

NOT SO BULLETPROOF

This wasn't supposed to happen. He had never been hurt before, so why now? Where was his patron Michael when he needed him? Peter retrieved the crucifix from his jacket and hung it around his neck, then he fainted with the pain.

Vinnie looked around him as Sebastian appeared around the corner. The Narzuk troops stood back when they saw the warrior priest with his crucifix. One Narzuk SS soldier jumped in terror as the clones looked on, puzzled. Sebastian fired at them, and they scattered in all directions. One nasty-looking Narzuk SS stood his ground, his sharp teeth chattering excitedly. As he approached the priest, Sebastian begged him to get closer,

'Just one more step you alien bastard.' Then he took the vial of holy water from his pocket and threw it on the alien, who screamed in pain as his flesh burned as though acid had been thrown on his chest and arm, his personal shield failing, clutching a black figurine around his neck, *but his god could not help him.*

Sebastian joined Vinnie and a weak-looking Peter who was lying on the floor.

Vinnie is in two minds, and he struggled with deciding what to do. He looked at his friend and then at the nuclear device.

The mission.

'Go plant the bomb, I will look after Peter—GO!' shouted Sebastian.

Vinnie put the heavy device on his back, and ran to the power plant, looking for a power conduit. Turning this way and that in frustration, he finally found it. The placement had to be right. Remembering his training, he opened the device panel, put the key in and turned it. A green light started flashing. He had ten seconds to enter a code. He entered the memorised code—1001—and then set the timer to a thirty-minute silent countdown. One final step: the red initiate button.

He paused. There was no going back now.

He pressed the red button.

He then hid the bomb carefully in a storage container, behind the power conduit before running back to his friend Peter.

'I'm not leaving you here mate!' Vinnie is almost in tears as he held his best friend, in his arms, memories of their good times together flooding into his mind, ignoring all the mayhem around him. He remembered the time Peter had saved him in the hot, dry Yemeni desert, carrying him for miles.

'Twenty-five minutes Sebastian!' shouted Vinnie.

Sebastian and Vinnie carried Peter, Vinnie still firing with his free arm. But then more alien soldiers joined the fray. Vinnie took a hit to his shoulder, then another to his leg. Vinnie staggered, fell but then managed to carry on. Just as he was about to give up, Mike turned the corner.

'Oi' Handsome, give us a hand here, Pete's in a bad way!'

Lucia joined them, and seeing the distress of Peter, she knelt down and stroked his face, kissing his forehead.

'We have saved as many women as we can. Let's get out of here!' said Lucia not looking up from Peter's face, who smiled weakly at her, then fell unconscious again.

Vinnie looked at his watch. 'Nineteen minutes thirty, hurry!'

Two women with pale green skin walked past, the only infected women they had seen. They looked pregnant. Their eyes looked empty and sad as if they were on drugs. The soldiers ignored them. Sebastian crossed himself again, but Mike was subdued.

'Call me old-fashioned, but I cannot shoot a pregnant woman, even if she is half-alien.'

'Amen to that!' replied Sebastian.

Vinnie shook his head thinking about Gill. Had she been impregnated by one of these alien bastards?

They arrived at the bay door, which was already open. Mike beckoned.

'I will give covering fire. Go!'

'Three minutes!' shouted Vinnie his wild eyes looking at Lucia.

Lucia transformed into a red-eyed vampire, her black leathery wings forming from her body. She grabbed hold of an injured Peter, then Vinnie, then flew out of the spaceship into the cold darkness. Mike and Sebastian helped some women to put on parachutes, as they jumped out of the open bay door. Abel and Arnoldo appeared in the open bay door, red-eyed and winged, terrifying the waiting women, but then they grabbed them and flew out into the darkness.

As the ground became closer, Lucia struggled with their weight, nearly dropping Peter. She steered her wings, her eagle eyes spotting a football park, a softer landing. They landed with a resounding thud on the grass, rolling over many times. As they were lying on the grass, they could see a massive explosion in the sky above as the spaceship spat fire and flames, and parts of the ship fall flaming to the ground, crushing whatever they landed on.

They could feel the heat on their faces as they gazed upwards. Peter was getting weaker as he looked at his injured friend Vinnie, who now supported him, as they half walked, half ran away from the impending danger. A piece of the ship fell only 100 yards behind them. They felt the earth shake as it landed. To Peter, everything seemed to be happening in slow motion, as Lucia—herself winded—screamed at them to hurry. Peter and Vinnie limped and ran, limped and ran for cover.

Above, there was an almighty groaning noise as the alien spaceship lurched thirty degrees to its side, flames still spewing from the monster ship. As they ran, Peter looked back to see the burning ship diving to earth and crashing, burying itself 500 feet into the ground, earth and concrete being piled up as it sank itself into the ground, moving towards them like a tidal wave.

They were in danger of being engulfed by the ship which glowed in the dark as explosions ripped it apart. Flames and debris were piling up where they had stood a few moments earlier. Peter could feel the heat on his back as they ran, and their hair was burning.

Lucia, sensing the danger, grabbed Peter and Vinnie, arched her back, summoned the last of her demonic strength, and flew up into the air, the heat from the explosion singeing their clothes, and carried them out of the city, out of danger. Peter looked at the enormous spaceship on the ground, among flattened buildings, homes, and roads, in flames.

Lucia, summoning the last of her strength, flew through the night until she was nearing exhaustion. Even as a vampire, she was reaching her limit. She spotted a wooded hillside, on the edge of the city, and swooped down.

On the hillside, an exhausted Lucia, Peter, and Vinnie watched the spaceship go up in flames in the distance. Peter, now so weak he could hardly speak, beckoned to Vinnie.

'Vinnie, in my bag—the healing device—give it to Lucia. Hurry…I don't have much time.'

Chapter 62

HEALING ON THE HILLSIDE

Peter is passing in and out of consciousness as Vinnie supports him, his back against a Bergen. He gives him a sip of water.

'Hurry Lucia, he hasn't got long!' Vinnie holds his best friend in his arms, his eyes watering. 'This damn sand gets in my eyes.'

Lucia reads the symbols on the alien device, translating them. She switches it on and smiles at Peter as she passes it over his wounds, back and forth, a beam of light penetrating his body, back and forth, back and forth. Peter falls into a deep sleep, as gradually his wounds heal. Lucia knows if it wasn't for his strong constitution, his Caius alter-ego, he would be dead by now for sure.

He is not a mere mortal.

She kisses his forehead.

'You will lose your reputation as Mr. "Bulletproof" at this rate.'

Then Lucia does the same for Vinnie's injuries. They all sleep for a few hours, then Peter stirs and opens his blue eyes, looking at Lucia, seemingly recovered as he takes a swig of water.

'This Caius really takes it out of me. One minute I'm Superman, the next, I feel half dead. But I'm alive, thank God.'

'There is always a price to pay,' Lucia crooned, wiping his forehead.

'Thanks, Lucia, at least these aliens are good for something,' looking at his healed wounds.

Peter looks at the direction of the spaceship, which is buried in the ground, bathed in flame, crippled, but 80% intact.

'I hope some women made it out alive.'

'I saved quite a few, and I saw hundreds manage to get out of da spaceship when it crash-landed.' Lucia cleaned Peter's wounds, which were miraculously healed. Peter sat up, looked around and drank some more water. He began to feel much better.

'I hope the kids are okay. They should be safe in the Brecons with Reg and Ron, right?' Peter is thinking aloud. 'But where is Jennifer?' deep down, he has a sick feeling in his stomach.

Lucia can instinctively feel Peter's anxiety and the faraway look in his eye. She is beginning to like Peter, and care for him. For a human, he is very brave, but was he 'The One?' *After all, he has been injured. Not so 'Bulletproof' after all.*

'Peter, let me see your Jennifer's picture again.' Lucia gazes at the picture, she seems familiar somehow, but the memory escapes her. The brown eyes and brown hair. So beautiful. Her mind then searches the earth for any sign of her. Thousands of people—women—flash before her eyes. Many of them look frightened and alone. Some of them are hiding on Earth, some in alien concentration camps, and some are hidden to her.

Minutes pass. Then, Lucia comes out of her induced meditation and shakes her head. She looks drained.

'Peter, da ships are shielded. I cannot see Jennifer, it is as if she has disappeared from my vision.' Lucia hesitates, memories rushing back of her World War Two experiences, and the time she rescued prisoners from a Nazi concentration camp. The faces of the victims still haunting her; gaunt, terrified faces, walking skeletons, dressed in striped uniforms.

'Peter,' she seems upset. 'Da alien filth have set up concentration camps, like the Nazis, during da war. Men, women, and children are suffering. I have seen IT!' Peter and Vinnie nod, remembering what they have seen already.

'What about Jennifer?' whispers Peter, his stomach churning.

'She is not in one of their camps. Unless they're shielded like da ships. I don't know. I'm sorry Peter!' says Lucia almost crying.

Vinnie looks at Lucia, pleading.

'What about my wife, Gill?'

Lucia does the same for Vinnie.

'Wait a moment. It is strange that I also cannot see your wife. I am weak,' Lucia pauses.

'We have seen transport ships…mainly women being taken on board,' says Peter sadly.

'By the alien bastards,' says Vinnie.

'Narzuk SS,' adds Peter remembering their uniform.

Lucia slumps by a pine tree, then falls down in the sandy soil, exhausted by her physic probing. 'I am weak. I need blood,' she gasps.

Peter shakes himself out of his thoughts. Now it is his turn to help his friend Lucia.

'Vinnie, you're the best hunter here. Go and find something for Lucia.

'But my leg still hurts.'

'Go on.'

'Cheers mate,' Vinnie replied.

Vinnie, muttering under his breath, gets out his hunting knife and walks off in search of prey. Remarkably, Lucia looks better after a few minutes' rest and looks at Peter, smiling, her eyes wells of desire.

'Is Vinnie really the best hunter or did you just want to be alone with me?'

Peter smiles at her intuition and looks into her blue eyes, and soft red lips.

'You really are physic, aren't you? I wanted to talk with you. Tell me more about being a vampire. How old are you?'

Chapter 63

AVENTINE HILL BY THE TIBER

Lucia playfully wagged her finger at him as she tut-tutted.

'Peter Da Bulletproof, it is very bad manners to ask da age of a vampire, but I forgive you,' she smiled. 'We do not want to be reminded of our curse.' Lucia held Peter's hand as she looked into his deep blue eyes.

'It was 2000 years ago that I became a vampire. I was living in Rome at da time. Cassian made me. He rescued me, and he took pity on me. I have been with him ever since. He has been like a father to me.'

'Do you like being a vampire?'

'Before I became a vampire I lived with my husband in Rome, in a villa in the Aventine Hill along da Tiber, near a port. We had a boy and a girl, they liked to play in da garden, running around, where we grew vegetables, and herbs—basil, rosemary and bay. We had two slaves, but we treated them well, as members of the family. I was very fond of a girl slave we had, brown hair. Strange, but she reminded me of your Jennifer.' Lucia smiled as she recalled the memory.

'My husband was a good man and a good father. He had lands to the north where he made wine. When he was younger he was a soldier in Caesar's army, a centurion.' Lucia paused her eyes wandering. You remind me of him,' Lucia smiled.

'Late one night, I was out walking with my husband, on da outskirts of the city, outside the city walls, among the hyssop and lavender, and grass, it was warm and humid. We walked and talked and walked, forgetting about da time.' Lucia's expression changed as she relived the memory.

'We found ourselves alone. Suddenly, out of nowhere, an alien craft came, one of da filthy Sumeri and they tried to kidnap me. My husband was killed trying to protect me.'

Peter for some reason felt sad but was not sure why, as if the memory was somehow shared.

'How did he die?' he asked.

'They stabbed him through the heart.'

'What was his name?'

'Caxus,' Lucia's eyes looked wet.

'Then out of nowhere, a creature in black came, with red eyes and wings, a demon, and killed da aliens, and rescued me. His name was Cassian. I was frightened of him at first, but later I learned to like him, like a father figure. I am grateful to him,' Lucia smiled.

'Later he made me. My senses were greatly enhanced. I could see for miles, smell freshly baked bread, from da next district, know what people were thinking—and I had a hunger for human blood, insatiable hunger. What I am now, a vampire, seemed the best option at da time. At first, I thought it was great, live forever, go wherever I want, the power to do whatever what I want, and no one to stop me. After a while, though, I began to get fed up avoiding da warm sun, it burned my skin. I lost what it was like to be human. I missed my family, my children. How could I explain to them what I had become? They thought I was dead. They would not understand.' Lucia paused, reliving the memory.

'Sometimes at night, I would stand outside my father's house for hours, just waiting for him to see me. He was good enough to take in my children, and I would spy on them, and listen to them talking.' A tear fell from her eye.

'One time, my father was on his own, he was drunk on wine, and singing to himself, an old Roman lament. I walked out of the darkness and spoke to him.'

'Father, it is me, your daughter, Lucia.'

He stared at me open-mouthed, then backed away.

'Get out of here demon! You're not my daughter!' he cried. I stayed in Rome, outliving my father, and my two children. Life seemed to have no point anymore.'

Lucia was quiet as she remembered gazing at the graves of her children, thinking how unnatural it was that she still lived, while her family were all dead. 'I am not human,' she thought.

'Da years, da centuries, weigh heavily on me. I remember everything—everything, do you understand?'

Peter nodded, in a way he did understand, for he was Caius, the Eternal Warrior, and he had lived many lives, loved many women, and fought many battles. The images still flashed in his mind of time past.

'I could hear the wings of a butterfly as it flew among the flowers. My strength, my God, I could run faster than a hawk. I was invincible. A bit like yourself, Mr. Peter da Bulletproof,' Lucia managed a smile.

'After the fall of da Western Roman Empire, Cassian and myself moved to Eastern Europe to try to forget all of da bad memories. We made a home in Transylvania. It is also our spiritual home. There are many vampires there.'

Peter touched Lucia's arm, and they move closer. 'I am sorry about your husband. Strange, but it felt as if I was there myself.'

'Humans live many lives, Peter. Once I die, I am gone, for I have no soul. I regret becoming a vampire now.' Lucia was tearful.

'I miss his love. I yearn for da light, but I live in darkness.'

Lucia started singing a love poem lament.

"Let me kiss your sweet lips again

So my soul is healed,

Let me see your face again

So that I am filled with joy and happiness once again,

Let us embrace again, so our souls are joined,

Till that day you live in my dreams.'

'There is always love as long as you believe in God, Lucia,' Peter said gently, stroking her long black hair.

'God has forsaken me,' Lucia replied a tear falling from her eye.

Peter and Lucia kissed and embraced, comforting one another. Peter searched his soul for how he felt. He should feel guilty, but he didn't, for some reason he felt like he was kissing Jennifer, but a different version of her, a distant memory of ancient times gone by— but then the thought was gone, a look of timeless yearning in Lucia's eyes. He felt a small stabbing feeling in his heart. He had a vision, an ancient memory of a walled city, and a hillside, but then it was gone.

Peter relished the animal passion of Lucia, her sweet red lips, the hard nipples of her soft breasts, and playful bites, as they wrestled on the ground. Afterward, they lay down and fell asleep in each other's arms.

Lucia was dreaming. She was in the bedroom of her Roman villa, long ago. The warm Italian sun afternoon beamed in, the smell of herbs drifted in from the garden, and there was a woman lying next to her, a beautiful woman with brown eyes and long brown hair. She had the charisma and beauty of a Greek goddess. They smiled and giggled, then kissed each other's naked body and soft breasts, moaning gently, as their tongues met. They did not rush, and their passion rose as their bodies moved together in a crescendo of passion. They lay there panting and kissed again, laughing as Lucia's husband, Caxus walked into the room and smiled. She admired his blue eyes and rugged handsomeness as he spoke.

'You are a beautiful sight, may the Gods be praised.'

'Join us, husband,' she smiled as Caxus lay down between them. She and the slave girl rubbed their hands over his firm, muscled body, smiling and giggling, like two young nymphs, enticing his manhood. He was middle-aged now but he still managed to satisfy her. Later, as they were lying there, out of breath but happy, she and the slave girl fell asleep together in each other's arms. Lucia was drowsy as she heard hear Caxus talking to someone.

'Who is it, husband?'

'It is Virgil, my old friend. I have not seen him for years, he has returned from his travels!' There was joy in his voice.

'Oh yes I remember your friend in Caesar's army. Bring him in here,' said Lucia yawning and covering her body with a cotton sheet. Virgil, tanned and rough-looking walked awkwardly into the bedchamber.

'Sorry to disturb you my lady.'

'Any friend of Caxus is my friend too,' she smiled. 'Where are you going?' she asked as she saw her husband getting dressed. 'We are just going for a walk, my dear,' said Caxus coughing.

She looked at him sharply.

'Do not go to Athena's my love,' for she had heard the stories during his time as a soldier. Caxus feigned innocence and Virgil shifted awkwardly.

'Promise my dear. We're just going to stretch our legs,' he smiled and she gave him that look. She would wait up 'till late that night.

Chapter 64

I Dream of Angels

Peter is standing on a little stone bridge over a gentle, silvery stream; the golden sun's rays beat through the green woodland. A breeze blows through the green conifers and the long, rich grass. Bluebells grow in abundance as he looks up at the blue sky, it is a place without time, without stress; it feels magical and serene. Everywhere is bathed in a golden light. Then in the silence he hears a rustle in the trees. Out of the conifers and ancient oaks approaches a figure like nothing Peter has seen before. The sun's rays shine on a beautiful woman in a shimmering dress. She has transparent wings on her back as she glides gracefully towards him, her long blonde hair flowing over her shoulders, her bare feet walking through the rich,

green grass. Her blue eyes pierce his soul as she approaches him, and kisses him gently on the forehead, then wraps a shining cloak around him, filled with tiny crystals.

'Peter, Prince Michael has sent me. I am the Angel of the Tears. You have suffered much torment, but please know that you are not alone. Each of these crystals in this cloak is a tear shed by the angels for the terrible suffering of mankind. Wear this sacred cloak, for it will give you strength and protection. I will always be with you for you are blessed. You are healed,' says the angel, wiping his forehead with some water from a nearby stream whose water is clear as crystal. Then she cups her hand and he drinks the cool liquid as she kisses him again on the forehead.

'You may ask me one question.'

'Where is Jennifer?'

'Follow Lucia, and she will lead you to her. Lucia, Jennifer, and Caius are as one. Now you must leave.'

Peter wakes and takes a sharp intake of breath, remembering his dream. Is there a connection between Lucia and Jennifer? He looks up as Vinnie strolls back to the clearing where they are camped. He has a dead coyote. Lucia's eyes open and she leaps forward, her physical appearance changing as she sinks her fangs into the animal's jugular and drinks until she is satiated, animal blood dripping from her fangs.

'Now you've had a nice drink, is there any meat left that we can cook for dinner?' Vinnie is looking forward to roast coyote that night. He retrieves the blood-drained carcass from the red-eyed, fanged Lucia, takes out his hunting knife, skins it, and removed the guts ready for roasting. Peter collects some brushwood and gets a fire going, hoping no alien craft will see it, though as truth would have it, he doesn't care, he could eat a horse, he was so hungry.

He salivates as they all sat around the fire watching the meat cook, warming their bones. After an hour or so, they use their knives to slice meat from the roasted coyote, the stars shining down on them.

'Not bad,' says Vinnie. Peter nods. He thinks back to when he and Vinnie used to camp out in the Welsh hills, cooking roast rabbit, telling jokes and getting drunk on cider: *the good times*. This would be fun at any other time, but his thoughts are now focused on Jennifer, and how to get back to the Mojave base; his strange dream now a distant memory.

'In the morning we need to get back to the city, find a vehicle and get back to base.'

Peter reads from his book. Lucia moves closer to Peter, now back to her normal self, red eyes replaced by blue.

'What is that book?'

'It's my little book of poetry. It helps me to sleep at night, especially on missions. Here...by Cummings.'

"Carry your heart with me…"

Peter recites the rest of the poem as they all sit in silence, deep in thought. Peter plugs in his headphones and listens to his favourite Led Zeppelin song Stairway to Heaven. As Robert Plant sings "and she's buying a Stairway to Heaven" Peter thinks about Lucia. Why is she helping humankind? Is she trying to redeem her soul, seeking forgiveness?

Is she trying to buy a stairway to Heaven?

Chapter 65

NOWHERE TO RUN

It was a dark and cloudy morning. Peter and Vinnie clung to Lucia's demon body as she soared through the air. Rainclouds hung low and visibility was poor, as Lucia struggled against the wind, the rain beating on her large leathery wings. She saw a spot through the rain, and they landed in the city, between some tall buildings. As soon as they landed, they realised that they were in the wrong spot. On all sides, there were buildings, with no visible exits. Peter was anxious. How can there be no exits? He must have an escape route. Standard SAS procedure.

An exit plan.

Lucia was out of breath.

'I could not fly any further, I'm sorry, I was disorientated. I don't know where we are!'

It was pouring with rain, as they donned their waterproofs, Lucia wearing a large hooded cloak.

'We're sitting ducks here!'

Peter could hear a familiar grinding noise as two alien robots appeared around the corner and headed their way.

'We've been spotted!'

They looked around for an exit. Through the driving rain, Vinnie spotted a narrow alleyway.

'Down there!'

They all ran down the alleyway but found it blocked off by a wall. They were hemmed in on all three sides, with the robots closing in. They turned round, the mechanical sound of the alien robots becoming louder. Vinnie looked panicked.

'How do we get out of this one? I've got no grenades left, no ammo!'

'Christ knows!' Peter exclaimed as his mind raced, looking for an exit.

Lucia shouted, 'Use your sword, the holy sword—it's our only chance!'

Peter's mind raced. In the panic, his memory failed him. His sword, the priest…call it three times…the name of the sword…the name? He stooped down, picked up some sand and rubbed it into his hands, earthing and balancing himself.

'Caliburnus!'

'Caliburnus!'

'Caliburnus!'

A sword appeared in his hand. It had a gold pommel and grip with an amethyst stone atop; the long silver blade gave off a bluish light. A dragon snaked down the blade. It seemed to breathe and move as Peter moved the sword in his hands. The sword and the dragon seemed to speak to him, it felt strong in his hand, and he felt empowered as he held it, the energy rippling through his body. At last, he was reunited with his sword. He felt complete. He was Caius, ancient warrior, but would the sword do his bidding, or would it control him?

He now stood defiantly facing the robot. His eyes shone blue like stars, and as he raised his sword the atmosphere changed. Dark clouds gathered as the sword shone like the sun and lightning sprang from it. Thunder rolled in the distance. A wind blew like the approach of a storm.

'Caius,' whispered Vinnie and Lucia as they looked at him, shocked by his change in appearance, growing larger; malevolent.

He instinctively knew what to do as he gazed at the oncoming robot. Its grinding gears suddenly stopped. It was charging its laser weapon, which glowed orange, getting ready to fire. Of its own volition, the sword stood upright in his hands, it was protecting him from the oncoming danger.

'Stand behind me, it's our only chance!' shouted Caius.

Lucia stepped away from the sword, a look of terror in her eyes.

'It is da Holy Sword…it is terrifying to me!'

'Get behind me Lucia, move!' Vinnie shouted.

As Caius raised his sword, the blue light from Caliburnus, the Holy Sword, expanded and all three companions are surrounded by a powerful blue light, shielding them. Caius felt a presence beside him, a powerful and overwhelming presence of pure power, omnipotent and benevolent. He felt protected.

Lucia, standing behind Vinnie, could detect the commanding presence and it terrified her to the bone, for she knew who it was. She muttered words to her own demon, but the presence in front of her was the Captain of Hosts, Commander of the Lord's Army, in charge of heaven's angelic army, and there was no escaping him. She knew that, ultimately, she would have to submit to his will. She shook in terror as the eyes of Prince Michael shone like blue fire.

Vinnie and Lucia looked at Peter and were shocked by the change in his appearance—as if he had aged, and grown larger and stronger, more powerful. They had seen it before, but it was worse this time, like a drug had got hold of him.

Caius dare not look behind him, at the supernatural entity, he just looked ahead at the robot through the blue haze of energy, the sword vibrating in his hands. It took all his strength just to keep it in front of him, possessing its own power, its own will. The robot raised its weapon arm and fired, the blast made a direct hit in front of Caius, but the blue light, emanating from the sword, protected them. He felt the heat from the explosion, but it had no effect on him. Smoke rose from Vinnie's hair as it smouldered, Lucia hid her face in her hands, and shut her eyes, for she dared not look at the entity.

The robot was recharging its weapon, which glowed orange. Caius, his warrior alter-ego, knew he only had one chance before the robot fired again. He quickly moved toward the robot, the humming and vibration from his Holy Sword increasing. As he stood in front of the alien robot, the sword—of its own will—swung round in a lightning swing and struck the robot at its neck, severing its head, which now bounced along the ground. Then it staggered, went around in circles a few times and then collapsed in a smoking heap.

Caius, the mighty warrior, now felt weak and dropped to the ground, blacking out. When he came around he wasn't sure how long he had been out, but he was Peter again, with a headache like the worst hangover ever, *and the sword had gone.* He coughed from the smoke from the robot and looked around, Vinnie and Lucia were pointing excitedly ahead of him. Another robot came around the corner. No sword, no PR7 ammo.

They were done for.

A sick feeling filled his stomach as he got up from his knees. He thought of Jennifer, 'goodbye my love, it was all worth it.' A sense of mortality filled his bones as he awaited his fate.

At that moment, a young woman in a nun's habit appeared from a hidden door in the wall. She beckoned to them. Peter and Vinnie stared, open-mouthed as the robot turned into the alleyway, moving inexorably toward them.

They sprinted for the hidden door and ran inside. The nun stood in the middle of the room, and the door closed behind them, of its own accord. She stood silently looking at them with her angelic face as they heard the sound of the alien robot going past the door. The

nun put a finger to her lips and smiled. There was an aura of peace and tranquillity about her, as if she came from a different world - *she had the Light of Christ about her.* Her eyes shone bright as she smiled at them.

Lucia, transfixed, stood rigid, looking like she had seen a ghost. The nun, silent and serene, pointed downwards. They turned and ran down a staircase. Peter turned to thank her, but the room was empty.

'Thank you, whoever you are—where is she?' thinking she looked like a younger version of Mother Theresa, but she had disappeared into thin air.

They tumbled down the stairs, down a passage. The door came out into a street by the edge of the city, which was deserted. Peter surveyed the scene: not a soul in sight, no refugees, no alien patrols. Then he spotted a piece of Heaven.

'There's a bar there. I need a beer.'

'Amen to that,' replied Vinnie.

Chapter 66

TIME FOR A PINT

Peter and Vinnie walked into an empty bar. The floor was covered in dust and rubbish, most of the furniture was lying in pieces, and the windows were dirty and smashed. Lucia stood a few yards away, keeping guard by the door, hiding from the sun. Vinnie went behind the bar and pours them both a tall, cold beer and smiled at the glass like a long-lost lover. He was pleasantly surprised that the hand-pull beer taps were still working. He put the two pints on the bar in front of Peter, who gazed at them as if he was looking at a million pounds in cash. They both sat on stools looking at their beer as if in a trance. 'Ice cold in Alex,' said Peter.

'Ice cold in Alex,' whispered Vinnie as they supped their beer. Lucia shook her head. 'This place is a wreck. Cigarette?'

'Yeah, trying to give up but I'll have one anyway. Who was that woman?'

Peter was curious as he looked into his beer.

Lucia turned around, her eyes wide.

'What is she, you ask? She is what I fear, yet she represents what I yearn to return to: da light.' She sighed and added, 'We are not alone in this fight Peter. There are other forces at work here.'

'The angelic entity…Michael,' said Peter while sipping his pint.

Peter and Vinnie sat in silence for a while, sipping their beer, and started to relax a little. Vinnie looked subdued as he looked at his friend.

'I suppose we should be celebrating, downing a spaceship, but I don't feel like celebrating much,' said a sad Vinnie looking into his beer.

'From what we have seen, both myself, and Lucia agree that the Earth ships are temporary holding areas for these women.'

'What makes you think that?' asked Vinnie with a loud burp.

'I just remembered. In that medical area, I saw some women with green tags being kept in one area,' Peter replied.

'Oh yeah, I remember now. What did the tags say?' asked Vinnie. Peter knew Lucia was listening.

'What did the tags say Lucia?'

'Green ones said Pass-Sector 16. The red ones said Fail.' She paused, then added, 'don't drink too much.'

'What happens to the women who failed?' asked Vinnie.

'I saw them going down a conveyor belt,' Peter crossed himself. Our best hope is that Gill and Jenny are still alive and being held somewhere,' replied Peter.

Vinnie's thoughts raced through his mind. Gill? Is she alive or dead? Or worse? Made pregnant by one of those alien bastards? An unknown child? The thought made him sick. He looked at Peter who seemed to read his mind.

'I was just wondering if Jenny is alive or dead,' Peter pondered. What if one of those alien bastards…you know.' Peter shook his head with worry, as Vinnie put his arm around his friend.

'Sector 16. We need to find out where it is Vinnie.'

'Maybe it's one of their camps?' said Vinnie beginning to feel the effects of the beer.

They were silent as Vinnie poured another beer. They sat gazing at their pints. Lucia looked at them, shaking her head, looking cross. 'Do not get drunk Peter da Bulletproof!'

Vinnie burped, 'I think she's nagging you mate,' Peter smiled, what would he do without Vinnie—and Lucia for that matter.

'Maybe Vinnie. Or maybe the mothership.'

'Wherever the fuck that is,' burped Vinnie.

'It's in Earth orbit. Difficult. We need it closer to Earth for a viable infiltration,' replied Peter, also giving a large burp. Lucia tutted. 'Somehow, we've got to get on that ship Vinnie. We need Lucia to navigate around the ship. She seems to understand these aliens—and their devices.' Peter downed his beer. At least they had an outline of a plan.

'We don't know they're on the mothership, Pete.' Vinnie finished his beer.

'You're right. We need to know for sure. Get them in Vinnie.'

Vinnie poured them another pint.

'I could kill a curry right now,' said Peter.

'Yeah,' replied Vinnie, having visions of a chicken vindaloo down Brick Lane. Lucia, arms crossed, gave them an even sterner look. Peter looked at Vinnie.

'Lucia said we are not alone. I had a dream, Vinnie…I think it was an angel.' Then he remembered the angel's words. 'She said Lucia would take us to Jennifer.'

Vinnie did not ridicule Peter as he normally would.

'Nothing would surprise me,' said Vinnie, 'that nun—she appeared out of nowhere. I fink she was protecting us. Those robots should have spotted us, but they didn't. Very weird.'

'We're either extremely lucky, or we are being protected,' Vinnie was not stupid *he had a sense of what was going on too.*

Peter leaned toward Vinnie.

'Vinnie, there's something else. In my dreams, there is a dark presence, like an anti-hero. Something evil, surrounded by flames, like an animal, but not an animal.'

'You must face this entity,' replied Vinnie.

'Yes, one day, I must face it.'

Lucia looked at Peter hearing every word he said. The professor is not telling her everything he knows about the Book of Borossus - *he is holding back.* Her friend Peter is fighting a struggle, and one day he must confront it, whatever it is—and she must be there for him.

They were shaken out of their thoughts by Lucia, looking at them like a schoolmistress, a stern look on her face. Vinnie burped again.

'Drink up. I think we've got company,' urged Lucia as she drew her sword with lightning speed.

Chapter 67

ERGTUK THE 82ND

An alien in a grey uniform stopped outside the bar and hesitated. He walked slowly towards them and opened the door. Vinnie pointed his pistol at the frightened alien, who put his hands up. Peter recognised it, not as a Narzuk, but one of the general troops; grey-uniformed, pale green skin, dark grey eyes, and not evil-looking like the black-eyed Narzuk rank and file and SS troops. However, this one did not have a blank expression, he looked intelligent.

'Oog zuk! Oog zuk! Help me! Help Me!'

Lucia hurled abuse at the alien in his own language, arguing with him, as she held her sword to his throat.

Peter was taken aback by the confrontation.

'Lucia, what are you arguing about with that alien?'

'I told him his mother was a whore.'

'What did he reply?'

'He says he doesn't have a mother, he is a clone.'

'Oh,' exclaimed Peter and Vinnie. Vinnie moved closer, ready to fire.

Lucia looked daggers at the alien. 'Do not feel sorry for him,' she hissed.

Peter lowered Vinnie's gun and walked towards the alien, curiosity getting the better of him.

'Lucia, I think the alien is trying to talk to us. I'm sure he said help me. Ask him what he wants.'

'Not a good idea.'

'Just do it please!'

Lucia conversed with the alien then looked back at Peter and then continued. The alien looked pitifully at Peter, pleading for help. Lucia moved close to Peter.

'He says he disagrees with what they're doing. Da Sumeri Elite invade planets and plunder it of all resources, then enslave da people. He does not want it to happen to your beautiful Planet Earth. Also, he thinks the traitor General Grimbald is an imposter, and he does not serve the interests of his people. He is not alone in this. Many of his comrades are unsettled. He says there are two alien factions: da black Narzuks, who are with Grimbald, and da greys, the regular troops, the clones, who carry out the orders of the black Narzuks. There are many of us. We outnumber the Narzuks a thousand to one. Some of da greys are not happy and are talking about open rebellion. Any greys who disobey the Narzuks are killed. There is a special unit called the Narzuk SS, they wear red armbands. We are afraid of them.'

'I've seen those!' said Peter.

'The regular Narzuks do not like their SS counterparts. They get better rations and pay. The SS are da ones responsible for the harvesting of human women for their breeding program. They are dangerous. Their master is Lord Grim-Uk.'

'Where do they take the women?' Peter asked in desperation.

Lucia talked to Ergtuk again in his native language.

'They take the women to the mothership—but only those who have passed processing,' said Lucia.

'The mothership!' said Peter and Vinnie together.

'Ask him his name,' urged Peter.

Lucia converses with the alien.

'He is Ergtuk the 82nd. He is an 82nd-generation clone, and he is asking for sanctuary.'

'What happened to Ergtuk the 81st?' asked Peter.

Lucia converses with Ergtuk, the grey alien again.

'Ergtuk, the original, lived for 100 years. Ergtuk the eightieth lived for twenty-two years. Ergtuk the 81st lived for 21 years. This Ergtuk is 18 years old.'

Ergtuk stared at Peter. Tears brewed in his eyes.

'Help me!'

Peter stared at him, uncertain of what to say, with every generation of clones, they live less and less. 'Tell him we will do our best to protect him, but he must help us in return.'

Even though Ergtuk was the enemy, Peter felt some sympathy for him. These clones seemed to be slaves of the evil Narzuks, blindly following all orders, perhaps not knowing the implications of these actions, but this clone seemed different. Peter remembered his history lessons: during the Second World War, the regular German army, the Wehrmacht, hated the Waffen SS, whose evil acts were carried out on Hitler's orders. The Wehrmacht had some sense of fair play and followed the Geneva Convention. However, Hitler's SS were responsible for many heinous, callous and illegal war crimes. There were some parallels here.

Lucia converses with Ergtuk who becomes agitated.

'He agrees to your terms.'

'OK, good.'

'If he's coming with us tell him to strip, and he will have to wear a blindfold. Make sure there are no devices on him.'

Lucia looked coldly at Ergtuk. 'I will interrogate him later.'

Peter was impatient to get going again. 'Let's get back to base and get some food inside us.'

Vinnie searched Ergtuk's clothes and found a small device. He put it into Ergtuk's face, Lucia's eyes were an angry red.

'What is this?' asked Lucia.

Ergtuk pointed up at the sky anxiously. 'He says it's a shielding device, if we switch it on, it will stop da fighters from getting a fix on us.' Ergtuk turned on the device and gave it to Peter.

'What if it's a homing beacon and he's trying to trap us?' Lucia was angry, as she looked at the frightened alien.

'General Grumpy said the aliens were trying to locate our Sirius base in Mojave.' Peter stared at Ergtuk, hands on hips.

'He could be a trojan,' Ergtuk seemed to understand and shook his head. Peter looked into Ergtuk's eyes, trying to gauge him, and then at Lucia. There were several giveaways to indicate if someone was lying, and Ergtuk was displaying none of them, but then again, *he was an alien.*

'We will just have to trust him—he could be very valuable to us. I'm sure the professor would like to speak to him.' Peter thought it was worth taking the risk.

Lucia smiled then stared coldly at Ergtuk.

'Peter, if da alien makes any moves, I will kill him. I will not hesitate.'

Peter almost felt sorry for the alien but also knew he could be very useful to the war effort. These aliens are not a united race, it seems some of them hate this bastard Grimbald as much as we do.

Vinnie found a vehicle, hotwired it, and they set off down the road, Vinnie at the wheel, next to Ergtuk. Lucia and Peter sat in the back to keep an eye on their alien passenger. Peter admired Vinnie for his many skills, including hot-wiring cars, and many other skills, which were not technically legal. But if you work for the Secret Intelligence Service *(the correct term for MI6),* those are the sort of skills you need, and Vinnie had those in plentiful supply.

Peter put the alien shielding device between the front seats as they combed the skies for enemy fighters. Vinnie found the way back to Route 58 which heads west across the vast and arid California Valley. The landscape looked parched as they drank their diminishing water supplies.

Ergtuk looked up, concerned, as an alien fighter passed overhead but didn't spot them. The device blinked as the cloaking engaged, and then went quiet again.

They passed old 1940s-style hotels. Some looked old and occupied, but many looked derelict and in need of repair. They passed a hotel with a lop-sided sign: The Minn-Iowa Motel. It looked like the desert had taken over it.

Later they passed the ruins of a giant radio tower, all that remained of a World War II auxiliary airfield, its grey buildings covered in graffiti, and nicknamed the Mojave Stonehenge. Vinnie wiped his brow and searched for water. Peter gave him his last drop.

'I'm cream crackered,' Vinnie looked out the window at the desert. Lucia looked puzzled as she hid from the sun coming through the car window.

'What is cream of da crackered?' Lucia asked in her East European accent.

Peter laughed. 'He means he's very tired, knackered.'

'Crackered, rhymes with knackered,' explained Vinnie.

'He can't talk proper English.' Peter smiled. He teased him mercilessly about cockney rhyming slang, but being best friends, that's what you do.

Chapter 68

THE LIFE OF ERGTUK

Peter blindfolded Ergtuk as they got near the Mojave Desert, but he did not complain. He thought these humans were thoughtful, resilient and compassionate—'human' qualities, especially the one called Peter. In the clone learning booths on his home planet, they were programmed twelve hours per day on everything they needed to know about Earth, and the human race, their history, their culture, their weaknesses and how to destroy them.

However, it wasn't until he actually met these beings that he started to know them. He liked Peter, but he didn't like the night-crawler they called Lucia, she seemed to hold a grudge against him. Then he remembered his history lessons in his learning booth, and the ancient war against the night-crawler vampires, dating back to the Sumerian empire, 7000 years ago.

This Peter seemed different from the other humans. He appeared to understand him more than the others did. Was he the one there were rumours about, who brandished a magical sword, obliterating all in his path? The only thing that frightened him were the night-crawler vampires, *their ancient enemy.* For all their advanced technology, they could not outwit them. Fiendishly fast, incredibly strong, telepathic; the vampires could read their minds, and so be one step ahead.

Ergtuk's home planet was Ergal Five, one of the planets orbiting the star Tau Ceti, only twelve light-years from Earth and visible to the naked eye. In cosmic terms, this is just spitting distance from Earth.

The planets surrounding Tau Ceti are two to six times bigger than Earth. Ergal Five is lying in what's commonly known as the star's 'Goldilocks Zone' a position that is neither too hot nor too cold, but instead exactly the right environment to support the prospect of liquid surface water, and therefore, life. Ergal Five is twice as big as Earth, and because of its size, the planet's gravity is stronger than Earth. The early inhabitants evolved with strong leg muscles and torsos to cope with the gravity. Later, as they became more advanced but physically weaker, they used gravity compensators to shield them from the gravitational effects.

Ergtuk the 82nd is a clone of the original Ergtuk. The original was a famous historian and accomplished engineer who wrote many popular books on the history and politics of his people, as well as designing spaceships. The problem was, as each generation of clones was manufactured to replace the ones that died, the DNA deteriorated to the extent that Ergtuk the 81st only lived 20 years, which did not hold out much prospect for Ergtuk the 82nd.

Ergtuk's first memories were waking in an enormous white room, full of other clones who were in various states of wakefulness. He looked around him at the other clones, who were equally curious about him. He knew his name was Ergtuk because that was part of his core memory.

Why am I here?

Who are these other people?

Why are they naked?

What is my purpose?

His core memory told him who Ergtuk the Original was.

But who was he really?

He decided from waking that he would be his own Ergtuk, be an original and not just a poor copy, like the rest. He would take orders but have his own agenda, create his own purpose in life—however, long that life was. He remembered his mother; she was beautiful, kind and loving. He recalled her face and smiled. It was a real memory. Then Ergtuk experienced a new emotion, one that he would learn to call happiness. But he found out that the memory was an implant. Later, he would experience other emotions like fear, loathing, and determination.

He was taken to a large hall with the other clones where he was fed a plate of various coloured pills; unappetising, he thought. The other clones didn't seem to mind, staring blankly at their food pills. A vague, core memory told him that Ergtuk the original ate real food, real meat, real vegetables and delicious fruit from his garden.

Was he wired differently from the others? He began to experience self-awareness of himself and his surroundings, a consciousness independent of his body. The other clones seemed to be eating the pills, but their faces were expressionless. Was he going to be a robot like them?

He had a friend, which was unheard of for clones. His name was Argvorn the 21st. They used to eat together. Then one day he was gone. When Ergtuk asked where he was, he was told that Argvorn the 21st had been placed in a punishment cell for seven days, for 're-education.'

In the learning booth, he was taught that he was a servi, a slave, and was a servant of the Sumeri, to obey orders and to serve his superiors, and not to question orders.

Ergtuk did not like being a slave. He had his own voice, but he was clever enough to keep it shut, unlike his missing friend Argvorn.

During Ergtuk's time he could see the size of the population of the Patricians decline, so the Patricians ordered more clones to be built. The cloned servi greys were programmed from birth to serve and obey the Patricians.

Ergtuk could see that society had become divided between the servi clones, or the greys, as they were commonly known, *(because they wore grey uniforms)* and their masters, the Patricians, including the Narzuk military. Ergtuk didn't like his military training. He wanted to be an engineer like the original, but he didn't have any choice. He was a clone. It was a year before he joined the military corps so when Ergtuk graduated from the learning booths he became a slave to a politician.

He soon learned that the Patricians, who were also landowners, and the oligarch businessmen, operated a system of nepotism, so only if you were a Patrician could you do business with other Patricians. Ergtuk could see that the greys and the Plebeians *(Sumeri working class)* were left out in the cold. The cruel Narzuks were part of the Patrician elite.

The sharp end of the stick.

Ergtuk learned a new feeling.

Resentment that they were treated so badly.

His Patrician master Gurvak looked down on Ergtuk because he himself was an original. Gurvak's wife Gurd-Im was trying to become pregnant, but with no luck. She was infertile, like most Sumeri women. Night after night Gurd-Im pleaded with Gurvak to try the latest new wonder drug. Gurvak coveted his fortune, made from buying and selling slaves, like Ergtuk. In the end, though, he relented, spending a third of his fortune on the newest and most expensive drugs. Miraculously she became pregnant, Ergtuk watched their happy smiles, but after three months, Ergtuk heard screaming in the middle of the night. Gurd-Im had aborted.

Ergtuk learned that the DNA cloning process sometimes creates 'oddballs.' Some of them originated from independent thinkers, such as Ergtuk the historian and engineer, creating 'original thinkers.' But there were many among the greys who were not happy, and who wanted more, they wanted rights like the right to live their own lives and not be slaves. Like Ergtuk.

In his booth, Ergtuk had learned the history of the Sumeri people. The leaders of the Patricians looked across the galaxy searching for a new home, new prospects, a new start. They could not believe their luck when they found Earth, a perfect climate, plentiful food and water, plentiful resources for the Sumeri to plunder. And best of all, a young and innocent emergent civilisation, in Sumeria *(as the aliens were later to call it.)*

It started with raiding parties. A ship would land in the dead of night and carry away the native Sumerian women for their experiments. Their initial attempt at cross-breeding human women with aliens was disastrous. Ergtuk cringed as he saw pictures of the results. The terrified women could not get pregnant with the alien sperm, *it just wasn't compatible*. But they didn't give up. After thousands of years of human kidnappings, suffering, and experimentation, they discovered they could make their alien sperm compatible with female human eggs by taking large quantities of certain fertility drugs and boosters.

They could now make a human female pregnant and create a half-human half-Sumeri half-breed. It was their hope for the future, but, Ergtuk thought, is this fair on these people?

The humans.

Ergtuk now had a conscience.

Chapter 69

DARK SIDE OF THE MOON

DARK SIDE OF THE MOON

The huge, ugly, black mothership was hiding behind the dark side of the moon. The gigantic bulk of the ship moved slowly over the rugged lunar terrain below and cast a giant shadow over the multitude of impact craters. It moved over the South Pole—over the Aitken basin, one of the largest craters in the Solar System. The massive bulk emerged behind the moon and headed back to Earth, accelerating. The small ball of Earth became large and loomed into view, white and blue, glorious and beautiful.

On the bridge of the mothership, General Grimbald lounged in his black Narzuk uniform. Alien centurion Imperial Narzuk Guards in red uniforms lined the perimeter of the bridge. On the massive deck of the bridge, just behind Grimbald, on a higher level, sat Marshal Zurg-Uk on a golden chair, his stiff black Narzuk uniform looking uncomfortable, but resplendent, with its gold braid, and decorated with medals. A white swastika was emblazoned on his sleeve. Zurg-Uk looked down with disdain at Grimbald. Resentment burned deep within what was left of his soul, as he glowered at the human imposter.

General Grimbald looked back at Marshal Zurg-Uk, they had retreated to the far side of the Moon after the attack on the Earth ships, and the Marshal had blamed him for it.

'We had 80 ships Grimbald—now we less than 40! Your incompetence has cost us dearly,' he shouted in front of the cowering bridge crew, averting their eyes from the Marshal.

Maybe he had been too harsh with Grimbald, after all, he was the emperor's pet. He would have to be careful with his words, even if they had lost half their fleet. They were now licking their wounds after the attack by the humans: *unexpected and surprising.* Skulking behind the Moon, Zurg-Uk wondered if this traitor to his own people could be trusted.

The humans had a saying for people like Grimbald: 'Teacher's pet.' Just because he was blood-related to Hitler, he was treated like royalty, and to top it all, the emperor had made them joint leaders of the Earth expeditionary force, and to add insult to injury, gave him the Order of the Black Warriors: their highest honour!

He, Marshal Zurg-Uk, chief of the military, should be leading this expedition, not this rat-faced upstart Earthling traitor, Grimbald. His resentment of this human traitor had taken him to breaking point. Just slip up once, my friend, just one more slip up, and you will live out the rest of your miserable life in the torture chambers of Doctor Vlad-Uk on Home Planet Ergal Five.

But then there was also Lord Grim-Uk to contend with. The Marshal suspected Grimbald, and the Narzuk SS chief had formed an alliance. Grim-Uk reported directly to the emperor, that's why they got better rations, more benefits. Yes, he could use the ship replicators, but replicators cannot replace real Sumeri food, it just isn't the same. It wasn't fair. He had to be careful.

Very careful.

He also had suspicions about the Narzuk SS agenda. Grim-Uk kept disappearing down to sector one. What was down there? The power outages were getting worse, and it wasn't just the poor state of the mothership either. Something else was going on behind his back.

General Grimbald wondered about the marshal. They did not see eye to eye, but he had a sense of honour he would give him that much, even if it was misplaced. But Grimbald had no room for sentimentality or sense of justice. No, he liked Grim-Uk. Cut from the same cloth, both were advocates of Nazi ideology and dedicated to the cause, he was a much better bedfellow. Grimbald wondered what evil deeds Lord Grim-Uk had committed to earn his medals and position. 'It takes a special kind of person to be totally ruthless,' he thought, and he was in good company. The needs of the many outweigh the needs of the one, that's how he rationalised his decisions, as long as those decisions were in his favour, of course. But at least he had Grim-Uk on his side, and he had royal blood, after all, being the nephew of Adolf Hitler. But Grim-Uk was busy on the planet with his harvesting program—and he was left alone with the Marshal.

He avoided the Marshal's glance as he pondered their retreat. The impudent humans. He had underestimated them.

He looked at the portrait of Hitler on the wall and admired his own shiny medal, the Order of the Black Warriors, given to him for his outstanding service to the Sumeri, presented by the emperor himself.

The marshal stood up. 'Where is Oluk?'

'He's on his way Marshal,' said a junior officer. 'Lord Grim-Uk has just docked also.' Grimbald smiled, and the marshal winced.

Oluk strode into the bridge, standing in front of Marshal Zurg-Uk, hands on hips looking annoyed.

'Marshal I don't know how you expect me to carry out these emergency repairs, I need at least three days. I don't have the men or the materials—it's ridiculous!'

If anyone else had spoken to him that way, he would have been executed immediately, but this was Oluk, the engineering genius who designed and built all their ships and was held in the highest regard by everyone, including the emperor. The marshal spoke with hands open.

'Oluk, old friend, we had to make a tactical retreat. The humans are fighting back, we have lost many of our ships. We cannot risk the mothership. It is an opportunity to make the repairs you keep talking about, but we must do it quickly. In two days we are planning a major attack which will destroy the humans, once and for all, and we will all be heroes, including yourself. We will sit at the dining table of our great emperor once again.'

Oluk bowed, 'It will be done in 24 Earth hours. Oh, and I installed the nuclear device detectors as you asked. They won't catch us off guard this time. They are accessed via the bridge console.'

Oluk strolled off the bridge, his genius mind working out the logistics of how he would make the repairs in time. Sticking plaster and Sellotape sprang to mind; *he liked these human expressions*. It had become a very popular pastime of the Patricians and Narzuks to study Earth culture and language, after all, he was a Patrician, but he had flatly refused to become a member of the Narzuk party—especially this SS faction, *they were fanatics*. He didn't like their politics. And he didn't like this human Grimbald who they were aligned with, he had a bad air about him. He thought this whole Earth expedition was a bad idea. The humans had a lot of spirit and guile, they were not a race that would be easily defeated, despite their technological inferiority; he felt unease as he planned his repairs.

And what did they have in sector one? He was detecting unusual power readings coming from that sector. It was making his ship even more unstable, and he didn't like it. There were rumours that the dreaded Narzuk SS had a secret. An unholy secret. In sector one.

Chapter 70

SECRET CONSPIRACY

The Marshal stood up and looked at the navigator, 'Head for Earth, United States.' He then turned to a nervous looking bridge officer, Erg-Ik. 'Are the detectors working? Have you calibrated them?'

Erg-Ik turned around, 'Yes, Herr Marshal, they are operational. We will detect any nuclear devices once they are activated.'

At that moment Grim-Uk walked in, smiled at Grimbald, then scowled at the marshal. He slouched down in his chair near Grimbald, grabbing a drink from a frightened human slave girl. 'It's a disaster Marshal, you have been too complacent. The imperial emperor will not be happy when I file my report!'

'Lord Grim-Uk,' Marshal Zurg-Uk, spoke at last to his rival, choosing his words carefully, 'We did not anticipate the Night-Crawlers; the humans and the vampires joining forces, but there's something else. I have heard rumours of a human, endowed with great powers who has been causing us problems. He is located in Los Angeles in the Western United States of America. I want you to find out more, and how we can neutralise this threat.'

'He is known to me Marshal, I have been thinking long and hard about him, and how we can use him. Or destroy him.' Then added, 'My trusted Deputy Himm-Uk, is on his way now.'

Himm-Uk entered the bridge acknowledging his brother.

'Brother Himm-Uk, we need to do something about this human, the one they call Caius,' Grim-Uk rubbed his red-stained eye and offered his brother a drink.

'We need to kill him, Lord Grim-Uk,' said Zurg-Uk.

'Do not be so hasty,' replied Grim-Uk, popping a pill. 'Perhaps we can convert him; convince him to come over to our side.' Grimbald nodded with enthusiasm as he watched Grim-Uk toy with a black figurine around his neck. He wondered why the Narzuk SS seemed much healthier than the other Narzuks, and it wasn't just the better rations either, they had an unholy light about them.

'We can offer him something. Power and wealth,' added Grimbald joining in.

The Marshal nodded. 'He would certainly be a great asset. A one-man army.'

'Brother Himm-Uk, do you think you can persuade him?' asked Grim-Uk, leaning forward in his chair.

'I will try, brother. I will try. I will leave immediately,' he replied. Himm-Uk left the bridge.

Marshal Zurk-Uk rose and put his hands on Grimbald's shoulders in a false show of unity. He needed to play his cards right, as the humans say.

'Soon, the humans will be begging for mercy. They shall be our slaves.' A confident Grimbald looked at a pretty human slave girl.

'Get me a drink, girl and take care of the Marshal here,' Grimbald shouted at the terrified slave girl who nodded, looking at the Marshal who smiled back. That will give me time to talk to Lord Grim-Uk. Alone, *there are many plans to be made.*

The slave girl knew what was expected of her. But her heart was filled with hate, taken from her family in London, and enslaved by these animals. Grimbald—she especially hated Grimbald, who forced her to come to his chambers at night.

The bastard Grimbald.

A smile lit inside of her. 'Just give me one chance,' she thought, and I will have my revenge.

Chapter 71

DANGEROUS CARGO

The huge mothership entered a high Earth orbit, the viewing screen showing the vista of the blue of the Earth. Erg-Ik, the nervous deck officer, looked up. 'Marshal, sir, we have been getting strange power readings: outages, from sector one sir. None of our troops will go near it. There are rumours, sir,' Erg-Ik looked nervously at Grim-Uk, the Narzuk SS Chief. The Marshal had his suspicions about Grim-Uk and his filthy SS. Rumour had it that he and his master Vlad-Uk worshipped a demon, an unholy entity that gave them unnaturally long life. The Narzuk SS had a secret sect—*no wonder God had turned his back on the Sumeri race. No wonder they were so unlucky.*

Zurg-Uk stood up to face Grim-Uk, his manner defiant. 'What is it you have in sector one Grim-uk?'

'Special cargo, Marshal,' replied Grim-Uk looking bored.

'Sector one is a special confinement facility. Is it dangerous?' All nicety gone from his voice. 'My chief engineer, Oluk wants it gone from the ship, whatever it is, and I would tend to agree with him.'

'You don't need to know, Marshal,' replied Grim-Uk, taking a sip from his drink. 'Remember, I report directly to the emperor,' an icy tone to his voice.

Zurg-Uk fell into a sullen silence. Special cargo indeed. Whatever it was, it was causing power outages in an already-unstable ship. He would go there personally to see what it was. He had heard the rumours. Doctor Vlad-Uk, Grim-Uk's mentor, had excavated deep down in the dark and forbidding network of caves below his torture dungeons and he had found something. Something very old and very powerful. It was shrouded in mystery; only a handful of people knew about it, and he wasn't one of them. *A Narzuk SS conspiracy, that was what it was.* But he wouldn't stand for it. He did not like hidden agendas.

Not on my ship.

The Marshal entered his private elevator on the bridge and inputted his code. Sector one. As he entered, the lights flickered. He was going to get to the bottom of this mystery, *there were too many hidden agendas on this military expedition.*

He watched the progress on the panel to sector one. There were 100 sectors on the ship and sector one was at the bottom part of the ship, only accessible by a few individuals. *That was how they planned it.* The elevator stopped at sector two. He would have to walk from here.

As he exited, he saw the derelict state of the corridors and facilities. Only half-built, with pipes and wires everywhere. Oluk had done a magnificent job in getting the mothership ready by the deadline, but anything not essential to the war effort was simply not done.

Shortcuts.

He switched on his torch on his laser pistol and clambered over some pipes and rubbish, making his way in the half darkness to sector one.

Environmental controls were not working. Shortcuts. Damned shortcuts. He breathed oxygen like the humans, but the air tasted bad. Stale and dirty. He coughed.

He suddenly felt a chill.

It wasn't just the faulty environmental controls, it was something else. There is no one about. Where were the Narzuk SS Stormtroopers who guarded this place? After all, they controlled this sector.

Silence.

There was a knot of fear in his stomach as he neared sector one. Then the lights dimmed and came back on again. Then went off again.

It is dark. Then it became colder—freezing cold. He heard a dull thud. Then it became louder, like something banging on a steel wall.

Then a sound like an animal.

But not an animal. Like it had intelligence.

Then he felt the corridor shake, and he fell over. As he retrieved his laser pistol and gets up again, he saw someone staggering through the dark corridor. He shined his torch on the face, a blood-stained face, then he saw a uniform: a Narzuk SS trooper.

'Leave now!' the trooper shouted in desperation. 'It has awoken, it cannot be contained!' But the Marshal's curiosity was stronger than his fear. He continued down the corridor as the commotion grew louder, even though it could spell his doom.

Then it goes quiet.

He tiptoed into sector one—the containment facility itself. He could hear a low, deep growling from inside the thick doors. There was a transparent panel in the door and a dim light from inside. He looked through the panel. There is something moving inside: huge, dark, animal-like, and a deep growl which made the corridor shake.

Then it turned and looked at him. Red eyes. Deep-set red eyes, with an unnatural animal intelligence. It lunged toward the door.

Zurg-Uk's heart skipped a beat as he stepped back from the thick door as it came away with a huge thud and landed on the floor.

It stood there, looking at him.

It was huge, hairy and muscular, some 15 feet tall, with glowing red eyes. On its head were two horns. Large leathery wings were on its back.

For a split second he stood there like a rabbit caught in the headlights. Then instinct took over, and he ran like his life depended on it, his heart pounding, his lungs trying to get oxygen from the stale air. He made it to the elevator and dragged the injured Narzuk SS trooper in with him. 'Bridge!' he shouted. The doors shut and the elevator sped away at tremendous speed, inertial dampers kicking in to soften the G-force.

He fell out of the elevator into the bridge. Grim-Uk and Grimbald stared at him.

'Erg-Ik, eject sector one—NOW!'

'All of it?'

Yes, do it!' Zurg-Uk commanded.

'I countermand that order!' shouted Grim-Uk.

'This is my ship Grim-Uk!' then he turned to Erg-Ik.

'Do it!' screamed the Marshal. 'And seal the bulkhead doors in sector two!' Ergik watched his screen as he tracked the detached section of the mothership descend to earth.

Zurg-Uk went up to Grim-Uk and lifted him up by the lapels on his uniform. 'You endangered the lives of everyone on this ship—my ship!' Grim-Uk was silent. He punched Zurg-Uk in the stomach, then left the bridge with the injured Narzuk SS trooper.

'Can we track it?' asked Grim-Uk talking to the trooper. 'Yes my Lord.'

Marshal Zurg-Uk slumped into his chair, trying to recover, grabbing a drink from a slave girl. 'You take command for a while Grimbald,' ordered Zurk-Uk, hand on head.

Grimbald looked at his empty glass, then at the viewing screen.

'Now we shall see who the master race is. Get me a drink, girl!'

A drugged human slave woman in a thin tunic approached the general. Her eyes looked vacant as she gave him his drink. Planet Earth zoomed into view, an astonishing blue vista that even Grimbald stared at it for a while. Marshal Zurk-Uk leaned forward to General Grimbald,

'We need to teach these humans a lesson on who is the superior race here, *deploy the destructor.*'

Grimbald smiled, 'Marshal, we have lost fifty percent of our Earth fleet. Let us exact revenge on the humans. What shall we destroy first? How about Texas? I never liked Texas, too many cowboys. Let's turn this planet into toast!' smiled Grimbald.

The massive mothership, entered the atmosphere, heading for the United States. On the bridge viewer was the South Eastern United States, the panhandle of Florida, in clear view. They veered west, and soon Texas appeared on the screen. Grimbald's eyes light up.

'Marshal Zurg-Uk, we shall build a glorious empire with our new race, we shall conquer Earth, the humans will be our slaves, doing our will! They will beg for mercy before I am finished with them.'

'Deploy the destructor General Grimbald,' ordered the marshal, ignoring his over-zealous speech.

Marshal Zurk-Uk watched as Grimbald moved a red lever. Underneath the ship, a huge half-mile wide panel slid back, revealing a laser-like weapon device a mile long. There was a low throbbing humming as the device gained charge. The throbbing became louder and more frequent.

'Thirty minutes to full charge, Marshal.' Erg-Ik watched the power display on one of his screens.

Chapter 72

CRY FOR HELP

Jennifer is in her pod in the massive cave-like structure of the breeding chamber listening to the screams of thousands of women around her. Some of them sound like they are in childbirth, she knows, she has two children of her own, and she has left them!

What was she thinking?

She drinks some water from the tube to cool herself in the humid atmosphere and thinks to herself,

'I will get out of here. I will get out. I need my hero my husband, Pete. I need the warrior, Caius. Come, my love, come get me. Rescue me.' The screams become dimmer and dimmer as she falls asleep from exhaustion. She is dreaming.

She is lying on soft green grass. Beside her flows a silvery stream, a golden sun's rays beat through the green conifers around her. A breeze blows through the woodland and the long, rich grass. Bluebells grow in abundance as she looks up at the blue sky, it is a place without time; peaceful and magical. All around her shines a golden light. Then in the silence, she hears a rustle in the trees. Out of the conifers and ancient oaks approaches a figure like nothing she has seen before. The sun's rays shine on a beautiful woman in a shimmering dress. She has transparent wings on her back as she glides gracefully towards her, her long blonde hair flowing over her shoulders, her bare feet walking through the rich, green grass. Her blue eyes pierce Jennifer's soul as she approaches her. She crouches down beside Jennifer and smiles at her as she helps her up. She strokes her hair and kisses her on the forehead.

'I am the Angel of the Tears. You have suffered much torment, but please know that you are not alone. You are protected. I will always be with you, for you are blessed.' She cups her hand, reaches down into the stream and cups some water. She gives it to Jennifer, and she feels the cool, healing liquid give her new energy.

'You are healed. You may ask me one question.'

'Where is my husband?' Jennifer pleads.

'He is searching for you. There is another helping him. You remember her from long ago because you loved her.' The Angel smiles and Jennifer is filled with hope and joy.

Jennifer is dreaming again. She is walking through a market. It is hot and noisy, an argument has broken out between a meat seller and the wife of a centurion, she covers her mouth as she walks past the meat stalls and buys some figs, grapes, and melons, making sure they are fresh. She gives the fruit seller some coins from her purse and hurries past a slave trader; the slaves are in shackles, looking miserable, dirty and malnourished. She makes her way out of the hustle and bustle of the market and starts walking up to the hill to the villa where she lives with her master and mistress. They are kind to her and treat her like one of the family. She is lucky to have been chosen by them.

She shivers as she remembers her traumatic kidnapping from her home in Gaul, put in a crowded wooden cage, like an animal, and the arduous journey in the stinking cart, to Rome and put up for sale in the slave market. She thought she would never stop crying, but now she has found a happiness of sorts.

She fingers the gold bracelet that her mistress has given her as she walks, and feels the warm sun on her brown hair as she knocks on the wooden gate. A guard opens it for her, and smiles, and she walks into a garden. Her mistress is sitting on a sofa enjoying the sun. She washes the grapes and puts them in a bowl. Her mistress looks at her with deep blue eyes, 'Come sit with me, Juliana.'

'Yes Domina.' She sits next to her mistress, who smiles at her.

'Juliana, are you happy?'

'Yes Domina…but,' a tear falls down her cheek.

'You miss your family?' She nods as the tears well up in her eyes and she starts to cry. Her mistress pulls her closer, as she kisses her head. 'There, there, you're safe now.' She runs her fingers through her brown hair, pulls her head up and kisses her on the lips, and wipes away her tears. Her heart beats faster as she kisses her mistress's soft red lips. Then Juliana runs her hands through her thick black hair. They both turn and look as the master, Caxus, sits opposite and drinks some wine. Juliana admires the tall, handsome charismatic man, wearing a toga. He is strong, clever and kind. A good master.

'Greetings Caxus, if you are well, it is good, I am well,' says her mistress as she pours herself some wine and squeezes Juliana's hand.

'Greetings Lucia, if you are well, it is good, I am well,' replies Caxus, as Juliana watches her mistress get up and sit on Caxus's lap and kiss him. Her mistress winks at her.

'How is your business, husband?' asks Lucia as she kisses him and gives him wine and grapes. Juliana admires Lucia's thick, black locks and curvy figure, like that of a goddess at the local temple.

'It is good, wife. Julius, the wine trader, has bought a year's worth of wine from my lands in the north. I got good coin.' He drinks more wine and wipes his brow with a cloth. 'I am hot, I need to change.'

'What do you think of our new slave girl, Juliana, husband?'

'She is pretty, nice hair,' as Lucia playfully wiggles her bottom in his lap and then kisses him with her red lips.

'I want to bed her Caxus, can I?' asks her mistress, looking at him with her sultry blue eyes. He smiles and nods as she gets up and takes Juliana's hand. She feels excited as they walk together through the garden, through the flowers and herbs; she can smell rosemary. She feels happy again; the happiest she has been for a long time,

Jennifer wakes with a start. Who is the beautiful woman with blue eyes in my dream? Where am I? She is not at home in Wales; she realises with a shock that she is being held prisoner on a spaceship. Her heart beats faster as she screams, 'Help me!'

Then her blood runs cold as she hears the screams of other women around her. Where is her warrior husband, Caius? Then she remembers the Angel of the Tears, and her words, and is filled with hope. *Her husband is looking for her. And another, whom she loved, is that the woman in her dream?*

Chapter 73

WAR STORIES

SIRIUS UNDERGROUND COMMAND
BUNKER IN MOJAVE

Peter and his team are sitting in the mess, eating breakfast. Lucia is sucking on a blood bag, her eyes blazing red. She sucks until she is satiated. They all look dishevelled and tired.

'We should celebrate. We downed a load of ships, so the aliens must be fearful now,' Handsome Mike tries to brighten the mood.

'They will be angry now, we have stirred up a hornet's nest,' Lucia speaks. They all nod.

'I'm not celebrating till I know my Jennifer is safe,' Peter glances at Vinnie. Vinnie looks back and carries on eating a large plateful of eggs, bacon, sausage, and beans. Colonel Stan Wight comes over wearing an apron.

'You boys need more chow?'

'More eggs please Colonel,' replies Vinnie. Peter looks at Stan.

'We're short staffed, so I'm filling in. Heard you boys downed the LA ship last night. Well done!'

'Thanks, Colonel,' replies Peter as Stan rushes back to serve a few other soldiers, half of them plainly injured. The mess looks half empty as Peter looks around not recognising anyone. 'Not many made it back from last night,' mumbles Peter.

Sebastian crosses himself and looks up. 'But we all made it back last night, thank the Lord,' said Sebastian.

'Amen to that,' replied Peter, 'what about your vampires Lucia?'

'Abel and Arnoldo were lost,' says Lucia sadly.

'I shall pray for them,' replies Sebastian.

Peter becomes more business-like. 'Just to bring you up to date. As well as bringing down the LA ship, the San Francisco ship was downed, but all our men were lost. San Diego and Seattle were destroyed, but New York and Chicago were a complete failure, as was Houston. No men apart from us have returned from these missions, so far.'

They all shake their heads.

'Vinnie, the Birmingham ship was destroyed, but the London mission failed. The good news is the London boys from our squadron made it out alive. I got a coded message from Artie, asking when I'm coming back. Vinnie, put it on our to-do list. When our business is finished here we destroy the London ship.'

Vinnie nods as he eats a sausage. 'As far as I can make out the aliens lost about half their ships worldwide. But most of our men and vampires were lost, in the effort,' Peter sighs, and Sebastian crosses himself again.

'Shame about Des and the boys,' says Vinnie.

Peter nods and yawns but he is in a philosophical mood.

'How can God allow this to happen?'

'Remember Peter, we have free will, and so do the aliens, but ultimately they must account for their actions, hence their souls are damned, like Lucia here,' Sebastian rubs his stubble as he speaks.

'Do we all have souls?' Peter chews through his sausage.

'Yes, each one of us is a tiny spark of His divine being. We are literally a chip off the old block. He sees the world through our eyes.'

Lucia is tearful.

'Is there any hope for me? Am I a part of God's plan?'

'We are all part of God's plan Lucia. There is hope for you, have more faith. There is no error here.'

They all sit in silence for a while.

'These yanks make a pretty good breakfast.' Vinnie is in a cheerful mood as he slurps his tea.

Peter looks at a tearful Lucia, touches her arm and tries to change the subject. Lucia looks up at him, her eyes wet as she brushes her long black hair off her face and manages a small smile.

'Lucia, how do you understand the alien language?'

'Professor Picard. I call him uncle, he taught me. It is very similar to ancient Sumerian cuneiform; very symbolic. The symbols have meanings like Egyptian hieroglyphs.'

'Was it difficult to learn? asks Peter, holding her hand.

'Yes, at first, but I had plenty of time on my hands—remember, I'm immortal.' She let the last word sink in as she looks hard at Sebastian, thoughtful and vindictive.

'The professor, why do you call him uncle?' asks Peter.

Chapter 74

WORLD ON A KNIFE EDGE

'It was during da Second World War when I met da professor, he was a boy then. After he lost his parents, Cassian and I sort of adopted him. I am very fond of him. It's a long story,' sighed Lucia.

'I'm listening,' replied Peter.

'Myself, Cassian, and the other vampire clans had decided to help the allies. Why did we help, you ask? We could not tolerate the idea of a world ruled by Nazis *da worst kind of demon.*'

'And you're a good demon?' Peter joked.

Lucia smiled and showed her fangs in a playful act and continued her story. Peter liked her East European accent, sometimes she would pronounce "the" as "da," but he didn't mind, he liked to listen to her talk—this beautiful vampire joined to him by destiny.

'It was 1941, the war was on a knife-edge. Da Axis Powers dominated the globe. In Europe, the German Empire extended west to the French coast, east to Russia, north to Norway and south to Tunisia. Da Soviet Union and British Empire teetered on the brink, and the United States finally entered da war after Pearl Harbor. Japan extended its boundaries from Vietnam to the Marshall Islands and from Manchuria to the equator.' Lucia cleared her throat and cast her mind back to the night of the raid.

'I remember it like it was yesterday. Da Vampiri, da Vampire Council, our government if you like, suspected the Nazis were developing secret weapons that could destroy the allies and send da world into darkness. The world was at a tipping point, and we had to act. There are many parallels with this alien invasion: da will to dominate, to conquer and to suppress freedom. Anyway, we knew they were developing a stealth bomber, a new kind of fixed-wing aircraft with an experimental jet engine. We knew they had a turboprop version but also a jet engine version we suspected could fly at 1000kph, making it faster than all allied fighters, and a deadly threat. Not only that, but a long-range version could reach New York. However, we encountered more than we bargained for.' Lucia held Peter's hand underneath the table as she spoke.

'We were on the edge of a pine forest overlooking a secret Nazi base, deep inside Nazi Germany. Heinrich and his wife Derica, the professor's parents were with us, German Jews working for da French Resistance. They had narrowly escaped from Germany with Louis Picard, my uncle, after the Nazi persecution of Jews in Germany in the late 1930s.' Lucia sucked on a blood bag, then continued.

'Around the large concrete installation was a high fence, and sentry posts every 200 yards. We could see a hangar and a runway running off the main installation. Da hangar looked bombproof. Our intelligence told us the walls were ten feet thick.'

Lucia started to remember every detail as her super senses kicked in. As a vampire, she was endowed with a photographic memory and could recall images and sounds, even smells, from thousands of years before.

It was pitch black, cold, but the sky was clear, one of those beautiful October nights when the stars seem to shine and the sky sparkles. It was the early hours before dawn when people were in their deepest sleep.

The dew was wet on the grass. She was wearing a leather suit, with a sword strapped to her back. On her waist, she carried a utility belt and knives on her thigh and shin. Cassian was shrouded in a dark leather cloak, bristling with weapons. She could hear a squirrel scurrying up a tree to its nest, which stopped and look at them and the scent of fresh pine needles and sap of the trees. All her senses were alive as Lucia urged the group to move back a few yards to the safety of the forest. She looked at Cassian, he was studying the sentries on the perimeter, looking for weaknesses. Lucia could smell the German sentry in his tower only 200 yards away. He had eaten garlic that night, she thought. She could smell his body odour. He had not showered in days. Lucia looked at his face; his eyelids were drooping. Heinrich and Derica seemed nervous, and their teeth chattered in the cold, but they were keen to meter out punishment to the Nazis.

'We must attack now!' said Heinrich.

'Patience,' replied Cassian. Heinrich looked at their vampire comrades, fear in his eyes. Lucia read his thoughts, *what sort of pact had the resistance fighters made with these demons?* He thought about his young son, Louis, hiding in the loft of his brother's house. He loved him so much. He was so smart, so studious; he knew that he would become a professor one day. Were they doing the right thing? Was this his war?

Lucia concluded their enthusiasm in hating the Nazis far outweighed their skill in fighting; she and Cassian had been reluctant to bring them along. Their mission was to destroy the prototype flying wing aircraft before it could go into production. But there were rumours of a bomb, a special kind of bomb, that the flying wing carried.

Cassian and Lucia thought about taking out the guards, but there were too many. Every 200 yards there was a sentry tower with at least two sentries and a machine gun pointing at the grass-covered no-man's land between the forest and the outer perimeter fence. But Lucia could see the nearest sentry in his tower, garlic breath, just 200 yards from the forest. They were in luck, just one sentry, and he was falling asleep.

'Now,' whispered Lucia. She and Cassian transformed into flying demons, red eyes aflame, leathery wings sprouting from their body as they picked up their comrades and flew silent as the night over the fence. Derica whimpered in terror but Lucia hissed, and she was quiet. With a flap of wings, they landed near the hangar. As they got their breath, two sentries came out of the shadows and challenged them.

"Halt! Wer da!" shouted the soldiers as they moved forward, Maschinenpistole 38 machine guns pointing at them. Cassian and Lucia leaped forward at lightning speed onto the soldiers, smashing them to the tarmac, as they broke their necks, then sunk their fangs into their jugulars, draining them of blood.

Heinrich looked on in horror.

'Quickly, we'll be detected!' hissed Cassian as he dragged the bodies around the edge of the building and put them into a bin. Lucia licked her lips and wiped the blood from her face, her eyes sparkling with a red light, a new energy. They looked at the solid steel hangar door. Even Cassian and Lucia together could not open it, for it was locked from the inside, so they realised that there must be another way in. They felt the walls of the hangar, Lucia's physic powers kicking in. They were definitely bomb-proof, at least 12 feet thick of reinforced concrete. This was the place. They needed to get inside. They made their way around the side of the solid concrete hangar fortress, looking for an entrance. They walked in the shadows around the hangar while keeping a lookout for any other guards. There seemed to be no entry, no doors: nothing. They hid behind a shed as the moon came out from behind a cloud, shedding light on the base.

A sentry patrol walked past and stopped five feet away as they stopped for a cigarette. Heinrich listened as the two German soldiers in heavy grey coats chatted about girls back in Berlin and how they would meet up and go to a nightclub, and then to a hotel, for all-night sex. As they laughed and chatted, Derica felt an itch in her nose. Heinrich looked at her and shook his head. The itch went away—then she sneezed. Cassian cursed. The two sentries swung around, looking in their direction, getting ready to fire their pistols.

'Achtung!' The soldiers saw their eyes glinting in the moonlight.

'We need one alive,' Cassian whispered to Lucia. In a blink of an eye, Lucia was behind one sentry, broke his neck and sank her teeth in, draining his blood. The other soldier just stared in shock as he saw the red demon eyes of Lucia the vampire. Cassian grabbed him and pulled him into the shadows. He looked at Heinrich.

'Ask him where the entrance to the hangar is, else I will break his neck and drain his body of blood, like his friend. Tell him now!'

The German soldier looked terrified as Heinrich interrogated him.

'You are leaning against it,' Heinrich interpreted. They searched the plain-looking concrete shed looking for an entrance, and the walls seemed smooth, with no doors or other openings. Lucia felt a depression in the wall, so she slid back a small panel and pressed a button – a steel door appeared, but it was locked. On the side was a number pad – Lucia stared at the terrified, sweating soldier who was desperate to cooperate. But he was shaking his head, pleading for mercy.

'He doesn't know,' said Lucia.

Cassian felt the panel and the ten keys, ranging from one to zero. Four keys had fingerprints on them - he could see and feel them. Cassian closed his eyes, and moved in time but not in space, until he could see images of Nazi officers entering numbers into the panel. Hazy at first, then clearer. Three, nine, zero, five. Cassian gently entered the sequence, and the door slid open silently.

'Quickly!' said Cassian. They were in a lift. Lucia looked at Cassian and Heinrich.

'It's on the lower levels, I think,' said Heinrich. There were four floor buttons, G, -1, -2, -3.

'Try minus three,' said Cassian. Heinrich crossed himself and touched the cross around his neck while muttering a quiet prayer. Lucia and Cassian stared at him.

'Pray to your God Heinrich, we pray to ours,' spoke Cassian who looked at Lucia. "We should not have brought them," he said silently.

Chapter 75

NAZI BOMB

Lucia's mind looked into Derica's as she shivered, 'I wonder what sort of God, thought Derica. Diabolical, quite likely.' The lift moved down, the whirring of gears disturbing their thoughts, wondering if there was a welcoming committee. The lift stopped. They looked at one another with trepidation.

The door opened. They stepped out into a cave-like structure, with lights built into the rock ceiling. About 100 yards away, they could see an aircraft that was in the shape of a huge wing, in one section with no fuselage as such, as in a typical aircraft. On the wing was a swastika and the cockpit was open. A technician was busy working on the huge wing of the plane. Two soldiers stood close by, guarding the plane. Lucia could see they looked bored as they were chatting and looking at what looked like photos of girls, laughing. They crept closer in the semi-darkness, hiding among crates of equipment. On their left, in an alcove of the cave, they could see what looked like bombs, large bombs. But they had a skull and crossbones insignia on them in black and yellow, signifying a warning of something.

'What sort of bombs are they?' thought Lucia. They were like nothing she had seen before. These were no ordinary bombs, there was something unusual inside of them. And it made her feel uncomfortable.

To their right was a glass office with large maps. Lucia recognised the United States. The New York area was circled. What does all this mean? They were taking in all this information as they crawled along the floor among the wooden crates, to avoid detection. The bombs were well guarded. Three more guards with SS uniforms walked around the corner and looked in their direction. One of them ran over and checked the lift. 'Achtung!' shouted the soldier as they looked around the cave.

Heinrich sweated and held Derica's hand. Lucia gave them a look of reassurance. Cassian whispered to Lucia, and she nodded. Cassian moved like lightning as he drew his sword, took out the two SS soldiers in a breath and sliced the head off the third. Cassian sank his teeth into one of the dead soldier's necks as Lucia leaped forward and knocked the two shocked soldiers unconscious. They did not deserve to die, she thought, they were not SS.

Heinrich attached explosive charges to the flying wing plane. As he finished applying them, Cassian came up, blood dripping from his mouth. Derica covered her ears, as loud sirens went off, shattering the peace.

'Set for 10 minutes, we need time to get out of here alive!' Cassian tied up the cockpit technician and two guards as he looked at Lucia. Her mind looked around for another exit; taking the lift now would be suicide. They were in a cave, and caves had tunnels. Tunnels usually go upwards as weak rain-soaked ground collapses, forming the tunnels. They could hear the lift coming down. They only had seconds to escape. Lucia's mind raced. She breathed in the air. Could she detect an airflow? Fresh air?

Which direction?

'Follow me!' she shouted as she ran towards the bomb alcove. At the back of the alcove was a thin gap in the rock, just wide enough for Lucia and Cassian to squeeze through. Heinrich and Derica took off their jackets as Cassian pulled them through the thin gap. They could hear shouts in the cave behind them. Although Lucia and Cassian could see in the dark, it was so hard to see in the pitch black that Lucia retrieved her torch. She led the way down a tunnel. She stepped through water, which had sharp rocks underfoot.

'Slow,' warned Lucia, as they crept down the tunnel.

Derica screamed as several large rats nibbled at her shoes. Cassian clamped his hand over her mouth, and all three looked wide-eyed at Derica, who now looked embarrassed. Cassian raised a finger as he listened for anyone following them.

He could hear faint shouts behind them.

'Hurry Lucia, we don't have much time,' Cassian urged. As they turned a bend in the tunnel, they stopped. There was a fork, two choices, left or right. The left one was flooded, but the right one seemed clear. Agitated German shouts become louder this time.

Derica started crying. 'Why did I leave my son? I'm sorry,' she said.

'This way, quickly!' urged Lucia as she grabbed Derica and dragged her along, choosing the right-hand fork. Heinrich looked at his watch.

'Four minutes—we need to be clear!'

Lucia led the way up the right-hand tunnel, which now inclined in an upward direction. She could see a faint glimpse of light ahead.

'Hurry!' she whispered.

Lucia could now see clear light ahead as she scrambled up the tunnel, leaving the others behind. She navigated a cleft in the rock and looked out into open air, through a narrow tunnel entrance hidden by bushes. As Lucia poked her head through, she could see the moon was full, which did not give the cover of darkness they needed to escape. Cassian joined her. Sirens were blazing, and soldiers were running everywhere.

'I think we're being followed up da tunnel!' said Cassian.

'We need to escape…Now!' replied Lucia.

'Ten seconds,' whispered Heinrich, as he joined them.

They felt a rumble in the tunnel beneath them. They saw flames erupt from a ventilation shaft, as the soldiers in the sentry towers turned the huge spotlights onto the base, searching for intruders. Suddenly, a shock wave from the blast hit them from behind, throwing them out onto the grass, into clear view of the spotlights.

'Cassian!' shouted Heinrich. Cassian and Lucia transformed into winged demons and carried their comrades high into the air, machine guns firing all around them, bullets spraying onto the ground. Lucia was hit, flinched a little, but kept flying high, framed against the full moon. Then from the forest, bats appeared in a huge mass, making a shrilling sound, and surrounded the machine gun turrets, swamping them and making the guns silent. They swooped down on the firing soldiers on the ground, who soon forgot about the escaping resistance fighters, as the bats bit and scratched at them.

Lucia and Cassian glided silently through the night until they reached the isolated house of Heinrich's brother nestling in the forest. They walked into the kitchen where his brother greeted them and prepared an early breakfast of bread, cheese, and ham. He looked with suspicion at the vampires who had now transformed back to their normal white-faced, blue-eyed appearance as they tended their bullet wounds, which were now nearly healed.

'When are you going to give up these nighttime escapades Heinrich? You have a son to think about,' lectured Heinrich's brother as they sat down on a plain wooden table and ate their breakfast. As they sat there in the sparsely decorated kitchen, the door opened slowly, and a little boy appeared, sleepy and carrying a book.

'Father, where have you been?'

'Louis, my son,' beamed Heinrich, 'We have been on an adventure, your mother and me,' Derica smiled.

'Louis,' Lucia approached the boy, stroked his head and smiled.

'I am Lucia, and my friend here is Cassian, what are you reading?'

'It's a book on mathematics,' replied the shy, young boy.

Cassian put his hand on the boy's shoulder. 'Louis Picard, you will grow up to be very clever,' he smiled.

'Another war, another time,' said Peter eating another sausage. They were joined by the professor in the mess, who kissed Lucia on the cheek and looked at Peter. 'Mon ami, it is good to see you alive and well.

'Lucia was just telling us of your time in World War Two. Fascinating,' said Peter.

'Oui,' the professor nodded wistfully. 'Lucia tells me you were hurt?'

'Professor, why was I injured? I'm Bulletproof Pete. I'm not supposed to get hurt!'

'From what you told me you became unbalanced when you had uninvited guests join your party,' probed the professor.

'Yes, Fred and Gregg joined us, looking for their women. It was not part of our mission parameters,' replied Peter.

'We rescued many women, we did good,' said Vinnie eating another egg. They all nodded.

'Amen to that,' said Sebastian.

The professor looked earnest as he spoke to the warrior. 'You must learn to control your emotions. You must not let anger or your ego control you, young Peter, else it will unbalance you.' The professor then paused, looked down and added. 'You have many challenges ahead of you.'

Lucia flashed a glance at her lover.

'What challenges?' asked Peter, then he knew the professor was hiding something.

The story is continued in -
CAIUS

DOMINION
First Blood Series Book Three

OUT NOW

(Buy it quick else Vinnie the Terminator will pay you a visit)

Sign up on my website for new book releases, free books, stories behind the books, competitions, news and gossip, sample chapters www.richardgmann.com

My blog www.richardmannblog.com

Follow me and Like my Facebook Page: facebook.com/richardgmann.author

Facebook Group: Richard Mann Author Sci-Fi Group
Follow me on Twitter: @richardgmann
Search Dominion First Blood on Google and Youtube

Review

If you like my book, I would be eternally grateful if you could give a ☺ review

Acknowledgements

My thanks go to Dennis Turla and Jose Pepitojr for their help with the book cover. To my patient wife Brenda as I spend endless hours in front of the computer on my book as she gently asks, when will it be finished? To my son, David for his suggestions on various things. For Celine Byford, Chris Robbins and Kevin Berney for their eagle eyes. To Allison Wright my editor, you are always right. And thanks to Led Zeppelin for keeping me sane during the long hours at my keyboard.

Appendices

Cockney Slang	Rhymes with	Meaning
Cream crackered	Knackered	Very tired
Pen and ink	Stink	Stinks
Tom and Dick	Sick	Sick
Adam and Eve it	Believe it	Would you believe it?
Boat race	Face	Face
Tom Tit	Shit	Going for a shit
Alan Whickers	Knickers	Women's Knickers

VAMPIRI COMMAND STRUCTURE

COUNT CASSIAN OF ROMANIA *1

LUCIA

| VISCOUNT VINICIUS OF BRAZIL *2 | LORD ASWERNE OF THE PHILIPPINES *2 | BARON TITAS OF GERMANY *1 | LADY VESILIA OF ENGLAND *1 | RAJA VAMDEVI OF INDIA *3 | SIR ELIJAH OF AUSTRALIA *1 | BARON ALEXANDER OF RUSSIA *2 |

*Notes number of legions commanded

Sumeri Alien Command Structure

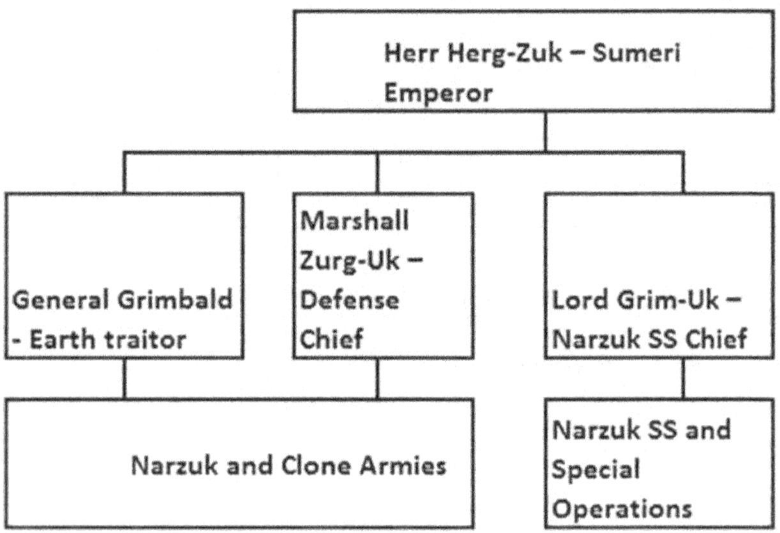

About the Author

Richard Mann grew up as an avid reader of books, even from an early age he loved the literary giants JRR Tolkien, Michael Moorcock, Frank Herbert and Douglas Adams. *(If you like these kinds of books you will love Richard's books).* He started writing at 16 and with a book called tales from Mellyms Tarc, with a character called Gluloidic. The dream of becoming a writer faded until a few years ago when he started writing again. During his twenties, he studied business studies and accountancy. During this time, he also studied Shaolin and Wing Chun Kung Fu and even started a school with a friend. He has worked as an accountant, a software developer in the City of London for banks and insurance companies and is now an author.

His mercurial work is action-packed, fast-paced, and guaranteed to keep the reader turning pages to the end. This wholly original book falls within the sci-fi post-apocalyptic, superhero genre with elements of thriller and horror. It combines incredible action, hair-raising scares, and big laughs. It will shock the reader into thinking about his own place in the world. Warning: This book may keep the reader up all night!

Richard is a Fellow Member of the Association of Accounting Technicians, Member of the Institute of Analysts and Programmers and a Member of the British Computer Society. He is in his late fifties, married, has two sons and lives in Berkshire.

The best way to keep up with his latest news is to
sign up for his newsletter.

www.RichardMannBlog.com

Feedback to the Author

If there is anything you would like to see in my books, please send me an email.

Give feedback on the book email: richardgmann@yahoo.co.uk
Follow me and Like my Facebook Page: facebook.com/richardgmann.author
Facebook Group: Richard Mann Author Sci-Fi Group
Follow me on Twitter: @richardgmann

Sign up on my website for my newsletter for book updates, new book releases, stories behind the books, competitions, news, and gossip. You can easily sign up by entering your name and email.

Book Movie Trailer

See the Movie Trailer for this book
Please share – Your friends will love it!
https://tinyurl.com/y8nksqmw
(or search Google for Dominion First Blood).

* 9 7 8 1 7 3 9 9 8 3 6 4 2 *